THE LOVE OF HER LIFE

Kate McCabe is married with two children and lives in Howth in County Dublin. She is a former journalist and has published several bestselling novels. Kate's hobbies include reading, music, travelling and walking along the beach in Howth while she thinks up plots for her stories.

ALSO BY KATE McCABE

The Music of Love
The Spanish Letter
The Man of Her Dreams
Magnolia Park
Casa Clara
The Book Club
The Beach Bar
Forever Friends
Hotel Las Flores

The Love of Her Life

KATE McCABE

HACHETTE
BOOKS
IRELAND

First published in Ireland in 2016 by Hachette Books Ireland

1

Cataloguing in Publication Data is available from the British Library.

ISBN 978 1 47360 971 6

Typeset in Cambria by Bookends Publishing Services.
Printed and bound in Great Britain by Clays Ltd, St Ives plc.

Hachette Books Ireland policy is to use papers that are natural, renewable and recyclable products and made from wood grown in sustainable forests. The logging and manufacturing processes are expected to conform to the environmental regulations of the country of origin.

Hachette Books Ireland
8 Castlecourt Centre, Castleknock, Dublin 15, Ireland

A division of Hachette UK Ltd
Carmelite House, 50 Victoria Embankment, London EC4Y 0DZ

www.hachette.ie

This book is for the four most important girls in my life:
Maura, Caroline, Elise and Karen

PART ONE
1978–1990

Chapter One

Ellie McCoy often remarked that the most important events in her life had come in threes. There were her three siblings, her three children, her three boyfriends, the last of whom, Joe Plunkett, was the man she had married.

And then there were her three best friends: Caroline Drew, Fiona Bradshaw and Mags Bannon. They had met in a single week in the autumn of 1978, and had remained firm friends even though their careers had taken them in widely different directions. Occasionally they had arguments and disagreements but they had never fallen out. They had provided support for each other whenever problems arose, offering sisterly advice when romances went sour, children got sick or work was too much. And today their friendship was as strong as ever.

Ellie smiled whenever she thought back to that innocent time. She had just turned eighteen and had received the precious letter she had been waiting for since she'd finished her Leaving Cert exams way back in June. With trembling fingers she had torn it open and her heart had leaped: she had secured a place at university in Dublin to study economics. That day there had been great rejoicing in the McCoy household.

She was the first person in her family to go to college and everyone had been delighted for her, particularly her parents, who had told her what a privilege it was. University would open up her career prospects. And Dublin was such a lively, bustling city with lots of interesting people to meet. What a lucky girl she was.

Ellie enjoyed the excitement and the congratulations but as the time approached to leave home, she began to have doubts. She had grown into a pretty young woman, who stood five feet seven inches, with a slim figure and dark, shoulder-length hair. She had buckets of confidence. But she knew almost no one in Dublin.

There were a couple of distant cousins she hadn't seen since her childhood, but she had no intention of contacting them. They had their own lives to live and, besides, Ellie wanted to be independent. But what if she was lonely? What if she didn't make friends? What if she failed her exams and had to return home with her tail between her legs?

Finally the time came to leave. One bright morning in October she boarded the bus from the little town of Ballymount in the Irish midlands, torn between expectation and foreboding. Her family came with her to see her off: her mother and father, her two younger sisters, Aine and Ciara, and her brother Sean. In one pocket of her travel bag was the address of a landlady in Harold's Cross, who had agreed to let her have a room and an evening meal for ten pounds a week. In another she had the letter from the university, telling her where and when to register.

She need not have worried. Her landlady, Mrs Bolger, turned out to be a plump, matronly woman, whose own daughter was working as a nurse in London. She immediately took Ellie under her wing and did her best to make her feel at home. And on her first day at university Ellie had another stroke of good fortune. As she joined the queue in the registrar's office, she fell into conversation with a petite auburn-haired girl.

'What are you studying?' the girl asked, as the queue inched forward.

'Economics,' Ellie replied.

The other looked impressed. 'You must be very bright to be accepted for that. It sounds terribly complicated to me.'

Ellie blushed. 'Not really. I'm just good at maths. What are you doing?'

'English literature. I expect it'll be a doddle. It's really just reading novels and poetry, writing essays and stuff.'

'I wouldn't bet on it,' Ellie said. 'I don't think any university course could be described as a doddle. I reckon you'll find they make you work quite hard.'

'What's your name?' the auburn girl asked.

'Ellie McCoy.'

'I'm Margaret Bannon. My friends call me Mags.'

Ellie had already taken note of her accent. 'You're a Dubliner, aren't you?' she said.

'That's right. And you?'

'I'm from Ballymount. It's in County Offaly. I don't suppose you've ever heard of it.'

'Of course I have,' Mags retorted. 'We studied geography at school, you know.'

They continued to chat till they reached the top of the line and Mags turned to Ellie. 'Do you know many people here?'

Ellie shook her head. 'You're the first person I've met.'

'Well, we'll have to sort that. What are you doing after you register?'

'I haven't decided.'

'I'm meeting a friend for coffee in the refectory. Why don't you join us?'

'I'd love to,' Ellie replied, welcoming the opportunity to meet new people.

'You know where it is?'

'Yes.'

'See you there, then. I'll watch out for you.'

After she had registered, and had been given her timetable of tutorials and lectures, Ellie made her way to the refectory. It was crowded with students, all chatting animatedly in huddled groups, and it took Ellie some time to find Mags sitting at a corner table with a dark-haired girl in a flowing linen dress. As she approached, Mags drew out a chair for her and introduced them.

'This is my friend Caroline Drew. We were at Holy Faith secondary school together.'

As she sat down, Ellie stole a glance at the new girl. She was wearing bright red lipstick and dark eyeshadow and had hooped earrings, like a gypsy fortune-teller. She looked very glamorous. 'Are you doing English literature too?' she asked.

Caroline raised her finely plucked eyebrows. 'I'm studying drama, actually. I'm going to be an actress. I'm planning to go into films.'

Ellie stared at her in awe. She had never met an actress before, not to mention a potential film star. 'Really? That sounds fantastic. I'll bet there was a lot of competition to get on that course.'

Caroline tossed back her mane of raven hair. 'It was way oversubscribed, and they turned down most of the applicants.' She shrugged. 'But I was lucky. I did a very good interview.'

'Oh, come off it,' Mags said, elbowing her friend in the ribs. 'You don't have to pretend. It had nothing to do with luck. You're very good. That's the reason you got the place.'

Caroline pulled a face. 'If you say so.'

And they all laughed.

***

It was a couple of days before Ellie met her third friend. By now she was beginning to find her way round the university campus and had attended her first lecture. She was coming out of the library one afternoon when she was stopped by a tall, thin, studious-looking girl, with a pile of books under her arm. 'I wonder if you can help me,' she said, in a polite English accent. 'I'm afraid I'm a bit lost. I'm looking for the students' union building.'

By coincidence, Ellie had arranged to meet Caroline and Mags there. 'That's where I'm going. Why don't you come with me?'

As they walked together, the girl introduced herself as Fiona Bradshaw and said she was studying medicine. By the time they arrived, Ellie had learned a lot about her. She was from London, had been educated at a private girls' school in Twickenham, and her father and grandfather were doctors. She was renting her own flat in Blackrock.

Caroline and Mags were waiting for Ellie on the steps of the union building. She introduced Fiona and they chatted for a few minutes. As the little party was breaking up, Mags said, 'We're meeting at three o'clock in the refectory for coffee. You're welcome to join us, if you like.'

'That's very kind,' Fiona said, her face brightening. 'I'd love to.'

It became a pattern. As the weeks passed, Ellie got to know more people. There were the students who attended her lectures and tutorials, and others she got to know in the library and at the clubs she had joined. But Caroline, Mags and Fiona were her closest friends. Before long they had formed a tight little circle and each day Ellie looked forward to three o'clock when they would meet in the refectory to chat. When December arrived and the university broke up for Christmas, she was surprised to find she was sorry to be leaving Dublin and going home to Ballymount.

**

The new term brought another development. One day as they were walking back from the library, Fiona said to her, 'I've been thinking. I've got a whole flat to myself. It has a kitchen, bathroom and living room. And I've got a spare bedroom. Why don't you come and share with me?'

'The rent must be enormous,' Ellie said regretfully. 'I don't think I could afford it.'

Fiona waved her hand. 'You don't have to worry about the rent. My dad takes care of that. He was so pleased I got a place in medical school that he's happy to pay.'

'So how would it work?'

'We'd share the expenses. Things like food, heating, electricity. What do you pay in your digs?'

'Ten pounds a week.'

'That should easily cover it. It's a lovely flat and Blackrock is a charming little town. It's only twenty minutes on the bus from there to here. I'd really appreciate your company. Why don't you come out and take a look at it?'

By now, Ellie had settled into Mrs Bolger's digs and was quite happy there. Although her room was tiny, the food was good, the rent was reasonable and her landlady fussed over her as if she was a member of her own family. But there were also drawbacks: the house was quite small, and there were other lodgers coming and going so there was little peace for her to study. And although she had her own key, Mrs Bolger expected her to be tucked up in bed by midnight.

'Okay,' Ellie said. 'I'll come this afternoon.'

When her last lecture was over, she met Fiona and they travelled out to Blackrock. She stared from the bus window at the beautiful gardens flashing by, with manicured lawns and tall, majestic trees. When they reached their destination, Fiona led Ellie along several streets till they came to the seafront and a large Victorian house staring out at Dublin Bay. 'Here we are,' she said.

'It's very grand,' Ellie said, looking up at the imposing building.

'Let's go inside and I'll show you around.'

They walked up the steps to the front door. Fiona took a bunch of keys from her handbag and let them in. They entered a large hall with a wide staircase facing them.

'The house has been divided into three flats,' Fiona explained. 'I'm at the top.'

They climbed the stairs to the top floor where Fiona selected another key and opened a door. They stepped into a room flooded with afternoon sunlight from a large bay window. Ellie was immediately struck by the scene before her. The room was furnished with a sofa and comfortable armchairs. A couple of impressionist prints adorned the walls. In a corner beside the windows, a pile of medical textbooks lay on a table.

'This is the living room. It's where I study. I find the view across the bay very calming – even when it's raining, which it seems to do a lot of the time.' Fiona laughed.

They left the living room and, in quick succession, Ellie was shown the bathroom, kitchen and Fiona's bedroom. Finally, Fiona pushed open another door and they entered a smaller room with a single bed, chest of drawers and a built-in wardrobe. From the window, there was another view of the sea. The floor was covered with a soothing blue carpet while a print of Picasso's *Guernica* stared down from the wall beside the bed. Compared with her cramped little room at Mrs Bolger's, this was luxury, Ellie thought.

'So, what do you think?' Fiona asked.

'I'm bowled over. It's fantastic.'

Fiona smiled and led Ellie back to the kitchen where she produced a bottle of wine from the fridge and poured two glasses.

'How much does this flat cost?' Ellie asked, still coming to terms with what she had just seen.

'I told you my father pays the rent but I believe it's one hundred and fifty pounds a month.'

'And you're willing to let me live here for ten pounds a week?'

'Because we're friends. I said I'd appreciate some company. I'm a stranger to Dublin and it can get lonely here, particularly at weekends. So what do you say? Will you take it?'

'Of course I will! I'm going to love living here.'

The following morning, Ellie told Mrs Bolger she would

be leaving at the end of the week. She felt guilty because the landlady had been very good to her but Mrs Bolger didn't seem surprised. 'You've found a flat, haven't you?'

'Yes,' Ellie admitted. 'One of my friends has offered me a room. How did you know?'

The landlady laughed. 'I've been in this business for twenty years and I've learned a thing or two about students. Most of them can't wait to strike out on their own. It's all part of growing up, I suppose.'

***

On Saturday morning, Ellie packed her bag, said goodbye to Mrs Bolger and set off for her new home in Blackrock. It was midday when she arrived and Fiona was waiting to let her in and help her unpack. When they had finished, she suggested they go out for lunch. 'It's a sort of celebration, the start of a new chapter, if you like. I've a funny feeling we're going to have a ball.'

Of course, once Caroline and Mags heard the news, they were envious and wanted to move in too. They thought it was the height of sophistication to be living in your own flat away from the watchful eyes of your parents. But there were no more spare rooms and, besides, their parents could see no good reason why they should subsidise a bohemian lifestyle in some student flat, particularly as they were already shelling out for college fees. But Caroline and Mags often stayed over at weekends, sharing a sofa bed in the living room.

Fiona's prophecy proved true. They *did* have a ball. The parties they threw, the handsome men, the love affairs that began and ended in that flat in Cumberland Terrace, Blackrock, became the stuff of university folklore.

And as time went by, Ellie's early fear of failing her exams and going back to Ballymount in disgrace proved unfounded. She was a good student, with an aptitude for economics, and easily passed each test that was set for her. She had settled down in Dublin and loved the excitement of university life and the buzz of the city. Only one thing troubled her: so far, she had failed to find a suitable man.

Chapter Two

Her first boyfriend was a young history student, called Henry Boylan, whom she met in the college library soon after she'd moved in with Fiona. He invited her to have coffee, then asked her out on a date.

Henry was tall and very handsome. He was a snappy dresser and had wonderful manners. He also had his own car, which was a novelty among students at that time, a second-hand Mazda hatchback. He was an only child and lived with his widowed mother in a large, red-brick house in Glenageary.

On their first date he took her to see a movie at the Carlton cinema in O'Connell Street. He bought her a box of expensive chocolates and held her hand. Afterwards he drove her back to Blackrock, and as she got out of the car, he delivered a warm, lingering kiss to her lips. Ellie thought it was all very romantic.

Soon they were going out every weekend and spending their evenings studying together in the college library. Before long, she was convinced she was in love. All her friends told her how jealous they were. Henry Boylan was a hunk. She was so lucky to have hooked him. Ellie floated around the campus on a pink cloud.

But, slowly, the dream began to dissolve. As she got to know him better, she realised that Henry had one big flaw. He was riddled with indecision. He couldn't make up his mind and was constantly asking her opinion on even the simplest things, like what tie he should wear. At first, she thought this was just politeness on his part, but eventually she realised that his good manners masked a distinct lack of self-confidence.

Ellie had always wanted a man she could look up to and respect, someone with firm opinions and a mind of his own. The magic between them began to evaporate.

Eventually he took her home one evening to meet his stern-faced mother, who interrogated her for an hour in the living room and never once smiled. Ellie felt she was on trial for the crime of going out with the woman's son. It was the last straw. How could she have any respect for a man who couldn't even choose a girlfriend without his mother's approval?

She met Charlie Timmons just after she had graduated. They had been introduced by one of Fiona's friends. By now, she had secured her first job as an economic researcher for a small firm of stockbrokers called Lombard and Brady, with offices in the city centre. Charlie was a trainee solicitor at a big Dublin law practice.

He wasn't as tall as Henry Boylan or as handsome but he didn't lack self-esteem. Indeed, Ellie discovered that he had an extremely high opinion of his own importance. At the beginning, Charlie was very attentive. He bought her flowers and presents, rang every day to ask how she was, remembered her birthday and held out her chair for her whenever they went to a restaurant. It wasn't till several months had passed that Ellie realised she was going out with a control freak who was so self-willed that it bordered on egomania.

Soon Charlie was insisting on having his own way in everything, and sulking if she objected. For the sake of peace, she put up with it as he dragged her all over Dublin to dinner parties with his lawyer friends and their snobbish spouses. But it grated on her. Why did she have to be the one who made all the compromises? Why couldn't Charlie occasionally do what *she* wanted?

She made up her mind to confront him. They were having dinner one evening in a smart Italian restaurant at the back of Trinity College. Charlie had chosen it and had even suggested what she should eat. As they were tucking into their veal *scaloppini*, Ellie said, 'Charlie, you and I have got to talk.'

He wiped some sauce from his chin with his napkin. 'What about?'

'Us.'

He grinned. 'What's to talk about? I think we're very well suited, don't you? I'm very fond of you, Ellie.'

'You've got to change.'

Now he laughed. 'Change? Me?'

'Yes. I'm fed up with the way you make all the decisions in this relationship. You never consult me. You never ask what I want. It's always your way. That sort of behaviour doesn't show much consideration for me.'

He waved his hand. 'You're imagining things, Ellie.'

'Am I? Would you like me to give you some examples? I can give you half a dozen straight off the top of my head.'

The smile was replaced with a scowl. 'Keep your voice down. People can hear us.'

'I don't care.'

'I didn't know you felt like this,' he growled. 'It's just that somebody has to make the decisions. It's easier if it's me.'

'And why is that?'

'Because I'm a man and men are natural leaders.'

Ellie felt as if she was going to explode. 'That's utter nonsense. You treat me as if I had no mind of my own. Why do you go out with me?'

'I like you. I enjoy your company.'

'You're behaving as if I was just something you carry around with you, like your briefcase. You don't treat me as a real human being. I'm fed up with it, Charlie.'

'A briefcase? What do you mean?'

'I mean you don't respect me.'

By now, several heads had turned in their direction.

'Okay, okay, calm down.' Charlie wiped his mouth again. 'I hear what you're saying. I'm listening.'

'You'd better be,' she said.

Within weeks, he had slipped back into his bad old ways and Ellie knew that Charlie was never going to change. The crisis broke one evening at a dinner party in Foxrock hosted by one of Charlie's senior legal colleagues. Ellie was practically ignored once the rest of the group heard she was a mere economic researcher and came from a hick town called Ballymount.

She endured it till the dessert course was served, when she shocked them all by standing up and announcing that she was going home. She would always remember their stunned faces as she walked to the hall, put on her coat and went out into the night in search of a cab. When Charlie had the nerve to ring the next morning to demand an apology, she told him to get lost and put the phone down.

There followed a period when Ellie found herself sinking into despair. She began to doubt if she was ever going to meet the right man. She'd had two unsatisfactory experiences but her friends kept telling her that was just the luck of the draw. She had to keep trying and the right guy would turn up eventually.

Sometimes she wondered if this was true. Was there really a Mr Right out there for every woman who wanted one? And would it be such a big deal if she never found him? She wanted someone loving and caring, someone with a bit of dash and verve, someone who knew his own mind but wasn't so self-centred that he turned into a monster, like Charlie Timmons.

She wanted someone she could respect and admire, a man with principles and standards, someone she could rely on. She wanted a man with a sense of humour, who would bring a bit of excitement and drama into her life. He didn't have to be startlingly handsome but he *did* have to be someone she could trust. She knew it was a tall order.

And what would she do if he didn't come along? Well, she would just get on with her life. There were plenty of women who didn't have men – she could think of dozens. And they all seemed happy with their lot. Her father's sister, Aunt Bridie, was a perfect example. She'd never married and never had children yet she had led a full and contented life. For fifteen years she had managed the local credit union in Ballymount, with a staff of eight assistants, and had made a big success of it.

She reminded herself that she had a good job and could look forward to a successful career. She would be quite capable of looking after herself. And, of course, she would always have her wonderful friends. If she didn't meet Mr Right, it wouldn't be the end of the world.

And then she ran into Joe Plunkett and everything changed.

Chapter Three

When Ellie first set eyes on Joe, he was a dashing twenty-seven-year-old reporter, whose career seemed destined for stardom. Despite his age, he was already head and shoulders above his colleagues. His reports were regularly splashed across the front page of the *Gazette*, Ireland's leading tabloid newspaper. And he was in constant demand from radio and television stations to provide background analysis of breaking stories and current affairs.

People said that Joe had his finger on the pulse of the nation. He appeared to have contacts in every area of public life from the police to the government to big business. One cabinet minister confessed that the first thing he did every morning when he got into his office was read the *Gazette* to see if Joe had written anything about him.

Joe was first with the news and his reports were always accurate. If Joe predicted that something was going to happen, the other papers scrambled to follow: Joe Plunkett never got his facts wrong. Already, people were saying that it wouldn't be long before he was scooped up by one of the big international broadcasting corporations for a six-figure salary.

Ellie first met him in Neary's at the top of Grafton Street on a balmy spring evening in 1983. She had come with Caroline, who was appearing in a play at the Gaiety Theatre just around the corner and had said that Neary's was a great place to meet interesting men.

The pub was crowded. Ellie pushed her way to the bar and managed to order their drinks while Caroline went off in search of seats. As she waited, she became aware that someone was speaking to her. When she turned, she found herself staring into a pair of dark brown eyes. On closer inspection, she saw they belonged to a man with a rugged face and jet-black hair. 'I beg your pardon?' she said.

'I said I don't remember seeing you in here before,' the man replied.

'That's because I've never been here before.'

He smiled. 'That explains it. I usually remember a pretty face.'

Ellie flushed. He was *chatting her up*. She couldn't believe it. She was barely in the door and a good-looking man was hitting on her already. Caroline was certainly right about this place.

The barman put her drinks on the counter. As she pulled out her purse, he waved her money away. 'It's already taken care of. Mr Plunkett paid.'

'Mr Plunkett?'

'The gentleman you were speaking to just now.'

She turned around but the dark-haired stranger was gone. Curiouser and curiouser, she thought, as she carried the glasses through the crowded pub to the seats Caroline had managed to find. 'You'll never believe what just happened,' Ellie said. 'This guy at the bar paid for the drinks. I've never had that happen to me before.'

'I told you this place is good!' Caroline laughed, sipping her gin with a contented sigh. 'Did he introduce himself?'

'No, and he was gone before I could thank him. The barman called him Mr Plunkett.'

'About six feet tall, broad-shouldered, dark hair?'

'That's him.'

'It must be Joe. He comes in here quite often.'

'You said that as if he was someone I should know.'

'And so you should. Joe Plunkett is only Ireland's most successful journalist. He's never off the television. Don't you ever read the papers?'

'Not as often as I should, obviously.'

***

Later that night, in bed, she thought about the incident. She was sorry now that she hadn't had more time to speak to the handsome stranger. She sometimes had to put up with men pestering her at bars when they were half drunk but Joe Plunkett had been entirely sober and seemed quite respectable. And he certainly hadn't pestered her.

Apart from telling her that she had a pretty face, which was a compliment, he hadn't attempted to press himself on her at all. Indeed, he had been very pleasant. Oh, well, she would have to mark it down as another missed opportunity. Since she had broken up with Charlie Timmons, missed opportunities were becoming increasingly frequent.

A few days later she was busy preparing an urgent financial

report when her phone rang. She picked it up and heard a man's voice: 'Ms Ellie McCoy?'

'Speaking.'

'This is Joe Plunkett, Ellie. Remember me? We met in Neary's?'

She caught her breath. 'How did you get my name ... and my phone number?'

He was laughing. 'That's my job, Ellie. Getting information is what I do for a living. Believe me, finding your name and number was much simpler than most of the things I'm required to do. Now, I hope I'm not disturbing you.'

'What do you want, Mr Plunkett?'

'For a start, I'd like you to call me Joe, like my friends do.'

'You haven't answered my question.'

'I want to ask you out for a date.'

'But we don't even know each other.'

'Isn't that the whole purpose of a date, to get to know one another? I told you I usually remember a pretty face and it's a long time since I came across one as pretty as yours. Now, what do you say? Will you allow me to buy you dinner some evening?'

He had caught her completely off guard and now she was confused. She should really put the phone down but something about his cheeky confidence made her hesitate. Then another thought occurred to her. What would happen if her boss, Mr Brady, came in and found her chatting to some strange man on the phone? She'd better get rid of him fast. 'I'm very busy, I have to go now.'

'Just say yes.'

'When are we talking about?'

'Tonight? What time do you finish work?'

'Six o'clock.'

'Why don't I see you in Neary's at half past? Will you recognise me again? I'll certainly recognise you.'

She heard footsteps approaching outside. Mr Brady was coming. She had to get Joe Plunkett off the line. 'All right,' she agreed. 'Half past six.'

***

Afterwards, when she had more time to think about it, she wondered if she had given in too easily. Did it make her appear too keen? That was always a bad way to start. But he had been so insistent. And he *had* bought her those drinks the first time they'd met. He was good-looking and well-mannered and, well, she'd been lonely since she'd dumped Charlie Timmons.

He had certainly gone to some trouble to track her down. She wondered where he had got her details. But perhaps that showed he was the one who was keen. Yes, that was the way she should look at it.

When she had a spare moment she rang Caroline to tell her but she was in rehearsals and couldn't come to the phone. Now Ellie couldn't wait for six o'clock to arrive, and when it did, she was out of the office like a shot.

As she was passing Bewley's in Grafton Street she went in and made straight for the Ladies, where she spent ten minutes brushing her hair and putting on her makeup. She wished she had something more glamorous to wear than her work clothes – white blouse, dark skirt and jacket. But when she'd got dressed that morning she hadn't known she was going to be asked out on a date.

When she had finished, she went into the café, sat for ten minutes and drank a cup of coffee while she watched the minutes tick away. She had already allowed him to bounce her into this date but she'd be damned if she was going to arrive before him. By the time she got to Neary's it was twenty to seven.

He was sitting alone at the bar. He got up as she approached and took her hand. 'Thanks for coming, Ellie. You look fabulous. Won't you sit down?'

He was just being polite. She knew she didn't look fabulous. The whole affair had been too rushed and unplanned. But it was gallant of him to say so. 'You don't look so bad yourself,' she remarked, letting her eyes roam over his face. He was wearing a light blue suit, with matching shirt and tie. And he was freshly shaved. He must keep an electric razor at work for occasions like this, she thought.

His dark eyes twinkled. 'Thank you. So what's your poison?'

'Gin and tonic, please.'

'Coming up.'

He spoke to the barman, then turned back to Ellie. 'How did your day go? Busy?'

'Probably not as busy as yours,' she replied, with a toss of her head. 'Now, before we begin, I want to know who gave you my name and telephone number.'

He put his hands up and grinned. 'I can't do that, Ellie. Golden rule of the newspaper business. I can't reveal my sources. I'd lose my union card if I did that.'

'You've got an answer for everything, haven't you?'

'Let's say I'm tenacious. I don't give up easily.'

'I know that already,' she replied tartly.

'So you're an economist. Ever think of going into journalism? There's a big demand for financial journalists right now. The pay isn't bad and you might enjoy it.'

She stared at him. He was beginning to sound like a private investigator. What else did he know about her? 'You really have done your homework on me, haven't you?'

He paused and gazed deep into her eyes. Ellie's heart fluttered.

'When I want something, I can be quite dogged, Ms McCoy. And, right now, I want you terribly.'

***

He brought her to a restaurant on Dame Street called Le Cirque. There was a burly man in a dress suit on the door, turning people away, but when he spotted Joe and Ellie, he quickly waved them through. The head waiter led them to a quiet table in a corner where they could see everything that was going on.

'Ever been here before?' Joe asked, as they took their seats.

She shook her head. It was way outside her price range.

'It's been getting great reviews,' he continued. 'The food is very good.'

Ellie looked around the room. It was eight o'clock and the restaurant was packed. She recognised several diners because she'd seen them on television – a politician in conversation with a group of sober-suited businessmen, a well-known fashion designer, a rock musician and various minor celebrities. 'They knew you at the door. Do you come here a lot?' she asked.

'Quite a bit. They've just hired an exciting new chef from Paris. I thought you might like it.'

They had barely sat down when a waiter appeared at their table to take their order. She was hungry so she ordered Caesar salad to start and followed it with prawns in a tomato sauce. Joe, who said he'd had a big lunch, went for grilled sea bass. Since he was driving, they restricted themselves to a glass each of Chardonnay.

Throughout the meal, the waiter was never far away, enquiring if they were enjoying the food, topping up their water glasses, ready to swoop at the slightest indication that they might require some small service. Ellie was convinced he had been told to look after Joe and make sure he was happy. When they had finished the main courses, they were offered dessert, which they declined.

She sat back with a contented sigh.

'Happy?' Joe asked, with a boyish grin.

'I most certainly am. That was terrific. I can see why you come here so often.'

He smiled. 'Do you dine out much, Ellie?'

'On my salary? You must be joking.'

'There are even better places I can take you, like Valentino and the dining room at the St Claire Hotel. They've both been awarded Michelin stars.'

She reached out and laid a hand on his. 'Joe, you've been more than generous and I'm grateful. I'll remember this meal for a very long time. But I couldn't impose on you.'

He leaned close and whispered, 'Let me tell you a secret. I'm not paying for this. The *Gazette* is.'

She was amazed. 'How do you mean?'

'I have an expense account for entertaining people who provide me with information. I pick up the bill and give it to the accounts department and they reimburse me.'

'So that's how it works?'

He nodded.

'And how will you describe me?'

'I'll put you down as a potential source in the financial sector.'

'Well, excuse me. If I'd known that I might have ordered a bottle of Dom Pérignon.'

'Maybe next time.' He laughed.

***

Outside, the evening air was crisp and fresh. There was a lively buzz about the streets. Lots of people were still around as the pubs were emptying.

'Where do you live?' he asked, as they walked along the cobbled pavements to the car park.

'You mean you don't know?' Ellie asked playfully. 'You seem to know everything else about me.'

'Give me time and I'll soon find out.'

'I live in Blackrock. I share a flat with a friend.'

'That's handy. I'm in Monkstown. I can drop you off on the way.'

It took them twenty minutes to get there.

As they said goodnight, he gently drew her towards him and pressed a kiss to her lips. His were soft and warm. She felt a thrill shoot down her spine.

At last, he released her and pushed open the door. 'Sleep tight,' he said. 'You'll be hearing from me.'

When she got into the flat, she found that Fiona had left a note saying she had gone out with some friends to a concert and would be home late. Ellie had a shower and slipped into bed. Outside her window, the streetlights were casting a soft glow into her room. She drifted off to sleep with thoughts of Joe Plunkett's kiss fresh in her mind.

Chapter Four

The next morning, on the bus into work, she went over the events of the previous evening, like a detective searching for clues. As far as she was concerned, the date had been a great success. The meal had been wonderful and Joe an entertaining companion, regaling her with jokes and little snippets of gossip. But how had he felt? Had he enjoyed it too?

'You'll be hearing from me,' he had said, as she got out of the car. She wished he had been more definite. It was the hint of another date but without any commitment. What if it was a polite way of giving her the brush-off?

She was already missing him and anxious to see him again. Once she got into her office, she buried herself in work in an effort to keep her mind occupied.

At eleven o'clock, Caroline rang. 'You were looking for me yesterday,' she began. 'Sorry I couldn't take your call but we were rehearsing all day, and when I finally got a chance to ring you back, you'd left the office.'

'I just wanted to chat,' Ellie replied. She was glad now

that she had failed to reach her friend. If she'd told her she had a date with Joe Plunkett, Caroline would want to know now when she was seeing him again and that would be embarrassing. Instead, she talked for a few minutes about the play and how the rehearsals were coming along.

'It's like working on a building site,' Caroline moaned. 'You've no idea. Everyone thinks acting's glamorous but it's bloody hard graft, I can tell you.'

'But it's all worth it,' Ellie said encouragingly. 'Keep thinking of the thrill when the lights go up at the end of the performance and the audience roars its approval.'

'And what if they boo us off the stage?'

'C'mon, Caroline, you know that's never going to happen.'

'Want to bet?'

They finished their conversation with Caroline promising to keep her a ticket for the opening night. Talking to her friend had cheered Ellie up. Caroline was forever complaining about her job but it was mainly for dramatic effect. Ellie knew she wouldn't swap her career for anything.

There were no more personal calls for the remainder of the morning. At one o'clock she nipped out for a quick break and ate a tuna sandwich at a snack bar near the office. When it came to six o'clock and time to leave, Joe Plunkett hadn't called. Ellie went back to Blackrock, picked up a Chinese meal on the way home and ate it with a glass of wine while she watched an old black-and-white movie on television.

Fiona came in at nine o'clock, exhausted after a long day at medical lectures and studying in the hospital. She had a cup of tea with Ellie, a quick bath and went straight to bed. Ellie followed soon after. She tossed and turned and tried to get comfortable but it was after midnight before she fell asleep.

Joe Plunkett didn't ring the following day or the one after. By now, she was growing desperate to hear his voice again. But as each day passed and she heard nothing, her hopes began to fade. If he was really interested in her, surely he would have called by now.

She felt a cloud of depression descend over her. It was becoming clear that the date had been a one-off. There would be no follow-up. She had been foolish, too eager, too easily impressed by his smart talk, his expense-account dining and his flashy man-about-town image. She had allowed herself to be swept away by his breezy manner and the compliments he had paid her. She had been too naive.

She knew she could always ring the *Gazette* office and ask to speak to him but her pride wouldn't allow her to do that. It would be too demeaning. Besides, it wouldn't work. If Joe really wanted to see her again, he had her number. Oh, well, she thought, I'll just have to put it behind me and get on with my life.

She worked so hard over the next few days that Mr Brady was moved to remark on her commitment and dedication. Every time the phone rang, she reached for it eagerly, hoping to hear his voice, and every time she was disappointed. Each evening, she went home feeling so tired that she had barely enough energy to eat before tumbling into bed and falling asleep. At least it had the effect of driving Joe Plunkett from her mind.

Then one evening as she was leaving the office she was startled to hear someone call her name. She turned. There he was, striding purposefully along the pavement towards her, the tails of his overcoat billowing behind him. She looked at him as if she was seeing a ghost.

'Ellie, I was hoping to catch you before you left work.'

'Where have you been?' she asked. 'Why didn't you call me?'

'I'm sorry, but I've been away. Have you time for a quick drink? I'll explain it all to you.'

Before she could answer, he had taken her in his arms and his warm lips were pressed to hers.

They went to a pub close by. It was empty, apart from a couple of men chatting over pints of Guinness at the bar. Joe chose a table and went to collect their drinks. She waited, trembling with excitement now that he was back again. All thoughts of recrimination had vanished from her mind.

'I owe you an apology,' he began, as he put down the drinks. 'I had to go off to Liverpool at short notice. I barely had time to pack my bags. That's why I didn't call.'

'You could have called me from there.'

'But I was busy. I'm working on a big story involving fraud and important people in the business world. It's going to cause a sensation when I publish it.'

'You don't have to explain, Joe. I know you have to do your job.'

'But I want to. There's something I must tell you, Ellie. The newspaper business is unlike anything else. It's chaotic. Events can happen suddenly and you just have to drop everything and go for it. I got a phone call that a contact in Liverpool had important information for me.'

'So, is it finished now?'

'Not quite. There's one more person I need to see.'

'Why are you telling me this?'

He took her hands and looked deep into her eyes. 'So that you understand the disruptive life you can expect if you get involved with me.'

***

After that, events moved very quickly. Joe had an apartment in Monkstown but it wasn't like the one Ellie shared with Fiona. Joe's home was in a modern purpose-built block and everything was spanking new. It had a large open-plan kitchen-cum-dining room, a living room with views towards Dun Laoghaire, a magnificent bathroom and two spacious bedrooms, one of which he had converted into an office so he could work from home. The block was in a secure complex with gates and well-tended gardens. What was more, Joe wasn't renting. He owned the apartment.

'It's magnificent,' Ellie said, while Joe was proudly showing her around. 'Who chose the fabrics and furniture? You didn't do it yourself, did you?'

He grinned like the Cheshire Cat. 'I'm afraid my talents don't extend to interior design, Ellie. I paid someone to do it for me.'

'Anyone I might know?'

'A young designer called Melanie Power.'

The name was familiar. Ellie was sure she had read about her in some of the fashion magazines. 'She certainly did a good job. It's beautiful. It's the nicest apartment I've ever seen.'

'Thank you.'

'It must have cost a packet.'

'It wasn't cheap, that's for sure. I had to take out a mortgage.'

'How much?'

He told her and she rolled her eyes. 'That's enormous. With a mortgage like that I wouldn't be able to sleep at night.'

He laughed. 'It's not so bad. I can manage it. I have to live somewhere and this is better than renting. No one can ever come along and throw me out.'

'So long as you keep up the repayments.'

'Well, there is that aspect,' he conceded.

Over the coming months, she spent a lot of time in Joe's apartment and then, one weekend, he asked her to stay over. She knew they had arrived at an important moment in their relationship.

That night when they went to bed, he drew her close. His lips explored her neck and throat and finally closed on her mouth. She trembled as he stroked her breasts and thighs. Her excitement mounted till at last he entered her. She gave a gasp and melted in his arms.

Afterwards they lay exhausted in the twisted sheets.

'Was that your first time?' he asked.

'Yes.'

'It was wonderful, the best I've ever had.'

'But you must have had lots of women.'

'Never one like you, Ellie.'

After that, she looked forward to the occasions when she could sleep with Joe. By now, she had introduced him to her friends and some of her work colleagues, and everyone agreed that he was the best-looking man they had ever seen.

'He's got this air of *je ne sais quoi*,' Caroline said, with a dramatic flourish of her hand.

'What on earth are you talking about?' Ellie asked.

'I don't know how to describe it. He radiates a sense of ... you know, excitement and mystery. Marlon Brando had it and Robert de Niro. Has he any brothers?'

Ellie tried to keep a straight face. 'Afraid not.'

'Just my luck. If you ever think of packing him in, do keep me in mind.'

Ellie was pleased that they all found him so attractive.

And it was true what Caroline had said about him being exciting. After her experiences with Henry Boylan and Charlie Timmons, Joe was like a gust of fresh air. She felt totally secure in his company and she trusted him. Joe Plunkett exuded the confidence of a man who was absolutely sure of everything he put his hand to.

***

Meeting Joe turned her life upside-down. It wasn't just the nights she spent at his apartment. Until she'd met him, her experience of Dublin social life had been confined to a few bars and clubs and occasionally a fancy restaurant to celebrate a birthday or some other special occasion. She simply didn't have the money or the connections for anything grander.

Now that changed. She learned that Joe didn't cook. He rarely used the dream kitchen in his apartment, except to make coffee and toast for breakfast in the morning. His fridge had some packs of beer, a couple of bottles of wine and a carton of milk. His shelves held nothing more exciting than a few packets of cereal and jars of instant coffee. There wasn't an egg or a single piece of fruit. Joe always ate out. And he always chose the best places.

When she asked him why he didn't cook, he said he didn't have time. Besides, the *Gazette* was picking up his restaurant bills. It was a perk of his job as the paper's star reporter. Why would he spend time messing about in his kitchen when he could wander into any place he chose and eat what he pleased?

'You might enjoy it,' she said. 'Some people find cooking therapeutic.'

'I get all the therapy I need with you.' He grinned, taking her in his arms and kissing her.

So, Ellie was treated to dinner at restaurants she had only read about in magazines: Gino's Italian trattoria in Dawson Street, the Suckling Pig in Booterstown Avenue, Chez Pierre, the famous French eatery on South William Street, and Karachi, an up-market Asian place in Baggot Mews.

Everywhere they went, they were treated like minor royalty and shown to the best tables. The chefs would come out of the kitchen in their whites and talk to them. The best liqueur bottles would be brought down from the shelf and they would be treated to complimentary drinks. Often, they weren't even presented with a bill. Having Joe Plunkett eat in their establishments was good for business so restaurant owners were always delighted to see them.

The same applied to nightclubs and concerts. They were given front-row seats when others were turned away. At clubs, they were ferried through the security cordons and offered glasses of champagne with the manager's compliments. Ellie was surprised at the number of occasions when Joe tried to pay a bill only to be told it was on the house. Eventually she grew used to it.

But she was about to learn that there was a downside to being romantically involved with Joe Plunkett. One morning, she had an excited phone call from Mags. 'Did you know you're in the paper?'

'What are you talking about?' Ellie sat bolt upright.

'The *Courier*, page seven. Maggie McConkey. She writes a column called "On the Town". You must have seen it.'

'I never read the *Courier*.'

'Well, you've got to today. They've even got a photograph. I must say, you look great.'

Ellie was off like a hare to the corner shop where she

bought a copy of the *Courier* and frantically tore it open. When she got to page seven, she gasped. At the top of the page there was a photo of Joe and herself leaving the Dolce Vita club on Harcourt Street several nights before.

MAN ABOUT TOWN HAS NEW WOMAN IN HIS LIFE

Many of our female readers will be fascinated to learn that dreamy Joe Plunkett, the handsome newshound, has found a new belle to mop his fevered brow after a hard day chasing fire engines. We can reveal that he is now squiring Ellie McCoy, an economic whizz-kid who works in the financial industry.

Joe, one of the city's most eligible bachelors, has been linked romantically with several of Dublin's leading ladies but now spends his nights discussing stocks and shares with brainy Ellie. Watch this space for further developments.

She snapped the paper closed. She was outraged that her personal life was splashed all over the *Courier* for everyone to read. What would her parents think if they saw it? They didn't even know about Joe. Or Mr Brady? If he read this he might not be pleased. At least the article hadn't identified the firm she worked for. She had to get hold of Joe and talk to him.

When she got back to her desk, the office was quiet, apart from the sound of typing coming from Mr Brady's room. Ellie went to her own quarters and quietly closed the door. Then she lifted the phone and rang Joe's number.

'Hi,' he said.

She lowered her voice to a whisper. 'Joe, it's me. There's a report about us in the *Courier* today. Have you seen it?'

'Oh, that.' He laughed. 'A Maggie McConkey special. She's always looking for ways to take a swipe at the *Gazette*. We're their main rivals. I wouldn't lose any sleep over it if I was you.'

'But I don't like my private business being broadcast all over town. Who I decide to go out with is of no concern to anyone but me. And you, of course.'

'I'm sorry, Ellie. But I can't really complain since I do the same thing myself every day. You'll get used to it, you'll see.'

'You mean there'll be more of this intrusion into my personal life?'

'I'm afraid so, as long as you're mixed up with me.'

'So can I expect Maggie McConkey to tell her readers what I had for breakfast?'

'Maybe not that bad but you're now in the public eye so you might as well get over it. There are worse things could happen to you. Lots of people would kill to get their names in the paper.'

'Well, I'm not one of them.'

There was a slight pause.

'You really are upset about this, aren't you?'

'Yes, I am.'

'I'll tell you what. I'm working on a big crime story. I've got to go down to Marbella to talk to a contact.'

'When?'

'This weekend. I'm going down Friday and back on Monday morning. How would you like to come with me?'

Chapter Five

Ellie caught her breath. The furthest she had ever travelled was to Brussels for an economics conference. Then she had had to spend most of her time indoors so had never got to see any of the city's highlights. A trip to Marbella sounded fantastic. It was May and the weather in Spain would be delightful. 'Are you serious? This isn't some practical joke?'

'Not at all. I'd love to have you with me.'

'How would it work?'

'It's simple. The *Gazette* is paying for my flight and accommodation. I'll book a double room at the hotel and pick up the cost of your air ticket. I'll put it on my credit card.'

'And no one will object?'

'Why should they? They don't care so long as I get the goods. I take it you have a valid passport?'

'Of course.'

'So why don't you go and clear it with your boss?'

They said goodbye and Ellie put down the receiver. She

stood up and straightened her skirt. Mr Brady's door was closed as usual. She took a deep breath, knocked and heard the call to enter. Gingerly, she went in.

Mr Brady was sitting at his desk studying spreadsheets, a thin, middle-aged man, dressed immaculately in a dark pin-striped suit and a gleaming white shirt. He looked up as she came in. 'Ah, Ellie, how are you this morning?'

'I'm fine.'

'I've some good news for you. The first quarter results have just come in and profits are up fifteen per cent. There will be a nice little bonus for you at the end of the month.'

'That's fantastic,' she said.

'It certainly is. As you know, we work as a team at Lombard and Brady and you've played your part in generating those profits so you're due your reward.'

Thank God I've caught him in a good mood, she thought.

'What can I do for you?' he asked.

'A friend has invited me to go on a short break to Marbella. It would mean taking Friday off and restarting work on Monday afternoon.'

He sat back and a smile creased his lips. 'Marbella. What a wonderful place. Have you been there before?'

'No.'

'You'll love it. I went there for my honeymoon. Mind you, that was several years ago. I'll always remember the quaint little bars, the moonlit nights, the friendly Spanish people. And, of course, the sun shone all day long.'

'So is it all right if I go? I'll work extra hours to make it up.'

'Not at all, a break will do you good. Besides, you've earned it. Did you say you're leaving on Friday?'

'Yes.'

'I'll get someone to cover for you. Now off you go and enjoy yourself. A word of warning, Ellie.'

'Yes, Mr Brady?'

There was a playful twinkle in his eye. 'Go easy on the sangria. It has quite a kick.'

She went back to her own office and rang Joe.

'So it's settled. I'll meet you after work today and hopefully I'll have all the details by then. You're going to enjoy this trip, Ellie.'

'I know – my boss has just told me so.'

She decided to find out more about Marbella so during her lunch break she visited several travel shops and picked up any brochures about Spain that they had to offer. Then she called into a café where she managed to get a table to herself. When the waitress came, she ordered coffee and a sandwich, spread the brochures on the table and began to read.

'Marbella: a gem of the Costa del Sol,' the first brochure declared, in an article packed with glossy pictures of golden beaches, palm trees, little whitewashed houses and dark-eyed *señoritas* with flowers in their hair.

Studying the brochures stoked Ellie's interest. It had been a long, cold winter. A couple of days in the sun would be wonderful, with nothing to do but relax and enjoy Joe's company. When she told her friends, they congratulated her on her good fortune.

'If you need someone to carry your bags, I'm always available,' Mags said.

'Me too,' Caroline added. 'We could sleep on the floor in your room.'

'I'd like nothing better,' Ellie giggled, 'but I'm not sure that Joe would.'

She couldn't wait for Thursday to come. Joe suggested she spend the night at his apartment so they could have a smooth start in the morning. After work, Ellie went home and packed her case. This was a short trip so she didn't need much: a couple of light summer dresses and something smart to wear in the evenings. And a camera, she mustn't forget that. Her friends would want to see the photographs.

She had already consulted the weather forecast, which predicted clear skies and warm, sunny weather. She might want to do some sunbathing but she had no swimsuit. I'll buy one when I get there, she thought. It might even be cheaper.

Once she had packed, she called for a cab to take her to Monkstown, where Joe was waiting. 'Have you eaten yet?' he asked, when she arrived.

'I had a snack at lunchtime.'

'Why don't I order in a pizza?'

'Brilliant.'

They shared a bottle of wine and watched television while they ate their meal. By midnight they were tucked up in Joe's comfortable double bed. He wrapped his arms around her and drew her close. 'Are you excited?'

'Of course! This is a double first for me.'

'How do you mean?'

'It's the first time I've been to Spain. And the first time I've gone on holiday with a man.'

His warm mouth pressed on hers. 'So we'll have to make it an experience you'll never forget.'

***

The following morning, she was woken by Joe humming in the shower. When she looked at her watch she saw it was ten past eight and light was pouring through the crack in the curtains. The bathroom door opened and he emerged in a cloud of steam. 'So you're awake. The shower is free. I'll go and make some coffee.'

She threw back the duvet and got out of bed. Minutes later, wrapped in a towel, she made her way into the kitchen. Joe poured a mug of coffee and offered her some buttered toast. 'How much time do we have?' she asked.

'Our flight leaves at eleven. If we get to the airport for ten o'clock we should be fine.'

'And when do we arrive in Spain?'

'Half past two, Spanish time. Then we've got a forty-five-minute drive to Marbella.'

She finished her breakfast and went back to the bedroom to get dressed while Joe made some quick phone calls. By nine o'clock, they had locked up the apartment and were driving to the airport. It was five to ten when Joe pulled the car into the short-term parking lot.

He immediately took charge, and around half an hour later they were boarding the plane. There was some fussing over seating and baggage but eventually the doors closed. They were told to fasten their seatbelts for take-off and the cabin crew ran through some safety procedures.

Ellie shut her eyes and said a silent prayer. When she opened them again they were airborne and the plane was passing over Howth Head. The green coast of Ireland was fast receding from view.

**

Málaga airport was busy and the vast arrivals hall was thronged with people. Once they had passed through

Immigration, Joe went in search of a trolley for their luggage, then made straight for the car-hire desk. Twenty minutes later, they were speeding west along the motorway towards their destination. It was afternoon and the sun was high.

Ellie watched intently as the landscape flashed by: little houses clinging precariously to the sides of the hills as if they could tumble over at any moment and fall into the sea, then long stretches of golden sand, waves lapping the shore.

'So, what do you think?' Joe prompted her. 'Are you impressed?'

'It's magnificent.'

'Good. And there's much more. Wait till we get to Marbella.'

'When will that be?'

He glanced at his watch. 'Another half an hour. Just relax and enjoy the scenery.'

It was siesta time when they got to Marbella. The town was quiet and the shops were closed. There was little traffic so it didn't take them long to reach their destination. Hotel Majestic stood on a little hill on the outskirts of the town, overlooking the sea. It was bright and modern, surrounded by green lawns and fountains. Outside the front door, a row of palm trees swayed gently in the breeze.

And flowers! Everywhere Ellie looked, there were tubs and hanging baskets of crimson geraniums, yellow nasturtiums and beds of bright red roses. She turned to glance over the sleepy town, with its shining steeples and gleaming rooftops. I'm going to love it here, she thought.

Their arrival had already brought an attendant in a striped waistcoat scurrying down the steps to greet them. He loaded their luggage onto a cart and they followed him into the cool interior. They found themselves in a large lobby with marble floors, comfortable sofas and more potted plants. A smiling receptionist with a name badge that read *Carmen* was waiting to greet them.

'We have a reservation,' Joe announced, producing their passports.

Carmen quickly checked their identification and asked them to sign the register. Then she presented them with room keys, a tourist map of Marbella and an information pack detailing the hotel's facilities. 'You are in room three one five,' she said, in perfect English. 'At the right-hand side of the hotel you will find the swimming pool and gardens. We have several bars, two restaurants and the Garden Café, which serves breakfast. Everything you need to know is in the information pack. Do you require assistance with your bags?'

'We can manage, thanks,' Joe replied.

'The lifts are over there,' she continued, pointing across the lobby. 'Your room is on the third floor. Welcome to Hotel Majestic. We hope you have a pleasant stay with us.'

Ellie couldn't wait to get to their room. Everything she had seen so far had impressed her. Once they arrived, Joe put down the cases and opened the door, then ushered her inside. They stepped into a spacious room tastefully furnished with sofa, writing desk, chairs and two beds. A large painting of a Moorish castle dominated one wall. More flowers stood in a vase on a side table.

She strode across the room, slid open the doors to the terrace, walked to the rail and gazed down. The gardens and the pool lay beneath her. Further out, she could see the ocean and the town. She turned to find Joe grinning at her. 'Does it meet your expectations?'

She threw her arms around his neck and kissed him hard on the mouth. 'Oh, Joe, it's wonderful.'

Once they had unpacked and put their clothes away, Joe said he had some calls to make, which would keep him occupied for a while. He explained that the man he had come to see was wanted by the police in the UK and was living in Spain to avoid extradition. As a result, he was very nervous about appearing in public. 'If you're hungry, we can order something from room service,' he said.

She shook her head. She didn't want to eat. She wanted to get out and enjoy the sun. 'I think I'll go down to the pool and relax. But first I've got to buy a swimsuit.'

She returned to the reception desk, where Carmen directed her to the hotel shop. It stocked a wide range of swimwear and it didn't take her long to choose a classy little bikini and some sun cream. Everyone had warned her about the hot sun and the importance of using protection. She paid, then returned to room 315, where she found Joe with a bottle of cava and two glasses.

'Look what I just discovered,' he announced, grinning like a child who'd received an unexpected Christmas present.

'Where was it?'

'In there.' He pointed to a small fridge beside the writing desk, which they had overlooked. 'We'll just have to drink it. It would be bad manners not to.' He filled two glasses and gave one to Ellie. 'To Hotel Majestic,' he announced, and kissed her again.

'And to us,' Ellie added, as the bubbles tickled her throat.

Chapter Six

About a dozen people were relaxing by the pool when she arrived in a hotel dressing gown, a towel tucked under her arm. It was almost four o'clock and the water was empty. She selected a vacant lounger and positioned it to face the sun. By now the temperature had risen and she decided to cool down with a swim.

She had a shower, then walked to the deep end and dived in. The water was cold but she quickly got used to it. When she emerged twenty minutes later, she felt thoroughly refreshed. She dried herself and, from her bag, retrieved the sun cream and a novel she had purchased at the airport. She applied the cream carefully, then stretched out on a lounger and started to read.

Above her, the sun was suspended like a ripe orange in the empty sky while a soft breeze fanned her skin. From the nearby palm trees, she could hear the gentle chirping of the birds. She thought of the bustling city she had left behind just a few hours earlier. It was as if she had been transported to a different world. Her friends would envy her if they could see her now, sunbathing in the garden of this beautiful hotel.

She made a mental note to ring them tomorrow, just a short call to say that everything was fine and they had arrived safely. She was so engrossed in her book that she didn't notice the time slipping by and when she checked it was almost six o'clock. The area around the pool was deserted and the sun was sinking below the tops of the trees. She got up and walked to the shower where she washed off the sun cream, then had another quick swim. When she got out of the water, she gathered her belongings and set off for room 315.

She found Joe sitting on the terrace, writing in his notebook.

'Enjoy your swim?' he asked.

'I had two. It was very relaxing.'

He smiled. 'That's a good sign. It shows you're starting to unwind.'

'How did you get on? Did you get hold of your contact?'

'I've arranged to meet him tomorrow afternoon. I'll have to leave you to your own devices, I'm afraid. He insists that I come alone.'

'That's all right. I'll find plenty to do.'

Joe put aside his notebook, stood up and stretched his arms. 'We need to think about dinner. We've had nothing to eat since breakfast and I'm starting to get hungry.'

'Me too.'

'Why don't we stroll into the town and find some place to eat, unless you want to have dinner here at the hotel?'

'The hotel can wait. Let's go into the town. I'm dying to see it.'

It took her ten minutes to slip into a cool linen dress and light jacket. Joe put on a pair of slacks and a golf shirt, and tied a sweater round his waist in case it got cool later. Finally, they locked the room and set off.

Their journey took them downhill along narrow cobbled streets, past tiny squares festooned with flowering window boxes. The town was awake again after the siesta, and from time to time, they caught the rhythm of guitar music from some gloomy little bar as they went past. After a while, they heard laughter. It grew louder till they arrived at the Paseo Maritimo, the promenade that ran along the seafront.

It was crowded with people: young couples strolling hand in hand, acrobats, other street performers, and souvenir vendors. On the pavement, people were sitting at tables, chatting as they ate and drank. By now, Ellie and Joe were ravenous. Each restaurant had a board outside displaying the menu, and there were so many that they were spoiled for choice. At last, they came to a place that looked perfect. It was set back from the Paseo in a little patio and had a menu broad enough to satisfy the most fastidious appetite. They went in, and an eager young waiter immediately showed them to a table, with a candle flickering in a little bowl. It was beside a wall with a wooden trellis supporting a trail of bright red and yellow flowers. The waiter was back at once, with a basket of bread and a dish of olives, to take their order. Ellie watched him. He was no more than eighteen, tall and slim with dark Spanish features and bright flashing eyes.

They decided to forgo starters and go straight to the main course. Ellie chose roast chicken and Joe ordered sirloin steak. To accompany the meal, they selected a bottle of Rioja from the wine list. Ten minutes later, they had steaming plates of food in front of them.

Joe's steak had been grilled on a barbecue, and when he

sliced it open, it was pink and bursting with flavour. Ellie had half a chicken, crisp and tender, the flesh white and succulent. Each plate was accompanied by dishes of salad and potatoes sautéed with garlic. Joe filled their glasses and they began to eat.

Their hunger lent zest to the food and soon they had finished. For dessert they had slices of almond cake. When the bill arrived, Ellie was surprised to find it cost half of what they would have paid for a similar meal in Dublin. Joe counted out the pesetas and gave the waiter a generous tip. The young man was so pleased that he was back again a few minutes later, bringing coffee and brandy with the compliments of the house.

'I really enjoyed that,' Joe remarked.

'Me too,' Ellie replied. 'Are all Spanish restaurants this good?'

'Not all. I think we've been particularly lucky tonight.'

'Why don't we come back tomorrow?'

He laughed. 'Slow down, Ellie. You're here to relax. Why don't we just wait and see what tomorrow brings?'

They finished their drinks and set off again along the Paseo. The crowds were increasing now and there was something of a carnival atmosphere. Laughter and music spilled out of the bars and cafés. A large moon had appeared and its pale light was shimmering across the water.

A warm sensation of contentment settled over Ellie. She grasped Joe's hand as they drifted along the seafront and slowly made their way back to Hotel Majestic. A church bell was tolling midnight when they finally got undressed and slid under the cool sheets in room 315.

***

The next day began early. Ellie woke at a quarter past seven to find Joe still sleeping peacefully beside her. She quietly drew back the sliding doors and stepped out onto the terrace in time to see the sun begin to brighten the sky. Within minutes, the birds were singing in the branches, and somewhere in the distance she heard a cock crow. There was only one thing to do. She would begin the day with a swim.

Back in the bathroom, she changed into her bikini, put on a dressing gown and grabbed a towel. Leaving Joe sleeping soundly, she tiptoed out of the room, went down to the ground floor and out to the garden. The grass was damp with dew as she made straight for the pool.

When she got there, she flung the dressing gown and the towel onto a lounger and, not pausing to check the water temperature, dived straight in. The water was icy, and when she surfaced, she gasped with shock, then giggled, and began to swim, a fast front crawl. Soon she had acclimatised and began to enjoy racing up and down the length of the pool. After about a quarter of an hour, though, she was feeling chilled so she got out, towelled herself vigorously, then put on the dressing gown to go back to her room. The sun was higher now and the air was already warming. It was going to be another beautiful day. On her way back, she discovered that the Garden Café was open and several people were sitting in the sunshine eating breakfast. She collected two coffees and a plateful of croissants and took them up to room 315 where Joe was awake.

'Good morning, sleepy head. I've already done thirty lengths of the pool – and look, I've got us some breakfast. Why don't you join me on the terrace?'

'You think of everything,' he remarked, climbing out of bed and making for the bathroom.

A few minutes later he joined her. By now, it was past eight o'clock and the gardeners had appeared. They were starting to trim the lawns and weed the flowerbeds. They sat on the terrace while Joe outlined his plans for the day. 'I'm meeting my man at one o'clock at a bar in Elviria. It's a quiet town further along the coast. He's paranoid about anyone spotting him.'

'How long will you be gone?'

'That depends on how much he's prepared to tell me. It could take hours. On the other hand, it could be over in ten minutes.'

'It's not dangerous, is it?' she asked, grasping his hand

He laughed. 'Not at all. The guy just wants to live quietly down here. He's not going to do anything stupid.'

'So why is he talking to you at all?'

'He wants to settle some old scores. These people always have an agenda. He feels he got blamed for things he didn't do.'

'Please be careful,' she said. 'Will you be back in time for dinner?'

'I sincerely hope so. What will you do while I'm gone?'

'Don't worry about me. I'll entertain myself.'

***

Joe left at twelve thirty to drive the short distance to Elviria. Ellie took her book and went out onto the terrace to read. But she soon grew restless. She decided to see some more of the town. She got dressed in a pair of shorts, a light top and sandals and put a baseball cap on her head, then set off down the hill.

It was siesta time again and the streets were quiet, but when she reached the Paseo, she found the beaches packed with sunbathers. She continued along the promenade till she came to a little park. A few minutes later she was in the centre of Marbella.

She took out her tourist map and consulted it. She was in the Casco Historico, the medieval part of the town. She set off again and soon entered a maze of narrow little streets crammed with boutiques and jewellery shops. A few minutes later, she came across a beautiful little square lined with orange trees and restaurants. She took out her camera and shot some photos.

By now she was peckish. She decided to have something to eat but not too much because she would be dining later with Joe. She sat down at a pavement table and consulted the menu. When the waiter came she asked for a plate of paella and a glass of wine. It turned out to be a tasty dish of prawns, chicken, peppers and rice. She finished the meal, paid her bill and started back for the hotel.

Joe had not returned so she decided to ring her friends. She picked up the phone and found herself talking to Carmen on Reception. 'I'd like to place some calls to Dublin please.'

'Certainly, Señorita.'

She gave her the numbers and sat down on the bed to wait. Shortly afterwards, the phone gave a loud ring. She lifted it and heard Caroline's voice.

'It's me,' Ellie said. 'I'm calling to say we've arrived safely.'

'What a lovely surprise!' her friend exclaimed. 'What's the weather like? How's the hotel? Is the food okay?'

'One thing at a time!' Ellie laughed. 'The sun is shining, the hotel is magnificent and I've just come from a lovely restaurant in a beautiful little square where I had a delicious lunch of paella and salad, washed down with a cool glass of wine. All in all, things aren't looking too bad.'

'Say no more,' Caroline said. 'I'm having a terrible day. I'm taking a break from rehearsals. And they are *not* going well. If that's not bad enough, it's raining. Where's Joe?'

'He's off interviewing somebody. That's the reason we've come.'

'And those dashing Spanish *caballeros* haven't tried to steal you away while his back's turned?'

'All the Spaniards I've met have been perfect gentlemen, and that's more than I can say for some of the gougers I've met in Dublin.'

'I envy you,' Caroline continued. 'I suppose when you return you'll be sporting a beautiful suntan?'

'I certainly hope so.'

'Tell me about the hotel. Are you able to sleep? It's not full of noisy holidaymakers, is it?'

'I'm sorry to disappoint you, Caroline, but the guests at Hotel Majestic are not the type of people who get drunk on the front lawn and sing football songs all night.'

'Well, that's a relief.'

'I'm hoping to call Fiona and Mags but just in case I don't succeed would you tell them I send my love?'

'Of course. God, I feel like packing my suitcase and coming to join you at once, but the bell's ringing for us to resume rehearsals. I've got to get back on the treadmill. *Adios!*'

There was a click and the call ended. Soon after, the phone rang again. It was Carmen to say that the other numbers Ellie had requested were not answering.

'Thank you for your help,' Ellie said. 'Would you put that call on the bill, please?'

She stretched out on the bed and stared at the ceiling. Talking to Caroline had made her realise just how fortunate she was. She was in Spain with a wonderful man. She hadn't a care in the world. Outside, the sun was shining, while back in Dublin it was raining. A daring thought came into her head.

She got up and went into the bathroom. She stood under the shower while she shampooed her hair and thoroughly washed herself. Then she put on her prettiest underwear and a little knee-length dress, sprayed on some perfume and sat down on the bed to wait.

***

It was after six when Joe came back. He was in jolly form after the interview with his contact. 'What a session,' he said, taking a portable tape recorder from his pocket and placing it on the writing desk. 'My man sang like a canary. I've got enough information on that tape to write a dozen front-page stories.'

She patted the bed. 'Come and sit beside me, Joe.'

He gave a puzzled smile.

'Don't you want to hear about my interview?'

'Not now. It can wait.'

'What's this all about?' He laughed nervously.

She flung her arms around his neck and kissed him passionately. 'I want to make love. And when we've finished I want to do it all over again.'

He grinned as she began to undo his shirt buttons. 'Well, if you absolutely insist ...'

Chapter Seven

That evening, after Joe had written his story and phoned it across to the *Gazette* newsroom, he drove Ellie a few kilometres along the coast to the luxury marina of Puerto Banús. She was still floating on a cloud of euphoria. She couldn't remember a time when she had been so happy.

'Puerto Banús is the Costa's answer to Monte Carlo, although it's not so grand. It's been specially designed to draw wealthy people down here to spend their money.'

They parked on the outskirts of the port and he led her along the marina. It was thronged with tourists taking photographs of the magnificent yachts and cabin cruisers whose white hulls gleamed in the evening light. Then he showed her the shops, their windows crammed with designer handbags, big-brand clothes and jewellery.

As they passed the bars and cafés, Ellie saw they were packed with thin, elegant women and well-dressed men laughing and drinking. On the pavement, the tables were crowded with tourists watching the sun descend into the sea.

At last they came to a restaurant called El Marinero, which Joe said meant the Sailor in Spanish. As the name suggested, it specialised in seafood. 'I thought you might like to eat here,' he announced, 'so I've taken the liberty of reserving a table.'

Ellie glanced into the restaurant. It looked terribly posh. 'Are we dressed properly? It's not going to be snobby, is it?'

'Not in the least. Our money is as good as anyone else's. Besides, this is a special occasion. Now you can tell your friends that you had dinner at one of the best restaurants on the Costa del Sol.'

As soon as they entered, the head waiter swooped. Joe gave his name and said he had already booked. They were immediately shown to a table beside the window where they could watch the crowds of sightseers passing by.

They were offered drinks while they studied the extensive menu, but, again, Joe restricted himself to a single glass of wine. After some deliberation, Ellie chose asparagus salad with shrimps to start with, and baked sea bass as her main course. Joe went for grilled sardines and lobster.

'You've been here before, haven't you?' she said, after they had ordered.

'Once,' he confessed. 'Tonight I thought we should celebrate a bit. The editor is delighted with my story. It will be the lead in tomorrow's paper. He told me to go off and enjoy myself. Besides, I've been neglecting you and wanted to make it up.'

'Oh, you haven't neglected me,' she said. 'You mustn't think like that. I'm having a ball.'

'What did you do today?'

She told him how she had walked along the Paseo as far as the old part of Marbella and taken some photographs to show her friends when they returned.

'Meet any interesting men?' he joked.

'Plenty, but I only have eyes for you, Joe.'

He leaned across the table and placed a kiss on her cheek. 'That's good to know.'

***

Their meal was a huge success. The food was excellent and the service superb. It seemed that every time Ellie turned around a waiter was at her side, asking if there was anything more she required. They had eaten so well that they refused dessert and the offer of complimentary liqueurs.

Outside, the port was as busy as ever and the sound of laughter carried on the warm evening air. By now, the moon was out and a handful of stars studded the sky. They walked hand in hand back to the car, and soon they were turning into the drive at Hotel Majestic. The lights were on at the Garden Café and some people were drinking on the terrace. Joe suggested they have a nightcap before turning in. It was eleven o'clock and Ellie was tired. It had been a long day. They ordered brandy and sat in the warm night air listening to the cicadas chirping in the bushes.

As soon as they returned to their room, she got undressed and slipped between the cool sheets. Five minutes later, she was fast asleep.

***

Joe had finished his assignment and all of the next day was free so he suggested they travel along the coast to visit the little village of Mijas. Ellie had her morning swim and they ate breakfast together at the Garden Café. Then they set off.

It was another glorious day. They drove for half an hour

till they approached the resort of Fuengirola, then turned inland. The road rose steeply as they began to climb into the hills until, suddenly, they rounded a bend and entered a little village of narrow, winding streets. Joe pulled into the main square and stopped beside the bullring. 'We've arrived,' he announced.

Ellie got out and stood blinking in the sunlight. The square was dotted with little shops selling leather goods and souvenirs. A handful of grizzled old men were drinking coffee outside a café. Across the square, a bus was disgorging a gaggle of visitors with backpacks and tourist maps.

Joe and Ellie started along a cobbled street and soon found themselves in another square with an ancient fountain in the centre. Ellie got out her camera and took some more photographs. Then Joe guided her to a viewing platform where a group of excited tourists had already gathered.

When she looked down, she was met with a stunning panorama. The surrounding countryside was spread before her like a canvas: fields, hills, streams, little whitewashed houses. The view stretched unbroken to the edge of the sea. She took some more photographs and turned again to Joe. 'This is absolutely breathtaking.'

'I thought you'd like it.'

They wandered to the end of the village, then turned back. By now, the restaurants were filling so they decided to have a light lunch. They found a place that appealed to them in another little square, sat down and ordered crispy bread rolls stuffed with ham and cheese.

She took Joe's hand. 'Thanks for asking me to come with you. I can't remember when I've been so happy. I'm only sorry our trip is ending so soon.'

'We can always return, you know. There's nothing to stop us. Next time we'll stay longer.'

'Just tell me when and I'll talk to my boss. Mr Brady is a big fan of Marbella. He told me he came here on his honeymoon.'

'Really? I've just thought of a slogan – "Marbella, where love is in the air". The tourist board could use that in their publicity material. I won't even charge them for it.'

***

When they got back to their hotel, Ellie spent the remainder of the afternoon relaxing beside the pool while Joe sat in the shade turning the pages of a detective novel he had found in the lobby.

That evening, they ate at the hotel restaurant, where they were entertained to a floor show by a troupe of flamenco dancers with swirling skirts and clacking castanets. Afterwards, they had a farewell drink on the terrace of the Garden Café. Then it was straight to bed in anticipation of an early start in the morning.

As they nestled together in their bed, he drew her close and kissed her and soon they were making love again. When it was over, they lay curled in each other's arms.

'I've been thinking about our situation,' he whispered. 'I'm growing very fond of you, Ellie.'

She caught her breath. 'Did you mean what you said about Marbella and love?'

'Sure. There's something special here. I could feel it. Couldn't you?'

'Oh, yes,' she said, her heart skipping a beat. 'Definitely.'

***

They were up early to settle the bill and drive to the airport. Ellie was sad to leave. She had been happy in Marbella. But she was certain of one thing: she had fallen in love. What else could explain the wonderful feeling that had taken hold of her?

She knew she had met the man she had been searching for, the man she had sometimes doubted she would ever find. Joe Plunkett had all the qualities she desired in a life companion. He was someone she could respect and admire, a man with principles and standards. Above all, he was a man she could rely on. She wanted to spend the rest of her life with him.

Chapter Eight

They arrived in Dublin to a steady downpour of rain from dark, leaden skies. After reclaiming their luggage, they hurried to the car park, anxious to reach the sanctuary of Joe's car.

'Welcome home,' he muttered, as he fired the engine and the wipers swept vigorously across the windscreen.

Ellie thought of the sunshine they had swapped for this grey, miserable day. Marbella and Dublin were indeed two different worlds.

'Cheer up, Ellie. We'll be back again, you'll see.'

He dropped her at her workplace and promised to ring later in the afternoon. She left her luggage in her office, tidied her hair then went to report to Mr Brady.

His face brightened when he saw her. 'Ah, Ellie, so you're back safe and sound. Did you enjoy your trip? I want to hear all about it.'

She told him about the places they had visited, what they had done and seen, while he listened attentively. 'You seem to have packed quite a lot into such a short visit. And I needn't ask about the weather. I can see that you caught a lot of sunshine.'

'There was barely a cloud in the sky. And I took your advice. I didn't have any sangria.'

He laughed. 'You've put an idea into my head. I might take my wife back there. Our anniversary is coming up soon. It would be nice to see the place again.'

She had barely sat down at her desk when the phone rang and Mags was on the line, anxious to hear all about the trip. She was followed by Fiona and, finally, Caroline.

'I'd say you're disgusted, coming back to this bloody awful weather. What a downer for you. Still, you had the handsome Joe to entertain you for a whole weekend. I trust he behaved like a gentleman.'

'And how is a gentleman supposed to behave, may I ask?'

'I hope he didn't try to take advantage of you, an innocent country girl all on your own in a strange land.'

Ellie grinned, enjoying the banter with her friend. 'I'm afraid I'll have to leave you guessing there. So, how are the rehearsals coming along? You sound terribly busy.'

'I'm worked off my feet, if the truth be told.'

'But that's a good complaint, isn't it? I thought you actors liked to keep busy.'

'That all depends, darling. My last part was a chambermaid in a bedroom farce. I got to speak exactly three sentences. How am I ever going to break into films unless I get greater exposure? And the competition is fierce. You've no idea. These actresses are getting younger by the week. Some of them look like they've just stepped out of their school uniforms.' She paused. 'I'm really pleased for you, Ellie. It looks like your relationship is moving up a notch. I can hear the sound of wedding bells approaching. Joe's a lovely guy and so good-looking. I know a lot of hearts will be broken when you marry him.'

'What?' Ellie exclaimed. 'Who said anything about marriage?'

'Well, that's the next step, isn't it? It's plain to see that he's terribly interested in you. We'll have a drink soon and you can tell me all the gory details.'

Ellie and Caroline finished their conversation, Ellie smiling to herself. So her friends had noticed that her and Joe's relationship was becoming serious. Well, she was in love with Joe Plunkett and didn't mind who knew. Her thoughts were interrupted when the door opened and Mr Brady's secretary came in with more spreadsheets for her to analyse.

***

She worked steadily all day. In her absence, Mr Brady had drafted someone from the accounts department to fill in for her but it had been no more than a stop-gap and now she had a large backlog to get through. When Joe rang at half past five to invite her to dinner, she had to turn him down.

He sounded disappointed. 'I'll just have to make do with a takeaway, I suppose.'

'That's more than I'm likely to get. I probably won't finish till nine o'clock so I'm looking at scrambled eggs and toast. That's if Fiona remembered to get in some provisions.'

'It'll do you good,' he joked. 'You've been eating too much rich food recently.'

***

In the days that followed, Ellie's mind kept returning to her conversation with Caroline. She found herself thinking in unguarded moments about the wedding her friend had forecast. Who would be her bridesmaids? And what sort of dress would she wear? How many guests would there be?

She wondered how she should react when Joe proposed. Would he go down on one knee and take her hand? And what about the engagement ring? Would he have it in his pocket ready to slip on her finger? That would be very romantic. But she would really prefer if they could go shopping together so she could choose one she liked. That was all part of the fun.

When her thoughts wandered like this, she quickly reined them in. So far only Caroline had mentioned marriage, although she suspected that all her friends had talked about it. She thought it would be only a matter of time before Joe popped the question.

She recalled the conversation they'd had on their last night in Marbella when he'd told her he was growing fond of her. She remembered the trip to Puerto Banús and the romantic dinner they'd shared. She thought of them wrapped in each other's arms in room 315. Ellie could read the signs better than Caroline and her friends. But she also knew that some men were painfully slow when it came to proposing marriage. She had read about it in magazine articles. She had even heard stories of girls who had been forced to take the initiative and propose to their boyfriends themselves. But Joe had plenty of spirit. He'd get round to it eventually. She just had to be patient.

He continued to call every day but now he was busy writing stories from the interview he had done in Spain. So it wasn't till the end of the week that they managed to see each other again. He rang her on Friday morning as she was stepping out of the shower.

'How are you?'

'Fine!'

'Have you adapted to the Irish weather again?'

'No, Joe, that's going to take a bit longer.' She heard him laugh.

'I wanted to catch you early before you go into work. Can we have dinner tonight? I've got something important I want to discuss.'

Ellie's heart skipped a beat. This could be it, she thought. This could be when he proposes. 'Sure, tonight's fine.'

'I'll pick you up at your office at a quarter past six. Does that suit?'

'Perfect. I'm dying to see you.'

'The feeling's mutual. Don't work too hard.'

She put down the phone and stared out of the window at the street below. There had been a note of urgency in his voice. Something important, he had said. This was definitely what she'd been hoping for. What could be more important than asking her to marry him?

The conversation had given her renewed energy, and now she couldn't wait to see him. She worked solidly till six o'clock when she went to the Ladies to tidy her hair and apply some makeup, then set off to meet him. He was waiting in his car at the corner of the street. When she got in beside him, he took her in his arms and kissed her passionately. 'You look fantastic, Ellie. You're going to turn all their heads tonight.'

She giggled nervously. 'Don't exaggerate, Joe.'

'I'm not exaggerating. I'm speaking the truth. That break in Marbella has done you the power of good.'

'That's nice to know. Where are we going?'

'A restaurant called Louis's Bistro.'

'I don't think I've heard of it.'

'It's a new place in Rathmines, not long opened. I've got a personal invitation from the owner, Louis Kilbride. It's been attracting some very good reviews.'

'And Mr Kilbride is hoping he'll get some more publicity if you turn up?'

'Probably.'

'Well, I hope he hasn't alerted your newspaper colleagues that we're coming. I don't want to read about it in Maggie McConkey's column in the *Courier*.'

He smiled sheepishly. 'Just relax. I think you'll enjoy it.'

***

Louis's Bistro was located at the corner of Leinster Road and Rathmines Road. It had a striped canopy above the front door and potted plants outside. Otherwise there was little to distinguish it from the many similar establishments in the area.

Joe parked in a nearby street and they walked the short distance to the restaurant. He had called in advance so the staff were waiting when they arrived and immediately shepherded them to a quiet table at the back, gave them menus and asked what they would like to drink.

The restaurant was small and cosy with about twenty tables, half of which were already occupied. It was simply furnished with subdued lighting and framed posters for absinthe and exotic French liqueurs decorating the walls. At once she felt comfortable.

The waiter returned with their drinks, which they sipped while they studied the menus. There was a good range of fish, meat and poultry dishes. Ellie had skipped lunch and now she was ravenous. She decided to have lobster bisque to start, then chicken cooked in wine with herbs. Joe ordered a hefty salad, then cassoulet.

They had just started to eat when a polite voice caused them to look up. A plump, dark-haired man in a chef's apron was beaming down at them. 'Hi, I'm delighted to see you, guys,' he said, and smiled at Ellie.

Joe put down his cutlery and introduced the proprietor, Louis Kilbride. He gave Ellie a warm handshake, then turned again to Joe. 'I'm pleased you could make it.'

'You're getting very good notices,' Joe replied. 'I thought we'd pop along and see what the fuss was all about.'

'Let's hope after tonight's dinner you'll understand.' He gave a small bow. 'I'm pleased to have made your acquaintance, Ms McCoy. If there's anything you need, please let your waiter know. Enjoy your meal.'

'You didn't say he was the chef,' Ellie said, when he was out of earshot. 'I thought he was the boss and somebody else did the cooking.'

'He does both. I'm sure it doesn't help his stress levels but at least he can't blame anyone if it doesn't work. And if it turns out to be a roaring success, he'll take all the credit.'

'And which is it going to be?'

Joe speared a forkful of salad. 'I'll tell you when we've finished eating. But on the evidence so far, the signs are good.'

They were pleased with their first courses. Moments after they had finished, their empty plates were whisked away and, soon after, their main dishes arrived.

The service certainly can't be faulted, Ellie thought. When she glanced around, she saw that most of the tables were now occupied and it wasn't yet eight o'clock. Another good sign that would make Louis Kilbride happy. 'So you had another busy day?' she asked.

'You can say that again. I have enough material from my Spanish interview to produce exclusive front-page reports for most of next week. The editor is delighted, of course, and our rivals are scratching their heads, trying to figure out where the hell I'm getting this stuff.' Joe made it sound like a competition between kids in the school playground.

'So the paper's investment in our Marbella trip is paying dividends?'

'Definitely.'

'You should ask them to send you again.'

'I might just do that. But let's wait and see how things develop. Sometimes stories like this flush out other informants who want to spill the beans too. So we get a bonus.'

They finished eating and Joe announced his verdict. The food was superb and so was the service. He predicted a bright future for Louis's Bistro. Ellie declined the offer of dessert but Joe ordered Tarte Tatin. Instead of liqueurs, they had coffee.

As the meal progressed, Ellie had grown increasingly anxious for Joe to reveal the important matter he wanted to discuss. But she was determined to resist the temptation to enquire. When he asked her to marry him, she wanted to appear surprised. So she waited patiently till the coffee had arrived.

Then he cleared his throat. 'I've been reflecting on our trip,' he said. 'Now, I appreciate that we were only down there for a few days but I think the whole thing went very well, don't you?'

'I've already told you, Joe, I had a wonderful time.'

'We never once had an argument or even a disagreement.'

'Of course not! Why should we argue when we were both enjoying ourselves so much?'

'Well, you might be surprised to learn, Ellie, that lots of couples have rows on holidays. It can be a very stressful time. People are forced into close proximity with each other and it can cause friction. But it didn't happen with us.'

'Joe, you know we get on well together. I don't think we've had one serious dispute in the fourteen months we've been going out.'

'That's what I'm coming to. We've proved we can do it, Ellie.'

This is it, she thought. Now he's going to ask me. She tried her best to remain cool. 'Do what, Joe?'

'Live together. What would you say to leaving your flat in Blackrock and moving in with me in Monkstown?'

Chapter Nine

She stared at him and felt the blood drain from her face. She couldn't believe what she'd just heard. Instead of asking her to marry him, he wanted her to live with him. That wasn't what she had been expecting at all.

She tried to hide her disappointment. She wished she could get up from the table and flee to the Ladies where she could figure out her response. But she couldn't escape. Joe was smiling at her, clearly oblivious to the turmoil raging inside her head.

'So what do you say, Ellie? I've got buckets of room and we'll be able to share all our free time. It will be just like getting married.'

Except it won't, she thought bitterly. If you want to marry me, why don't you say so? She struggled to remain calm. She mustn't do or say anything that would let him know how she really felt, at least till she had time to consider what to do. 'This is a shock,' she said. 'I had no idea.'

'I know. But it only occurred to me after we got back from Spain. I'm surprised I didn't think of it sooner. So will you agree?'

She bit her lip. She felt trapped. There was no easy way to do this. 'I can't, Joe. I need time to consider.'

His face fell. 'But what is there to consider? It's fairly straightforward. You just pack up your stuff and move in with me.'

'Well, there's Fiona, for one thing. I can't just walk out on her after the last few years. Then there are all the people I have to alert to the change of address.' She knew her excuses sounded feeble but he had caught her completely off guard. 'I wish you'd given me a hint, Joe.'

He drained his coffee cup and put it back firmly in the saucer. 'I thought you'd be pleased, Ellie. I've never done this before, you know. You're the only woman I've ever asked.'

She had hurt his feelings. But she had been disappointed too. She reached out and took his hand. 'Let me have a week and then I'll give you my reply.'

'It's not me, is it?' he asked.

'How do you mean?'

'You do care about me, don't you?'

'Of course I do. Why do you think I continue to see you?'

That seemed to mollify him. He waved his hand and the waiter came hurrying with the bill. When they got outside, it was raining again and they had to splash through the puddles to the car. Fifteen minutes later, he was depositing her outside the flat in Blackrock. He drew her close and kissed her before pushing open the door. 'I'm holding you to your promise, Ellie. I'll expect your decision within a week.'

***

When she got into the flat, Fiona had gone to bed so she had a quick shower and went to her own room. But she couldn't sleep. Joe's shock announcement kept washing backwards and forwards inside her head, like a piece of flotsam caught in the tide.

One thought crystallised in her mind. If he wanted her so much, why didn't he ask her to marry him? That was what most men would do. Instead, he had offered this halfway house. There could only be one explanation and it cut her to the quick. Despite his declarations of affection and the fancy meals, Joe wasn't sure that he loved her. This thought hurt her so deeply that it was hours before she drifted off to sleep.

The following morning when she came down to the kitchen, she found Fiona sitting at the table drinking coffee. 'What's the matter?' her friend asked. 'You look like you've been awake half the night.'

'So I have,' Ellie replied. She felt an overpowering need to talk, to pour out her heart to her friend. And she knew that Fiona would be calm and receptive. 'I had a strange proposal from Joe last night.'

'Strange in what way?'

'He asked me to go and live with him.'

'Really? And how did you respond?'

'I told him I needed time. He caught me unawares and there are so many things I have to think about. You, for instance. What would you do if I left?'

Fiona waved her hand vaguely. 'Oh, don't worry about me. I'd miss you, of course, but I'd have no problem finding a replacement. Caroline's been dying to move in here. Is that all that bothers you?'

'No.'

'Are you worried what people might say if you lived with

him? It's not unusual, you know. Lots of couples are doing it.'

'I don't care about people.'

'So what is it?'

Ellie took a deep breath. 'If Joe really loves me, why didn't he ask me to marry him?'

Fiona was silent for a moment. Then she said, 'I'm afraid only Joe can answer that. You've been seeing him for over a year, haven't you?'

'Fourteen months.'

'That's certainly enough time for him to know his mind. Look, Ellie, I'm not qualified to give advice on something like this but one thing I have learned. Making major decisions in the heat of the moment is not a good idea. You did the right thing by asking for time. I suggest you talk this over with him. Ask him straight out why he won't marry you. There might be some perfectly valid reason.'

'Like what? He's already *got* a wife somewhere?'

'That wasn't what I meant.'

'So what could be holding him back?'

Fiona shrugged. 'I don't know.'

***

She felt better after she'd talked to her friend. She had a quick breakfast and set off for work. Now that she had decided to have it out with Joe, she would waste no time.

But before she got the opportunity to call him, he surprised her. She had barely settled at her desk when the phone rang. She picked it up and heard his voice. He sounded cautious.

'Hi,' he said. 'How are you this morning?'

'I'm fine.'

'Look, I've been thinking about last night. I handled things badly and I want to apologise. Is there any chance we could meet again so I can set the record straight?'

'Of course. When?'

'Today. We can grab a quick lunch somewhere. I know a quiet spot. It won't take long. Can you get away?'

'Sure.'

'Good. I'll pick you up at one o'clock.'

He'd sounded relieved as he ended the call. Something's happened, Ellie thought.

***

Joe was waiting in his car when she left the office and they drove the short distance to the Jackson Hotel in Merrion Square. It radiated old-fashioned comfort and style. He led her into the lounge. It was almost empty and they found a quiet table in a corner beside the window. When the waitress came, they ordered the bar lunch.

Joe waited till the waitress had gone, then said, 'About last night, I'm sorry if I sounded abrupt. I didn't prepare properly. You probably felt like you'd been ambushed.'

She let him continue. There was a lot at stake in this conversation. She loved Joe and didn't want to lose him, but she was determined not to live with him unless she was sure that he loved her too.

'The truth is I've been thinking about our situation for some time,' he went on. 'And I've come to realise that you matter an awful lot to me, more than any other woman I've ever known. The trip to Spain brought matters to a head. I just thought it would be a natural step if we lived together.'

Ellie couldn't restrain herself any further. 'Does that mean that you love me?'

'Of course I love you.'

'Then why didn't you ask me to marry you?'

'Because I was afraid you might turn me down.'

'Really?'

'Yes. Remember shortly after we met and I had to rush off to Liverpool? I told you that life with me would be unpredictable. I don't work regular hours. I'm always on call. I can't guarantee to be home for dinner every evening. I can't forecast what I'll be doing at the weekend. That's an awful lot of uncertainty and disruption to expect a wife to take on board.'

'Is that the only reason?'

'Of course.'

'So why don't you try me?'

He stared at her in amazement. 'Are you serious?'

'I've never been more serious in my life.'

He glanced around, then got down on one knee and took her hand. 'Will you marry me, Ellie?'

She was so lightheaded with relief that she felt like shouting her response all over the lounge. 'Oh, Joe, I'd marry you in the morning.'

Just then they heard a polite cough. The startled waitress was standing beside them with their food.

Chapter Ten

Of course Ellie didn't marry Joe in the morning. It took a bit longer than that. The following weekend, he brought her to a jeweller on Grafton Street and invited her to choose an engagement ring. She looked at the trays the assistant placed before her, dazzled by the glittering array he was offering.

'Pick one you really like,' Joe urged. 'Don't worry about the price. This isn't something we do every day of the week.'

It took her a while to decide – they were all beautiful – but in the end she chose a large diamond, with two smaller stones, set in gold.

'Is that the one you want?' Joe asked.

She slipped it onto her finger and stretched out her hand to admire it. It sparkled in the light. 'Yes, please.'

'We'll have it,' he said to the jeweller, and took out his chequebook.

***

Her friends couldn't wait to see the ring. Ellie was the first of the quartet to get engaged and they were very excited.

She organised a little celebration party for them in a pub in Blackrock.

'It's beautiful.' Mags sighed. 'Oh, how I envy you.'

'So I was right,' Caroline said, triumphant. 'I predicted when you returned from Marbella that it wouldn't be long before we'd hear wedding bells. It was plain to me that Joe was going to propose.'

Ellie exchanged a glance with Fiona. 'You missed your true vocation, Caroline,' she joked. 'You should have been a fortune-teller.'

They all laughed.

'And there's a bonus for me,' Caroline continued. 'I've spoken to Fiona and she's agreed to let me have your room when you leave.'

'That calls for another round of drinks,' Ellie said.

***

Choosing the ring was only the start. There was another major bridge to cross. Ellie had to introduce Joe to her family, and so far they didn't even know of his existence. She had kept her relationship secret for fear that it might fizzle out and then everyone would feel sorry for her.

She decided to do it immediately. By now Mr Brady and everyone in the office had been told the good news. It would be a disaster if her family discovered by the bush telegraph. She chose the following weekend but first she had to call them to let them know.

Her mother answered the phone.

'Hi, Mum,' Ellie said, in her best chirpy voice. 'I'm ringing to tell you my good news.'

'You've won the lottery?'

'No, it's better than that. I've got engaged.'

'Mother of God!' her mother exclaimed.

There was one decent hotel in her home town, the Ballymount Arms. Joe booked a single room and on Saturday morning they drove down in his car. When they arrived at her parents' house, they found it packed with aunts, uncles and neighbours, anxious to get a look at Ellie's fiancé.

Joe had had his hair cut and was wearing his best suit, with a white handkerchief peeping out of the breast pocket. Ellie thought he looked quite dashing. So did the rest of the McCoys, particularly Ellie's younger sister Aine who, at twenty-two, had developed a keen interest in such matters.

After Joe had been introduced and everyone had shaken his hand, Mrs McCoy announced that a buffet lunch was waiting in the dining room. Mr McCoy uncapped a bottle of whiskey, filled their glasses and proposed a toast. Then someone produced an accordion and the singing started. Ellie stole a glance at her mother and saw her wipe a tear away with her apron.

It was after midnight when Joe eventually got away to his room at the Ballymount Arms while Ellie shared a bed with Aine in the family home. The following day, after breakfast, they drove back to Dublin.

**

Now the planning for the wedding began in earnest. There was no doubt who Ellie's bridesmaids would be. Mags, Caroline and Fiona were the first friends she had made when she came to Dublin. And she couldn't pass over her sisters, Aine and Ciara, who seemed to be as excited about the wedding as Ellie. They would be bridesmaids too. Joe asked his brother Eddie to be best man, and three newspaper colleagues, Jim Enright, Paul Delaney and Pat Duggan, to be his groomsmen.

Ellie's parish church was to be the venue, so they had to talk to the priest and fill in various forms to say they had never been married before and were duly baptised. Then there was the selection of wedding guests. This threatened to be the most difficult of all. Joe knew so many people and so did Ellie's family: there was the danger that someone would be left off the list and they would have made an enemy for life. By the time the first count was completed, the list had grown to almost two hundred.

By tradition, the bride's father was expected to pay the wedding costs, which were already looking exorbitant. After thinking about it for a whole week, Joe took Ellie aside. 'This is starting to get out of hand. It's going to cost a fortune. I can't expect your dad to pick up the bill for my wedding.'

'Maybe we could cut the list a bit more.'

'I don't think so. It's been pared back already. Besides, I want to do this properly. But I have another suggestion. What if I offer to split the costs with your father? It's only fair. If I'm not mistaken, it's only a matter of time before your sisters will be getting married too. At this rate, your dad will be in the bankruptcy court.'

'Let me have a quiet word with him,' Ellie said.

After some huffing and puffing, Ellie's father was persuaded to accept Joe's offer. Then Ellie bent her mind to the pressing matter of the ceremony. She had never realised the amount of planning that went into such an event. The wedding was scheduled for the second week in September so, after agreeing the date with the priest, she had to book a venue for the reception, which, given that it was the only decent hotel in the area, meant the Ballymount Arms.

But when she spoke to the manager, she got a shock: he had to tell her that another event was already scheduled for the same day. So she had to go back to the priest and ask if they could bring their wedding forward by a week. Luckily, he was a good-natured man, who saw the humorous side of the situation.

'Are you sure the hotel is free for that date?' he asked.

'Oh, yes, I've already checked.'

'That's good. I'm glad you've got your priorities right,' he replied.

Now that the church and the reception had been booked, Ellie had to turn her attention to the dresses for herself and her attendants. At least this part was enjoyable and she had the support of her friends, who went shopping with her and helped her decide. Then there were the myriad issues such as the wedding cake, the cars to transport the bride and her party to the church, a photographer to record the event, someone to sing at the service, the church organist, flowers, the menu for the wedding lunch and a band to play at the reception.

By now the guest list had been finalised. After some judicious pruning, they had managed to get it down to a hundred and seventy, which Mrs McCoy swore was the fewest they could invite unless they wanted people to stop talking to them. Now they faced the task of getting all the invitations delivered and the replies collated so they could give the hotel an accurate number.

Most of this burden fell on Ellie and her family but there were two more tasks, which inevitably involved Joe. One was the choice of a wedding ring. They returned to the shop where they had purchased the engagement ring just a couple of months before. This time Ellie knew exactly what she wanted – a plain gold band. Ten minutes later she had made her selection and Joe had the ring safely tucked away in his inside coat pocket.

Now there was only one thing left – the destination for the honeymoon. But Ellie had been thinking about this quite a lot and had already made up her mind.

'So where do you want to go?' he asked.

'There's only one place it can be.'

'Where?'

'Don't you know?' she teased. 'Shall I give you a couple of clues? Sunshine, flowers, flamenco dancers?'

'Let me guess. Does its name begin with M?'

'The talents you possess. Now you're a mind-reader.' She laughed. '"Marbella – where love is in the air". You coined that slogan, remember?'

***

It was impossible to keep the wedding a secret for long. All Ellie's colleagues and friends knew, as did most of the town of Ballymount. The same applied to Joe and his pals in the media. So, just when Ellie thought that everything was finally under control and nothing could go wrong, he rang to tell her that the gossip columnist, Maggie McConkey, was running a piece in the *Courier*.

She rushed from her office to the corner deli to pick up a copy then quickly flicked to page seven. There, below a grinning photo of the columnist, she read:

HEARTTHROB JOE TO TIE THE KNOT

A little bird tells me that hunky Joe Plunkett, one of Dublin's most eligible bachelors, has agreed to walk down the aisle with his long-time companion, Ellie McCoy.

Joe, one of the city's most successful newshounds, is to wed McCoy, an economic guru who works in the financial sector, in a lavish ceremony in her home town of Ballymount.

Friends tell me that sexy Joe fell head-over-heels for the dark-haired stunner when they met at a theatrical party. Since then they have been inseparable. They plan to honeymoon in Las Vegas.

Ellie gasped. The nerve of the McConkey woman! This was the second time she had intruded into her personal life. Ellie had never courted publicity and didn't welcome it. As far as she was concerned, her private life was just that – private. What was more, Ms McConkey hadn't even checked her facts. Ellie hadn't met Joe at a theatrical party and the honeymoon wasn't scheduled for Las Vegas. Where did the woman get this stuff?

She was so enraged that she rang Joe immediately. 'I've read that report and I'm fuming. Is there anything we can do to stop this nonsense?'

'Not a lot,' he admitted.

'She can't even get a few simple facts right. How did she get into journalism in the first place?'

'Calm down, nobody takes her seriously. It's just a bit of fun.'

'Fun? She's telling her readers we're going to Las Vegas for our honeymoon. And all this hunky Joe and dark-haired stunner stuff. Is there some way we can get them to print a correction or an apology?'

'I wouldn't waste my breath trying. Look, the best thing is to ignore it, pretend you didn't see it. If I'd known you were going to get upset I wouldn't have told you.'

'I would have found out anyway. Someone would have made sure to let me know.' Another thought occurred. 'She's not going to turn up at our wedding, is she? Maybe bring a photographer with her.'

'I hadn't thought of that,' Joe admitted.

'If she does, I swear to God, I'll have her arrested,' Ellie snarled.

***

By now, the honeymoon had been booked – two weeks at Hotel Majestic, Marbella, and the air tickets had been paid for. Ellie sat down with Fiona, who was very disciplined and organised, and together they ticked off the remaining items on her list: the dresses, the lunch menu, the cars, the band, the photographer, the cake, the flowers. Everything appeared to be in order.

'You must be exhausted,' Fiona said.

'I am. When this is all over I'm going to sleep for a week.'

'On your honeymoon? Have you told Joe? I'm not sure he'll be too pleased.' Fiona laughed.

'I'm joking, of course. I'm deliriously happy. But I'll be glad when it's all over.'

'I'm going to miss you. The flat won't be the same without you.'

'But you'll have Caroline to replace me. She'll certainly bring a bit of drama with her. Besides, I won't be far away and we'll always keep in touch.' She paused. 'I've just had an idea. First thing I must do when I get back from Marbella is organise a dinner party for you guys. You should see the magnificent kitchen Joe has. It's time I started putting it to good use.'

With everything under control, there was now a brief pause when Ellie was able to draw her breath. But in the middle of August, it all took off again. There were rehearsals for the wedding ceremony, final fittings for the dresses, a last check on the menu and the cake, then the hen party.

Fiona and Mags had arranged a weekend trip to Galway for Ellie's friends and colleagues, where they ended up in a nightclub and ran into a bunch of rugby players out on the town. It turned into a very late night, and by the time they returned to Dublin, Ellie was still slightly hung-over.

***

At last the big day arrived. Ellie and her bridesmaids had spent the night in her parents' house while Joe and his party stayed at the Ballymount Arms. The ceremony was scheduled for two o'clock, and Ellie was up at eight. After a quick breakfast, the dressmaker came to make last-minute adjustments to the outfits. She had barely gone when the hairdresser arrived.

Meanwhile the house was in a constant state of flux, with visitors and well-wishers. The flowers were stacked in the hall and the dining-room table was festooned with cards and telegrams. At half past one, Joe phoned from the hotel, to say his party was ready and about to depart.

The tension mounted. First Mrs McCoy and the bridesmaids left for the church. There was a short gap and then the car arrived for Ellie and her father. When she stepped outside the front door, the sun was shining. A handful of well-wishers cheered and the official photographer came forward to take some pictures. Then they were off for the short drive to the church.

When they arrived, they found it was packed with wedding guests – family friends, work colleagues, old neighbours and former schoolmates. Ellie felt a lump rise in her throat as the organist started to play the *Bridal Chorus* and she began the slow progress down the aisle on her father's arm to where Joe was waiting.

As she approached, he stepped forward and took her hand. Mr McCoy slipped into his seat in the first pew. As he looked into her eyes, Joe whispered, 'Love of my life, now and for ever.'

Chapter Eleven

After all the fuss with the wedding preparations, Ellie was desperate to get down to Marbella once more to begin their honeymoon – just Joe and herself on their own for a whole fortnight with nothing to disturb them. As a precaution, she had made him swear not to divulge their location to anyone at the *Gazette*. They were incommunicado, which was exactly how she liked it.

She soon discovered that the weather in September was much hotter than it had been in May. Each afternoon a languid heat settled over the town, forcing people to head for the beach or the coolness of the shade. Otherwise everything was exactly as she remembered it: the stillness of the early morning, the dawn chorus of birds, the dew on the grass, the clear blue skies, the sparkling sea, the flowers ...

They quickly settled into a routine. Ellie usually rose about seven o'clock and went down to the pool, leaving Joe to sleep on. She swam for twenty minutes, then picked up croissants and coffee from the Garden Café on her way back.

They would eat breakfast on the terrace while they planned their day.

Mostly, the mornings were devoted to sunbathing and the afternoons spent reading and relaxing or making love in the big double bed. Some days they ordered a light lunch from room service, on others they ventured as far as a little bar just outside the hotel, which served delicious tapas and glasses of cool white wine.

Joe had hired a car so in the evenings when the temperature began to fall, they escaped into the hills where they ate wonderful meals in quiet little restaurants: lamb roasted on a spit or grilled lobster and prawns fresh from the sea, with ripe figs and mangoes for dessert. Afterwards, they would sip their coffee while they gazed along the coastline as far as Gibraltar and watched the sun sink like a ball of fire into the sea.

They made a couple of longer trips, setting off in the early morning for Ronda and Granada where they viewed the Alhambra Palace and the stunning Moorish architecture. On another occasion, they passed a pleasant day in Seville, visiting the magnificent cathedral and other attractions before spending the night in a comfortable pension and travelling back to Marbella the following morning.

But even on his honeymoon, Joe was restless for news. The hotel shop sold English papers, flown in especially for the tourists. They usually arrived about noon and he fell into the habit of going down each day and buying the *Mail* and the *Telegraph* and devouring them on the terrace while Ellie read her novel.

'You're like a drug addict with withdrawal symptoms,' she chided. 'You have to get your news fix every day, don't you?'

He held up his hands and laughed. 'Guilty, Your Honour,

but in my defence I must plead the necessity to know what is going on in the world so that when I return to work I don't look like an absolute idiot.'

She didn't mind that he read the papers from cover to cover. She had him all to herself and that was what mattered.

***

The days merged gracefully into each other, all bright skies and sunshine with rarely a cloud. It felt liberating to relax without clanging alarm clocks or ringing phones to distract them. Ellie called home to talk to their friends and families and posted some cards with pictures of whitewashed villages and sun-drenched beaches. But otherwise they spent the entire time wrapped in each other's company.

She felt totally content. Any doubts she had about living with Joe had long since vanished. She adored him and knew her love was reciprocated. He was an easy-going husband: attentive and caring. And he was a wonderful lover. She had only to fall into his arms and curl close to him to feel herself melt with desire.

After the first week was over, the days seemed to pass more quickly until suddenly their departure date was looming. On their last evening, Joe suggested they should go somewhere special for dinner.

'Have you got anywhere in mind?'

'Why don't you decide?'

'I know,' she said. 'Why don't we go back to that little restaurant where we had that wonderful meal the first time we came here? You remember, down on the Paseo?'

'You mean the place with the patio?'

'That's right. The food was good and it'll be a pleasant walk.'

'All right,' Joe replied. 'But I suggest we go early before it fills up.'

That evening, they were dressed and ready to leave at six o'clock. It was still warm and Ellie had put on a light dress and sandals. Joe was wearing chinos and a golf shirt. They set off through the narrow streets till the sound of laughter and music drew them closer to the Paseo.

They found it packed, as before, with crowds of tourists, and hucksters trying to sell cheap jewellery and souvenirs to them. At last they came to the place they were looking for. And they were in luck. There were several free tables, including one near the trellis where they had sat the last time they were there.

They went in and sat down. Ellie glanced around. Nothing had changed, right down to the candle flickering in its bowl. They had scarcely arrived when the young dark-haired waiter was at their side to present them with menus.

'*Buenas tardes, Señor, Señora.* May I bring you something to drink?'

They ordered beer. A few seconds later the waiter was back with a bowl of olives and a basket of bread. He eagerly pointed out the special dishes of the day. They chose fish – sole for Ellie and grilled prawns for Joe – and ordered a bottle of white wine to go with it.

She sat back and breathed in the heady scent of the flowers cascading from the trellis. Joe placed his hand on hers. 'Our last night,' he said. 'The time has flown. Are you sad to be leaving?'

'A little. I'll always have happy memories of Marbella. But I'm also excited to be starting our new life together.'

'Me too,' he said, with a twinkle in his eye. 'It's going to be an adventure.'

The meal proceeded at a leisurely pace. The fish arrived and was as good as the waiter had promised. Outside on the Paseo, a queue was forming as people waited for a table to become available.

They finished with coffee and Joe called for the bill. When the waiter brought it, Ellie asked his name.

'Francisco,' he said.

'You speak very good English.'

His face lit up. 'Just a little,' he protested modestly.

'No, you speak very well. Do you work in the restaurant all the time, Francisco?'

He shook his head. 'Only in the summer. I am training to be a teacher.'

'Do you live here in Marbella?'

'Yes, and you?'

'We live in Dublin.'

'Ah, Irlanda. It is beautiful there. I have seen photographs. Everything is so green.'

Ellie laughed. 'And cold and damp. Don't believe everything you see in photographs. We've had a lovely meal, Francisco. *Muchas gracias.*'

He bowed, took the money and fumbled in his pocket for change.

'The change is for you,' Ellie said. 'For the good service.'

He thanked her, took a card from his shirt pocket and pressed it into her hand. It bore the name of the restaurant and a phone number. 'So you can tell your friends,' he explained. 'Do you have a card also? I collect them. It is my hobby.'

Ellie fished in her bag and gave him one of her business cards.

'What a nice young man,' she said, as she linked Joe's arm and they started back along the Paseo.

They had gone only a few paces when she heard Francisco's voice again. They turned to find him hurrying after them with a single long-stemmed rose. When he caught up with them, he pressed it into her hand. She looked into his dark brown eyes and handsome face. 'That's very kind, Francisco.'

He gave a little bow. 'Only for a special lady. *Adios*, till we meet again.'

'What a lovely gesture,' she remarked to Joe, as they continued their walk. 'Who said the age of chivalry is dead? Not down here it isn't.'

***

The next morning, they were up at eight o'clock, packed their cases and, after a quick breakfast, drove to Málaga airport to catch the eleven o'clock flight to Dublin. As she watched the Spanish coastline disappear, Ellie gave a little sigh. In the years ahead, she would always look back on her honeymoon as one of the happiest times in her life.

Chapter Twelve

Once she got back, Ellie was anxious to put her stamp on Joe's apartment and turn it into their new home. Not that there was very much to do. Until she had come on the scene, it appeared that he had done little more than sleep there. The apartment was spanking new and a professional designer had decorated and furnished it.

But there were certain improvements she was keen to introduce. She proceeded to buy some additional furniture for the living room, a new carpet for the bedroom and some modern paintings for the walls. This was all accomplished within a fortnight of their return. Then she turned her attention to the next item on her agenda: housetraining her husband. This would not be as easy as buying new furniture.

Ellie had spent the last six years living with Fiona, who had been the perfect flatmate: quiet, tidy and considerate. She always left the kitchen sparkling clean, the cooking utensils scrubbed, the floor swept and everything put away in its proper place. It was the same with the bathroom and the other shared spaces.

Joe had been living a solitary bachelor existence without female oversight for most of his adult life. As a result, he had developed some bad habits. She bridled at his tendency to leave discarded clothes on the bedroom floor and teacups unwashed in the kitchen sink, not to mention keeping the bathroom windows closed when he took a shower so that all the surfaces were covered with steam. These were small things but they began to get on her nerves.

She realised that she would have to go about changing his ways with tact and diplomacy. The situation was fraught with difficulties and could easily blow up into an argument if she didn't take care.

She began by scolding him gently whenever he did something she didn't approve of. Matters improved for a while but he quickly slipped back into his bad habits. After repeated attempts, she decided it was time for a serious talk. One evening, she raised the subject. 'Joe, I don't want to be a nuisance but I think we need to draw up some house rules and stick to them.'

He was sitting in an easy chair, turning over the pages of the evening paper. 'House rules?'

'Those clean shirts in your wardrobe. How do you think they got there? Do you think they did it by themselves?'

He put down the paper and stared at her. 'I'm afraid you've lost me, Ellie. What on earth are you talking about?'

'I picked those shirts up from the bedroom floor where you had left them and I put them in the laundry basket for washing. But I shouldn't have to do that. I don't expect you to go around picking up *my* clothes.'

'But *you* don't leave your stuff lying around.'

'Exactly,' she said, with emphasis. 'And neither should you. The same applies to glasses, cups and plates. When you lived on your own, you could do as you pleased, but now there are two of us and we have to introduce some rules. For one thing, it's not very hygienic.' By now, she had his full attention. 'The bathroom is another example. Why don't you open the window when you take a shower so that the steam can escape instead of fogging up the mirror and condensing on all the cold surfaces?'

'There's an air vent. It's supposed to take care of the steam.'

'Well, it clearly isn't working very well. The last time you came out of the bathroom it was like a scene from the Jack the Ripper movie. I couldn't see the wall for the fog.'

'Okay, I hear you.'

'And please don't leave the hot water running. It's like burning pound notes. Have you seen the electricity bill recently?'

He put the paper down, a little too sharply, she thought, before she had a chance to mention some other matters that were irritating her.

'All right, I get the message. Can we change the subject, please?'

She decided to let it rest. She could always return to it another day.

The next thing was to utilise Joe's magnificent cooking facilities. He had one of the finest kitchens in south Dublin and all he used it for was making breakfast. The cupboards were practically bare, except for basic breakfast provisions. The first weekend they were home, she insisted on cooking Sunday lunch.

'There's no need,' he protested. 'The Grove Hotel does an excellent carvery lunch. And there's no washing up afterwards.'

'And they provide it for nothing?'

'Don't be ridiculous. There's a charge but it's modest. And I usually put it on my expenses.'

She gave a deep sigh. She could see she was going to have another battle on her hands but this was one she was determined not to lose. 'Joe, this isn't simply about convenience or cost. This apartment is our home and one of the joys of a home is cooking meals.'

'I'm thinking of *you*,' he said. 'I don't like the idea of my wife slaving over a hot stove.'

'But you can help me. It's fun, Joe, not a chore. Once you get started, I'm sure you'll enjoy it. Now why don't you let me cook you Sunday lunch?'

He shrugged. 'Okay, if you insist. We'll give it a go.'

There was a large supermarket in Blackrock. On Saturday morning after breakfast, Joe drove her there and waited in the car while she went shopping. She went first to the butchery department and selected a nice leg of lamb, then potatoes, onions, carrots, peppers and broccoli, a chocolate cake and a selection from the salad bar.

She finished by visiting the wine department and selecting half a dozen bottles of claret and Chablis. Joe helped her put it all into the boot and they drove back to Monkstown.

On Sunday morning he helped her prepare. The lamb went into the oven first. Then they chopped the vegetables and she began to set the table. 'You don't have any candles, do you?'

'Whatever for?'

'The table. Candles lend a touch of style to a meal.'

'You're out of luck.'

'I don't suppose you have a tablecloth either.'

'Afraid not.'

Among the wedding presents they had received, there was a set of table linen. Ellie took it out and spread the cloth on the table. 'Now,' she said, 'doesn't that look better?'

'I suppose so,' he admitted.

They sat down to eat at half past one, after Joe had listened to the radio news. She watched nervously as he sliced into his lamb and put a forkful in his mouth.

'Umm,' he said. 'Not bad. Not bad at all. In fact, it's very good.' He proceeded to eat all the food on his plate, and then they had coffee and cake. When the meal was finished, he gave a satisfied sigh. 'That was marvellous. You're a woman with hidden skills, Ellie. I'm going to enjoy exploring them.'

She smiled sweetly. 'Me too.'

***

She had promised Fiona that as soon as she got back from her honeymoon she would have the girls round for dinner so they could see the apartment. But Caroline was appearing in a successful play at the Gaiety and it was several weeks before they found an evening that suited everybody. Finally they settled on the second Saturday in November.

She had a word with Joe and told him of her plan. 'You're welcome to join us, if you want. But somehow I don't think you'd enjoy spending a whole evening with four women.'

'Oh, I don't know about that,' he joked. 'I quite enjoy female company. But you'd prefer if I was out of the way so you can indulge in some serious girl talk. Don't worry about me. I'll go down the pub and meet some of my pals. When do you expect to be finished?'

'We won't be late. They should be gone by midnight at the latest.'

'That's fine then, just fire ahead. Don't make too much noise and upset the neighbours.'

Ellie pulled a face. 'As if,' she said.

She returned to the supermarket and stocked up. This was her first serious attempt at a dinner party and she wanted it to be a success. She knew that some of her friends had pernickety tastes so she had to settle on a menu that would suit them all but wouldn't be so elaborate that it would take hours to cook.

In the end, she opted for a starter of smoked salmon. For the main course she decided to cook chicken breasts in a mushroom sauce served with pasta and green beans. She gathered together the ingredients, then made a detour to the bakery section where she found the perfect dessert – coconut pie. She collected two and proceeded to the checkout.

When she got back to the apartment, Joe was watching football in the living room.

'What time are your friends coming?'

'Six.'

'I'll stay to welcome them and then I'll be gone. Is that okay? It won't look rude?'

'Not at all. I'm going to be tied up for a while. Can I get you a beer?'

'No.' He waved his hand. 'I'll be fine.'

She went into the kitchen, rolled up her sleeves and put on an apron. She had read in a magazine article that the secret of a successful dinner party was preparation. In that case, she would leave nothing to chance.

For the next forty minutes, she worked steadily, topping

and tailing the beans, weighing the right amount of pasta, laying the smoked salmon on a bed of chopped lettuce with wedges of lemon, and pre-cooking the chicken over a slow gas. Then she returned to the dining room and quickly set the table with their best glasses and cutlery, then added the candles and napkins she had recently acquired. By the time, Joe came in to ask if he could help, the table was laid.

It was now half past five. She turned off the cooker and went to have a shower and get dressed. She had barely poured herself a glass of wine when the bell sounded and Caroline and Fiona were on the doorstep.

They came in with gifts of flowers and wine.

'Oh, my God!' Caroline looked as if she was about to swoon with ecstasy at the sight before her. 'This place! It's easily the most fantastic apartment I've ever seen. Why don't you get a photographer round from *Dublin Society* magazine to take some pictures?'

Joe and Ellie exchanged a smile. They were well used to Caroline's flourishes.

'We decided against,' Joe said. 'It's an invitation to thieves to come round some afternoon and rob the place while we're at work.'

'You're right,' Caroline conceded. 'I didn't think of that.'

Joe bent to kiss their cheeks and waited while they took off their coats. Then Ellie led them into the living room where the fire was lit and offered them some wine. There was another squeal of delight from Caroline when she saw the carpets and furnishings. 'I didn't know you had such elegant taste,' she said to Joe. 'This is really something else.'

He suppressed a laugh. 'Most of the credit should go to Ellie,' he replied gallantly. 'She's the creative force in this marriage.'

Just then the doorbell rang once more. Joe excused himself and returned a minute later with Mags. 'Sorry I'm late,' she said, smiling at everyone and pressing another bottle of wine into Ellie's hands.

'You're not,' Fiona said. 'We've just arrived. Come and sit down.'

Joe filled her glass and hung around for a while, then put on his coat, kissed them all goodbye and left for the pub.

***

Although Ellie was the first of the friends to get married, the others were now in relationships at varying stages of development. Mags was progressing steadily in her teaching career and for the last six months had been dating a lawyer called Peter O'Neill. There were vague whispers of a possible engagement.

Caroline had drifted in and out of so many relationships that the others had lost count. Now she was seeing a script writer. She was a striking woman, with her dark features and sensuous figure, and seemed to attract men like moths to a flame, but they never lasted. She blamed this on the fact that her boyfriends were mostly involved in the theatrical world. Others, less charitable, said it was down to her personality. Living with Caroline would be like living with a ticking bomb. You just never knew when it would go off.

'It's very difficult to hold down a relationship when you're running around like a headless chicken from one rehearsal to another and your partner is doing the same,' she would say. 'It's not really conducive, you know.'

'So why don't you look outside the theatre?' Mags asked.

Caroline rolled her eyes as if this was the most idiotic

suggestion she had ever heard. 'But, my dear, apart from you lot, they're the only people I know.'

The one who had surprised them all was Fiona. For a long time she had struggled to find a boyfriend. But just four months ago, she had met another young medical student, Gerry Denvir, and romance seemed to be blossoming.

Once Joe had left and the women were alone, the interrogation began. This was the first opportunity they'd had to be together since Ellie had come home from Marbella and they were keen to cross-examine her.

'I want to hear all about the honeymoon,' Mags insisted. 'I know the weather was fantastic but what about the rest of it?'

Ellie recounted the daily routine, the places they had gone, the sights they had seen and the meals they had eaten. She produced the photographs they had taken, which were passed around and studied intently.

'It looks fantastic,' Mags said. 'What was the name of the hotel again?'

'The Majestic.'

'I must remember that,' she said, to general laughter. 'In case the opportunity presents itself.'

Caroline refilled her wine glass. 'Well, the honeymoon was clearly a success but now for the key question. Tell me truthfully. Is marriage all it's cracked up to be?'

The others looked at her in horror but Ellie seemed to take it in her stride. 'Oh, I definitely think so,' she replied chirpily. 'I'm deliriously happy.'

'You're lucky. You got the gorgeous Joe.'

'Looks are only part of the story. There's a lot more to it than that.'

'But looks certainly help.'

'Of course that's what attracted me to Joe in the first place, that and his charm. Remember that evening in Neary's? You had a hand in introducing us, Caroline.'

'So I did,' Caroline replied, looking pleased with herself. 'Maybe I should open a dating agency. But tell me, is everything going smoothly? He doesn't grab all the bedclothes for himself, does he? He doesn't snore and keep you awake? He doesn't take the last chocolate biscuit?'

Ellie burst out laughing. 'Joe is very considerate.'

'So you haven't had any disagreements?'

The others frowned as if Caroline was crossing a red line. But Ellie brushed aside the question. 'Every married couple has disagreements,' she said, recalling her recent attempts to housetrain Joe. 'My own parents used to have issues from time to time. People wouldn't be human if they didn't. But the trick is to reach a compromise. Besides, I'd got to know Joe pretty well before I married him, so I knew what to expect.'

Caroline was ready with another question but Mags moved quickly to deflect her. 'I love those wall prints,' she said, turning to Ellie. 'They really set off this room. Where did you get them?'

They sat chatting for about half an hour, then Ellie took them on a tour of the remainder of the apartment. It was punctuated with more extravagant squeals of delight from Caroline. At last they arrived in the gleaming kitchen and adjoining dining room. This time it was Mags who gasped. She went around the kitchen, taking great interest in the appliances and the layout. 'I love it,' she said. 'This is exactly what I want. Look at the space and the lighting. Just think of the wonderful meals you could produce in a kitchen like this.'

'Thank you,' Ellie said. 'Let's hope my efforts live up to your expectations. If you'd all like to sit down, we'll eat.'

She guessed they were hungry and she was right. They quickly devoured the starter and moved on to the main course. By the time they got to the dessert, everyone was in a jolly mood and the laughter around the table could be heard out on the street.

'Let me help you with the washing-up,' Caroline offered, when Ellie had removed the plates and cutlery from the table.

'Stay where you are, I've got a dishwasher for that,' she said, emptying the scraps into the bin and putting the dishes into the machine. She produced a box of chocolates that Joe had given her and passed it around the table. 'Now, Fiona, tell us more about this Gerry Denvir you're seeing. What does he specialise in?'

'Yes!' Mags put in. 'I want to hear all the gory details.'

By the time Joe arrived back from the pub at half past eleven, the dinner party was still in full swing. Later, when the guests had been deposited in taxis to take them home, Joe and Ellie sat together in the living room.

'Your party seems to have been a big success,' he said. 'Pick up any salacious gossip?'

'We may have another wedding soon.'

'Oh?'

'Yes. I think it's only a matter of time before Mags announces her engagement.'

He drew her closer and nuzzled her ear. 'Just look what you've started.'

Chapter Thirteen

That was the beginning of Ellie's career as a dinner-party hostess and now that she had gained the confidence to cook for other people, it wasn't long before she gave another party. This time, she invited her father and mother and Joe's parents. That evening, too, proved quite a success. Her parents used the opportunity to do some shopping in Dublin and spent the night at the apartment before travelling back to Ballymount.

In the weeks and months that followed, she hosted parties for work colleagues and some of Joe's friends from the newspaper business. They got to know another young couple who lived in one of the ground-floor apartments and gave a dinner for them. These ventures led to more invitations, and soon scarcely a weekend went by without Joe and Ellie attending or hosting a party. But the core of her social circle remained her three friends.

Later, Ellie would remember this period as a special time. She and Joe were young and madly in love. They had a busy social calendar and successful careers. Joe continued to be the star reporter on the *Gazette* and in constant demand for radio and television shows. Ellie was promoted to chief economic analyst at Lombard and Brady and given a pay rise.

Now Joe's mortgage, which had seemed enormous when Ellie first met him, shrank in significance. They had money to spend on clothes and household items, holidays and entertainment. They fell into the habit of taking short weekend breaks every couple of months and one extended holiday in the summer. And they had each other. With each passing month, Ellie found she was deeper in love with Joe. But things were about to change.

***

One Sunday morning, about eighteen months after they were married, Ellie woke feeling nauseous. They had been out to dinner the night before and hadn't got back till the small hours. She threw back the duvet and rushed to the bathroom in time to throw up into the washbasin. Then she sat down on the toilet seat while she waited for the nausea to pass.

'Are you all right in there?' Joe called from the bedroom.

'Yes. Just give me a minute.'

Eventually, she got up, rinsed her mouth and washed out the basin.

'What was it?' he asked, as she got back into bed beside him.

'Stomach upset. I expect it was something I ate last night.'

'The fish,' Joe announced. 'I thought it tasted a bit odd. You've got to be very careful with fish. Are you feeling okay now?'

'Yes,' she said, snuggling closer. 'I'm much better, thanks.'

'Stay on in bed and I'll make you a cup of tea.'

That morning sickness was the first sign that she was pregnant. The next sign came a week later when she missed her period. It had never happened before. Her cycle had always been regular. Now she began to get anxious.

Starting a family was not on their agenda. Before they got married they had discussed the issue and had agreed to wait. They were young and there was plenty of time. Why not enjoy themselves for a few more years before assuming all the responsibilities that came with children? Now it appeared that something might have occurred to change their plans. She spoke to Fiona and asked her opinion.

'Have you been under any stress recently?'

'Nothing beyond the usual.'

'And you're on the pill, aren't you?'

'Yes.'

'You didn't forget to take it by any chance?'

Ellie had already asked herself the same question. 'I can't remember.'

'Okay, if you miss the next one, go and see your GP at once.'

Now Ellie awaited her next period with some anxiety. Personally, she would be happy to have a child and she knew her parents would be delighted. But how would Joe react? She circled the date in her diary and counted down the days. When the time arrived and the period didn't, she knew for certain she was pregnant.

But it still had to be confirmed. She went to her GP, who examined her, took a urine sample for testing and promised to ring with the result in a day or two.

She was at work when the call came.

'It's positive,' the GP said. 'You're pregnant. Congratulations.'

'Thank you,' Ellie said, slightly bewildered by the speed of events.

'I'm going to make a hospital appointment for you,' the doctor continued. 'Have you any preference as to which one you'd like to attend?'

As soon as she put the phone down, she rang Joe. 'I've got some news. Are you sitting down?'

'Sure, go ahead.'

'We're going to have a baby.'

There was a long silence. Then: 'Did I hear correctly? You're telling me you're pregnant?'

'Yes.'

'There's no possibility—'

'Absolutely not,' she cut him off. 'I've done a test and my GP's just called with the result. I'm definitely pregnant.'

She heard Joe chuckle and breathed a little easier. 'That's fantastic, Ellie. I'm over the moon.'

'You don't mind? It changes all our plans.'

'So what? You know how to make God laugh, don't you? Make plans. It's the best news I've heard for a long time.'

***

The only other person she told was Fiona and she swore her to silence. It was a special secret she shared with Joe. Telling others would take away some of the magic and she wanted to hold onto it for as long as possible. She was delighted by Joe's reaction and pleased that he wanted the baby. At night, he would lie in bed and stroke her belly or lie with his ear pressed against it, listening for a heartbeat.

'The little beggar's in there somewhere. What do you think it will be, a boy or a girl? Will we place bets?'

But the time came when she began to put on weight and couldn't disguise her condition any more. First they told their parents, then their friends, and finally the people at work. Everyone was pleased for them and wished them well. As word spread, cards began to turn up in the post with pictures of storks carrying bundles in their beaks.

Ellie tried to stay calm. Joe was the one who got excited. He started fussing over her, making sure she was eating properly and taking her folic acid supplement. He checked her weight too, insisting that she take things easy and didn't tire herself.

'At last I'm getting the attention I deserve,' she joked. 'I should have got pregnant sooner.'

It turned out to be an easy pregnancy. She attended for prenatal checks. She went to classes for first-time mothers. She took her vitamins and did everything the doctor prescribed. She read books and talked to mothers with three, four and five children to pick their brains. She carried on working until two weeks before the baby was due because someone told her that the maternity leave would be more valuable after the baby was born.

***

It was a seven-and-a-half-pound boy. Everyone who saw him said he was the image of his father, which pleased Joe. Ellie's mother said he was going to grow up to be a footballer. More like an all-in wrestler, Mrs Plunkett said.

Ellie couldn't keep her eyes off him as he lay in the cot beside her bed. 'You're the best-looking baby in this entire hospital,' she whispered. 'You're so beautiful, I could gobble you up.' He gazed into her face, then screwed up his eyes and began to bawl for his feed.

She remained in the hospital for another four days. By now, she was desperate to get home. Eventually Joe arrived to drive them back to Monkstown. He took the baby in his arms and kissed him. 'Have you thought about a name for him?' he asked.

'What about calling him after your dad? His name is John, so we could call his grandson Jack?'

'Dad will love that,' Joe said.

She was entitled to eighteen weeks' paid maternity leave and a further eight unpaid. People told her she was going to need it all, and they were right. She quickly discovered that looking after an infant was a full-time job, even though Joe and his parents helped as best they could.

Jack was a placid child who slept a lot, but by the time Joe got home in the evenings, Ellie was often so tired she could barely keep her eyes open.

Eventually the maternity leave expired and it was time to go back to work. 'You don't have to,' Joe said. 'We can easily afford a few more months of unpaid leave. Why don't you rest a bit longer?'

But Ellie was desperate to return. There were aspects of her job that she missed, particularly the contact with other adults. Talking to a baby all day had its limitations. 'I think I'd prefer to go back.'

'If that's what you want, it's your decision.'

'Who will we ask to look after Jack?'

'My mother. She's dying to take care of him.'

'Are you sure? It doesn't seem fair.'

'But she wants to do it. And she's got plenty of experience. She raised four of us. Besides, we'll have him every evening and weekends. It'll be fine. You'll see.'

So Ellie left Jack with his grandmother every morning on her way into work and picked him up in the evening. Everything went smoothly, and for several months she seemed to have the best of both worlds.

But, gradually, she found she was missing her baby and longing for her working day to end so she could get home to see him. However, Fate had another surprise in store for them. A few months later, she missed another period and discovered she was pregnant again.

This was another unplanned event. On one rare evening they had left Jack with Mrs Plunkett overnight and treated themselves to dinner at one of Joe's favourite haunts, the Valentino in Dalkey. It was just like the old days before Jack had come along. When they got back to Monkstown, the apartment sounded eerily still, no crying baby demanding their attention. They undressed frantically and fell into bed.

Later, Joe lay back on the pillow and threw his arm across his forehead. 'My God, that was marvellous. I'd almost forgotten how good it can be.'

'Yes, it was,' Ellie agreed. 'We should do it more often.'

'Maybe if I asked my mum nicely she might agree to take him again next weekend.'

'Poor little mite! We're making it sound like he's a burden to us.'

'Well, you have to admit, Ellie, it's easier when we don't have a hungry baby screaming at us.'

***

The second baby was a girl and they called her Dee, which was short for Deirdre. Unlike her brother, she was a demanding little creature, who slept little and cried a lot. Now Ellie had to deal with two babies, and even with the help of her own parents and her in-laws, she found the constant washing and feeding a struggle.

As the time to return to work drew closer, she began to think carefully about the situation. Did she really want to go back? She didn't need to work. Joe was earning a good salary, which was more than adequate to meet their needs, and if she stayed at home, she could devote her full attention to the babies. One evening after they had got the children to sleep and were having dinner, she raised the subject with Joe.

'Are you sure you won't miss working?' he said. 'You did the last time.'

'I probably will but I think I'll be happier. Children grow up so quickly, and I don't want to look back with regret. I'd prefer to stay at home till they're older and going to school. Then we could review the situation.'

'Ellie, it's your call. Whatever you decide to do, I'll stand beside you.'

'In that case, I'll leave.'

When she explained the situation to Mr Brady, she found him very sympathetic. 'To be honest, Ellie, I don't know how you managed when Jack was born. I don't think I could have done it. We'll miss you, of course. You've been a dedicated and effective member of staff.'

This time they threw a farewell party for her with champagne, a cake and a good-luck card that everyone signed. Mr Brady made a little speech. Then Joe came to pick her up and she left Lombard and Brady for ever.

Chapter Fourteen

After Deirdre was born, Ellie decided to have one more child and then the family would be complete. Afterwards, she would joke with her friends that this baby was the only one that had been planned. The child was born twelve months later, another girl. They named her Alice, after Ellie's mother.

She had soon discovered that looking after three babies really was a full-time job. She worked much harder than she ever had when she was at Lombard and Brady. And it never ended. She couldn't switch off the lights, lock the door and leave everything till she came back the following morning.

It was an endless round of washing, feeding, nursing and soothing. She would fall into bed at night exhausted, only to be woken by one of the children crying to be fed. Then there were the endless trips to the baby clinic, the doctor, the chemist, the supermarket, the post office, the bank, not to mention the usual household tasks, like cooking meals and cleaning the apartment.

She had some help, of course. Mrs Plunkett lent a hand whenever she could. Her own mother was eager to assist but she was too far away in Ballymount to be of much use, although she came up to Dublin often. Fiona put her in touch with a young woman called Rose, who had trained in childcare and came to the apartment three days a week. But most of the burden of child-rearing still fell on Ellie's shoulders.

Even though she was now the busy mother of three young children, she kept in close contact with her friends. Mags had got married and had a little girl. She lived nearby in Booterstown and often came over to visit. They would sit in the kitchen and exchange gossip over cups of tea and biscuits while the children played noisily in the living room.

She heard regularly from Fiona and Caroline. Fiona was now a junior doctor, engaged to Gerry Denvir and a wedding date had been fixed. Caroline remained unattached, despite a passionate affair with a costume designer, which everyone was certain would result in a trip down the aisle. In the end, he went off with a young actress half his age, and left poor Caroline broken-hearted.

***

The time came when they had to think of moving house. The apartment, which had seemed the height of sophistication when Joe had first shown it to Ellie, was too cramped with two adults and three growing children. They needed a house with more bedrooms and a garden where the children could play.

Joe spoke to the property editor of the *Gazette*, who put him in touch with an auctioneer called Barry Forsythe. He came out one weekend to look over the apartment and assured them they would have no difficulty in selling it. There was a shortage of good properties in the area, and apartments like theirs were in vogue with retired couples who were downsizing. They would even make a handsome profit on the sale.

Armed with this information, they set about house-hunting. Each Saturday afternoon, they packed the children into the car and went off to view potential homes. At first Ellie enjoyed these excursions, but she soon grew tired of tramping up and down people's stairs and peering into their bedrooms. But they persevered until they found what they wanted.

It was a four-bedroom detached villa across the bay in Clontarf. Ellie knew it was the house for them the minute she set eyes on it. It had a garage for two cars and gardens front and rear. The location was perfect: it was close to the city centre, within easy reach of the *Gazette* office, and there were good schools locally for the children.

She was relieved that the search was finally over but there was still much legal and financial work to be done. Soon after, Barry Forsythe came through with the news that he had a client for the apartment in Monkstown. There followed a hectic round of visits to solicitors and bank managers to sign documents, but eventually everything was complete.

One Saturday morning, a removal company arrived and carefully stacked their belongings into a van. By the afternoon, they were in possession of their new house. Joe opened a bottle of champagne and proposed a toast.

'I hope you realise this is the last time I'm doing this,' Ellie said. 'I plan to die in this house.'

'Don't be so dismal. You're too young to die.' He laughed. 'You're going to live to a ripe old age.'

***

It was several weeks before Ellie had arranged the house to her satisfaction. She got the decorators in, bought some extra furniture and hired a gardener to get the lawns into shape. When everything was ready, she threw a housewarming party.

It was a warm autumn evening and the house was packed with colleagues, neighbours and friends, chatting, laughing and admiring Joe and Ellie's new home. At one point, Ellie decided to go outside for a breath of air. The sky was clear and the stars were out. As she stood in the garden, she heard footsteps behind her and turned.

'Mistress of all you survey,' Mags said. 'Your new house is beautiful, Ellie. I wish you happiness in it.'

'Thank you.'

'Do you remember that first day we met? We were in the queue to register at university?'

'How could I forget? I didn't know a soul when I came to Dublin. You were the very first friend I made in the city.'

'I bet you never believed you'd end up owning a magnificent home like this, did you?'

'Of course I didn't. I wasn't thinking any further than the end of the week when I'd get back to Ballymount to see my mother.'

Mags smiled. 'We were so innocent back then. But life's been good to us, hasn't it?'

'We've been very fortunate.'

'Sometimes I get this nervous feeling that everything's going so well it can't last. Do you ever feel like that?'

Ellie shook her head. 'I try not to think too far ahead. Joe has a saying that you shouldn't plan because it makes God laugh. I think he might have a point.'

'So you're an optimist?'

'I suppose I am.'

'And people call economics the dismal science.'

Ellie laughed. 'Not this economist. If anything, I think that things will just continue to get better.'

Chapter Fifteen

Soon it was time to think of the children's education. Ellie made some enquiries and found a Montessori school close by, which had an excellent reputation. She spoke to the principal and enrolled Jack, then Dee and finally Alice.

They all loved school and the opportunity to mix with other children. Before long, they had made friends and were being invited to birthday parties. For the first time in years, Ellie thought about re-entering the workforce.

She mentioned it to Joe.

'If it's money you're concerned about, you should relax. We're financially secure. And I've just been given another rise.'

'It's not just money, Joe. It's also personal satisfaction. I studied hard to become an economist and it's a pity I'm not putting my knowledge to some use. Besides, now that the children are at school I've got time on my hands.'

'I've always supported your decisions. If you want to return to work, go right ahead.'

She brushed up her CV, went out and bought herself a smart business suit, then registered with an employment agency. Before long, she was attending job interviews. She knew she would be competing with bright young graduates fresh out of business colleges, but she had something they didn't. She had been chief economic analyst with Lombard and Brady. That experience had to count for something.

The first few attempts ended in failure. But she didn't allow it to get her down. She was confident that if she knocked on doors long enough, one would open. Then one day she was invited for interview with a firm of investment consultants called Mallory and O'Keefe, in the Dublin docklands. They were looking for an economic analyst.

She was called for a second time and sensed she was getting closer. This interview was a bruising encounter and lasted for almost an hour, but when she left, she had a feeling that success was within her grasp. At the third interview, they offered her the job.

That night, she and Joe hired a babysitter and went out to celebrate. Ellie felt flushed with success. It gratified her to know that Mallory and O'Keefe valued her so much that they were prepared to pay her a handsome salary to work for them. But she knew the job would require some skilful juggling. The children still had to be taken to school every morning and someone had to look after them when they got home in the afternoon.

She decided to hire Rose full time, and expanded her duties to include housework. Ellie dropped the children at school in the morning on her way to the office. Rose picked them up at midday, gave them lunch and kept them occupied till Ellie got back in the evening. In the mornings she did the cleaning and shopping. The arrangement worked perfectly, and Ellie was able to concentrate on her new career.

Mallory and O'Keefe was a small firm, relatively new, and eager to carve out a niche for itself in the growing financial industry. From her first day, Ellie was treated as an equal and given responsibility. Her job was a key one: to assess economic trends and use the information to devise investment strategies for the company's clients.

She enjoyed being back at work. It was a tight-knit team and each member had a particular role in the success of the whole operation. Ellie was older than most of the others, who were in their mid to late twenties, but she quickly established good relationships with her colleagues.

Her hard work soon began to yield results, and as the firm's reputation grew and spread, she was promoted. First she was appointed senior analyst, and when the firm merged with a smaller outfit and it was decided to hire some more economists, Ellie was made chief analyst and given a company car.

PART TWO
2010

Chapter Sixteen

The years had flown by so fast. It seemed to Ellie that one day she had been sitting at the kitchen table helping the children with their homework and the next they had grown up, formed relationships and begun finding their careers.

Jack had inherited his father's good looks and his interest in publishing. He was working for a digital media firm in Ringsend and living with his girlfriend, Mollie Brennan, in an apartment at Sandymount.

Dee was employed in a busy advertising agency, having started her career in the commercial department at the *Gazette*. She had just married her childhood sweetheart, Tony Mulhall, another advertising executive, and was living close by in Raheny. Of all the children, Dee was the most organised.

Her sister, Alice, was completing a post-graduate degree in computer science at Trinity College and was still living at home: she had wisely concluded that it was the cheapest accommodation she was likely to find in Dublin.

Joe continued to dominate the Dublin newspaper scene. He

had received many tempting offers of management positions but had turned them down, insisting that he would die of boredom sitting behind a desk all day, pushing pieces of paper around. He was now in his mid-fifties, still dashing and charming, still regarded as the sharpest investigative reporter in Irish journalism.

He continued to break exclusive stories, despite having several young reporters snapping at his heels. He was still called on by radio and television stations to explain some complicated political development or the background to a gangland killing. And he was still prepared to drop everything and fly off at a minute's notice to talk to some contact who had promised to spill the beans on a major scandal.

So, when he announced one day that he had to go to London for a couple of days to talk to some people, Ellie had taken it in her stride.

'When will you be back?'

'That depends. It shouldn't take more than a couple of days. Don't worry, I'll keep in touch. I'll call every day.'

He had packed his bag, set off in a taxi for the airport, and Ellie had gone into work. That had been two days ago. He had kept his promise to stay in touch. She had spoken to him just that morning and he had sounded his usual cheerful self.

She often thought that her life couldn't get any better. She loved her job, she loved her husband and family, and she loved her house in Clontarf. It was almost within shouting distance of her office just across the Liffey. And she still had the close friendship of her three friends, which had strengthened and deepened over the years.

She was thinking of them as she drove home from work. Mags was now the deputy principal of a large girls' secondary school in Donnybrook. Her husband, Peter, was a busy lawyer and they had one daughter, who was hoping to go to university to study languages. Fiona and Gerry Denvir had busy careers as hospital consultants. They lived in a wonderful house in Ballsbridge and had two teenage sons.

Caroline was the only one who hadn't married or had children. She'd had a number of tempestuous relationships but none had survived. She was picking up acting work wherever she could find it in television or on stage. Her dream of a film career was fading although she hadn't entirely abandoned it.

This year, they would all turn fifty. They must organise a special celebration. Ellie knew they would be keen on the idea – everyone except Caroline. She hated birthdays and recently had begun to chip years off her age when she was interviewed for newspaper articles. But Ellie was sure they could persuade her.

The thought crystallised into a decision as she approached her house. She would start calling them this evening as soon as she had finished dinner. Alice would be out with her friends, which meant that Ellie would be eating alone – a TV meal heated in the microwave. As compensation, she would treat herself to an extra-large glass of pinot noir.

She turned into her driveway and noticed a strange car parked beside the garage. As she drew closer, the doors opened and a man and a woman stepped out. She immediately recognised the grey-haired figure of Tom Matthews, managing editor of the *Gazette* and Joe's immediate boss. The woman was younger, in her early forties. She was Paula O'Brien, Tom's personal assistant. What are they doing here? she wondered.

They waited till Ellie had turned off the engine and got out of the car. Then they began walking towards her. Tom had his hands outstretched and there was a nervous look on his face. Ellie immediately sensed that something was wrong.

'I tried ringing you at work but you'd already left. So I thought it best if we came straight out to the house.'

'What is it, Tom?'

'It's about Joe.'

'What about him?'

He took a deep breath. 'We had a call from the Excelsior Hotel in Knightsbridge forty-five minutes ago. It's not good news, I'm afraid.'

Her pulse missed a beat. 'Why? What's happened?'

'He had a heart attack this afternoon.'

'Oh, my God, I'll go there at once.'

Tom placed a restraining hand on her shoulder. 'It's too late, Ellie. He's dead.'

She felt her legs go weak. Tom wrapped his arms around her and held her tight. 'You need someone with you, Ellie, a family member. Tell us who to call.'

But she wasn't listening. Joe was dead, the man she had loved for most of her adult life, her rock, her pillar, her soul-mate. It wasn't possible. A bizarre thought hurtled into her brain. Everything important in her life had happened in threes. What else was coming down the tracks?

Chapter Seventeen

Tom Matthews turned to his assistant. 'We'll have to get her inside, Paula. Check her handbag and see if you can find the keys.'

He kept his arm tight around Ellie's shoulders while Paula rummaged in the bag. At last she extracted a keyring, walked to the front door and managed to open it. Then she returned to Tom and together they helped Ellie into the hall.

The living room was on the right. They steered her through and sat her on the sofa. She looked at them with glassy eyes.

'How do you feel?' Paula asked. 'Can you breathe freely? Here, let me loosen your collar.' She fiddled with the buttons on Ellie's shirt. 'Is that easier?'

Ellie mumbled something. She wished they wouldn't keep asking her questions. She was in a daze. She couldn't comprehend the awful news she had heard.

Paula stood up. 'I'll make tea,' she said. 'It will do you good.' She went off to find the kitchen.

Tom sat down beside her. 'You're not looking well, Ellie. Maybe we should get you a doctor.'

'No doctor,' she said, grasping his hand. 'I'll be all right. Just give me a few minutes.'

'What do you want me to do?'

'Call Dee.'

'Dee's your elder daughter?'

'Yes.'

'How do I contact her?'

'There's a black phone book in the hall.'

Paula was back with the tea, a glass of water and some paracetamol she'd found in the bathroom cabinet. 'Here,' she said, and gave Ellie the glass with the pills.

Meanwhile Tom had returned with a small black book and was rapidly leafing through the pages. 'I've found her,' he said.

He took out his phone and went back into the hall.

'Are you feeling any better?' Paula asked.

'A little.' The initial shock was passing and now the cold reality was setting in. Joe was dead. Her life would never be the same again. 'Do you know how it happened?' she asked.

'Not really. Tom took the call from the hotel manager. It seemed Joe was working in his room when he collapsed. By the time they got the doctor, it was too late.'

Ellie's eyes filled with tears. She would never again see his smiling face, never hear him laugh. Never feel his warm body curling up beside her in bed at night. She felt the hot tears trickle down her cheeks. Then her chest was heaving and she was sobbing uncontrollably.

***

Later, when she tried to piece it together, the evening appeared as a series of disconnected fragments. The doorbell sounded, and Dee came bustling in. She went straight to her mother, hugged her tightly and didn't speak for a few moments. The two women sat holding each other.

At last, Dee wiped her eyes. 'I'm so sorry, Mum. I don't know what to say. What was it?'

'A heart attack.'

'Oh, my God.'

'I can't believe it,' Ellie said. 'He was the fittest man I knew.'

'Now listen, Mum, there's an awful lot to do. We have to organise the funeral and get death notices into the papers. Someone will have to go to London and bring him back. They'll want somebody to identify the body. They may want to hold a post-mortem. Would you prefer me to do it?'

In her shock, Ellie hadn't even thought of the funeral. 'What about Tony?'

'He'll come with me. We can get time off work. It won't be a problem.'

'Would you mind, Dee? I don't think I could handle it.'

'Consider it done. Now, who took the call from the hotel in London?'

'Tom Matthews.'

'I'll go and talk to him,' Dee said. 'I've already called Jack and Alice. They're on their way. Don't worry about the funeral. Just leave everything with us. We'll take care of it.'

She got up and went off in search of Tom.

Suddenly the house was full of people. There was Jack, a sombre image of his dead father, with his girlfriend, Mollie, clinging to his arm. Alice appeared, tearful and distraught, then Jim Enright and Paul Delaney, Joe's newspaper buddies who had been groomsmen at their wedding. Joe's brother, Eddie, arrived, with the parish priest and a couple of neighbours to give their support.

They crowded around and offered their condolences. The women kissed her and held her hand while the men told her how sorry they were. Meanwhile, someone had taken over the kitchen and organised sandwiches and tea. Ellie saw Mags and Fiona coming into the room. She struggled to her feet.

'This breaks my heart,' Mags said. 'Where is the justice in this world?' All at once, they were embracing and the tears were flowing.

'Is there anything I can do?' Fiona asked. 'Is there something you need?'

'I don't think so,' Ellie replied. 'The children are here and Dee has offered to take over the funeral arrangements.'

'Well, that's a relief.'

'Caroline is working tonight but she'll call later,' Mags added. 'She's distraught. She asked us to give you her sympathy.'

They sat talking together while the house continued to fill. By now word was spreading and Joe's journalist friends were calling. Mags and Fiona eventually left, saying they would return tomorrow. Before they departed, Fiona pressed something into Ellie's hand. 'Those are sleeping tablets. You might need them. Try to get some rest, Ellie. It's very important. The next few days are going to be tough. And remember to call me if you want to talk.'

She struggled through the remainder of the evening. Jack and Mollie had decided to stay over to keep her and Alice company. By ten o'clock, most of the visitors had drifted away. Ellie went to bed. As she slipped under the sheets, she opened the packet that Fiona had given her and took out a small white pill. She wanted desperately to sleep, but most of all she wanted the oblivion that the tablet would bring.

***

When she woke it was late morning and Alice was standing by the bed with the phone in her hand. 'Dee's on the line. She's calling from London.'

'Hi, Mum,' Dee began. 'How do you feel this morning? Did you get any sleep?'

'Yes. Fiona gave me a tablet.'

'That was good thinking. Now, listen. I'm getting things under control at this end. A doctor examined him and certified the death as cardiac arrest. There's no need to hold an inquest. I have the medical certificate and I've also identified Dad, so there's no problem with releasing his body.'

'When are you coming back?'

'We're still working on that. I've engaged a firm in London and they've been excellent with the paperwork. I've also hired Talbot's, the Dublin undertakers. As soon as we get clearance, Tony and I will travel back with Dad's body and some people from Talbot's will meet us at the airport and transfer Dad to their premises, unless you want to bring him to the house.'

Ellie thought of the constant stream of visitors the previous evening. It would be even worse if Joe was here, laid out in his coffin. She couldn't face it. 'I think it would be better to take him to the funeral parlour.'

'Okay. Now, we've also been in touch with the church and the funeral can go ahead more or less straight away. The undertakers will look after the death notices. That leaves only one thing to settle. Do you want a burial or a cremation?'

Ellie struggled to think. Her head was muddled. And she

was still drowsy from the sleeping tablet. 'We don't have a grave.'

'The undertakers can organise that.'

'What would be best?'

'It's your choice, Mum. Cremation is easier and cheaper.'

'Don't worry about the cost. I want it done properly.'

'Speaking for myself, I would prefer to be cremated.'

'Then tell the undertakers to go ahead and arrange it.'

'Fine. I'll keep you informed. Now, don't be worrying, Mum. When I saw Dad, he looked at peace. I don't think he suffered any pain. There are many worse ways to go.'

There was a click and Dee was gone.

Ellie got up, had a shower and started to get dressed. Downstairs in the living room, there was a pile of wreaths and flowers from friends, along with sympathy cards. Alice had prepared some food but Ellie merely picked at it. As soon as they had finished eating, the phone started ringing again.

First it was Caroline, weeping and talking about the tragedy of it all. Joe was her third friend to go in the past fortnight. It was all too much. 'It's awful dying alone in a foreign city like that. I just can't take it in.' She continued for about ten minutes before Ellie managed to get a word in.

'I appreciate your support, Caroline. I'm very grateful.'

'I couldn't come to the house last night. I had to go on stage at eight o'clock. But I was thinking of you all the time.'

'I know you were.'

'I'll be at the funeral. When is it?'

'It hasn't been decided yet. Dee and Tony are in London arranging to bring Joe's body back. I'll let you know when it's all finalised.'

'I'll send flowers. What would you like?'

'No, please, don't do that. We've got so many flowers there's nowhere to put them all.'

'Well, if you say so. I'll keep in touch with you. My God, Ellie. This is a cruel world.'

As soon as she'd managed to get Caroline off the line, the phone rang again. It was Hugh O'Leary, the chief executive at Mallory and O'Keefe. 'I'm calling to offer our sympathy,' he said gently.

'Thank you, Hugh.'

'How are you coping?'

'It's not easy. It's been a terrible shock. No one was expecting it.'

'I understand. Is there any news about the funeral?'

'Not yet.'

'If there's anything we can do here, don't hesitate to call. And forget about work. Just take as long as you need. We can talk about your return when things have settled down a bit.'

Right through the rest of the day, the phone continued to ring. Eventually Jack said, 'Why don't you have a nap, Mum? We can handle the calls.'

She went back upstairs to the bedroom, drew the curtains and slipped under the sheets. It felt strange to be in bed in the late afternoon. Her eyelids grew heavy and she felt herself drifting off. A few minutes later, she was fast asleep.

***

It was two more days before Dee and Tony could bring Joe's body back from London in its sealed coffin. By now, the worst of the trauma had passed and Ellie was slowly coming to terms with her loss. The flight was due to land at six o'clock.

She travelled out to Dublin airport with Jack, Mollie and

Alice, and when she got there she found Mags and Fiona, Joe's parents and a small knot of his colleagues waiting for them.

Meanwhile, her own family had arrived from Ballymount and were staying at a nearby hotel. They were all in shock, particularly her parents, who had been very fond of Joe. When her father shyly approached and took her in his arms, she saw there were tears in his eyes.

Once the paperwork had been cleared with the airport authorities, Joe's coffin was put into a hearse and taken straight to the funeral parlour, where it was to remain overnight before being brought to the church. Notices of the funeral service had been placed in the media.

When they arrived at Talbot's, a larger group of people was waiting. The coffin was carried into a small chapel and they took their seats while a priest conducted a short service, then spoke quietly with Ellie and the family. This was the signal for the congregation to come forward and offer their condolences. Some pressed sympathy cards into Ellie's hands. Eventually they drifted away and only the family remained.

'There's something I want to do,' Ellie told Dee. 'I want to look at his face one last time. Would you speak to Gerry Talbot?'

Dee got up and approached the funeral director. They held a short consultation. Then he gestured for her to come forward. Two of his staff undid the screws that held down the lid of the coffin and lifted it off.

Joe was dressed in a neat suit, shirt and tie and his hands were joined at his breast as if in prayer. Ellie bent forward and kissed his cold cheek. Then she stood back and took one last look at her dead husband.

What Dee had said was true. Joe did look at peace. There was even a hint of a smile on his face.

***

The funeral was one of the largest seen in Dublin for many years. The *Gazette* had gone to town on Joe's death with two pages of articles and photographs. An obituary detailing his career was signed by the editor. There were tributes from public figures, sports personalities, musicians, entertainers and people in the arts world. Joe had been a very popular man.

Even the politicians had joined in. A statement from the minister for justice said that Joe Plunkett had played a leading role in the fight against organised crime for which society owed him a debt of gratitude. The leader of the opposition declared that Joe had been a tireless crusader who had never been afraid to write the truth.

The funeral mass was to begin at ten o'clock and afterwards the cortège would proceed to the crematorium where there would be another short ceremony.

Ellie, in a dark skirt and jacket, set off at nine thirty with the children to the church. When they took their seats in the front row, the coffin had been placed before the altar, surrounded by a bank of flowers. Already, all the seats were taken and there was a large crowd outside, along with several press photographers and a television crew.

Ellie stared straight ahead. New emotions stirred in her breast: pride and gratitude that so many people had offered their support in the last few days and had turned out now for Joe's farewell. Just then the organ sounded and the choir began to sing 'Amazing Grace'. The funeral mass began.

**

After the two ceremonies had concluded, there was a lunch for the mourners in a nearby hotel. During the course of the meal, a woman approached and introduced herself as Patsy Devine. Ellie recognised her name as a features writer with the *Gazette*. 'I wanted you to know that Joe was the most wonderful colleague,' she said. 'He was so kind, so very loyal and helpful. Everybody loved him. We're going to miss him terribly.'

'Thank you,' Ellie said.

'I lost my own husband eighteen months ago,' the woman continued. 'If you don't mind me giving you a piece of advice, the best thing is to keep busy. Don't sit around brooding. You must fill your days with lots of things to do, or you'll go crazy. That's how I got through it.'

Chapter Eighteen

In the weeks that followed, there were so many things to sort out that Ellie didn't need Patsy Devine's advice. There were forms to be filled in, solicitors to meet and legal documents to sign, bills to be paid and letters to write to all those who had been kind and supportive since Joe's death. With the help of Dee and Tony, she emptied his wardrobe and handed his clothes to a local charity, then gave his books to some of his friends.

Eventually, when these tasks were completed, Jack and Mollie returned to their apartment in Sandymount, and only Alice remained at home. Ellie was relieved that it was over. She had come through the most harrowing time in her life and now she was exhausted. The phone calls stopped and an empty silence pervaded the house. It was time to return to work.

One day, she rang Hugh O'Leary and told him of her decision.

'Are you quite sure?' he asked. 'I told you there was no need to rush back.'

'But I'm not rushing, Hugh. I've had marvellous support from my children and together we've tidied up all the loose ends. I'd welcome the opportunity to concentrate on something else now.'

'Well, if that's what you want, we'd be very happy to have you back with us. When do you want to start?'

'Is next Monday all right?'

'Sure. I'll look forward to seeing you, Ellie.'

She put down the phone. Had it been her imagination or was Hugh O'Leary a little reluctant to have her back? But that was ridiculous. He was just being thoughtful, as a good boss should. She shook away the idea and began to plan her return.

She went shopping for new clothes and took the family for lunch at a restaurant in Howth village to thank them for the way they had rallied round her after their father's death. She had lunch with her friends. Joe's departure had left a hole in her life and she wondered if she would ever be able to fill it, but she had to get back into the world. She knew Joe would have been the first person to agree with her.

On Monday morning, she was up early and at her desk for eight thirty. There was a little bit of awkwardness at first, as her colleagues came to welcome her, but it soon passed. By the end of the week she had settled back into her familiar routine.

Work was like a comfort blanket: the daily routine of the office gave her a sense of security. She buried herself in weighty economic papers, often working late as she drew up charts and wrote investment reports based on the information she culled from the statistics.

But at the end of each week when the staff repaired to a nearby pub for a few drinks, Ellie didn't go with them. It didn't seem right to be socialising, with Joe barely cold in his grave. She thought it would be unseemly.

She found it strange to return to a silent house and an empty bed, and to eat her meals alone. Her domestic life had always been disrupted by the nature of Joe's work, but she had known that whenever he went off at a moment's notice to chase a story he would eventually come back to her. Now she missed the hurly-burly, Joe's laughter and jokes, even the mornings when he was grumpy because he had been drinking with his mates the night before and had a hangover.

Alice was still living at home, but she was often out at night and away at weekends so Ellie couldn't help feeling lonely. She would look at Joe's favourite armchair in front of the television and remind herself that he would never sit in it again.

Sometimes the phone would ring and she would answer, half expecting to hear his voice. Or she would start to lay a place for him at the dinner table only to remember that he wasn't coming back. Every corner of the house held memories of her dead husband. When she went to bed at night, she would lie awake thinking of him. Often he visited her in her dreams. She was finding it difficult to accept that this was how her life was always going to be.

Of course, she still had Caroline, Mags and Fiona, and they kept a close eye on her. They took her out to the cinema or the theatre and invited her to their homes for meals. But no matter how hard they tried, it couldn't compensate for not having Joe. The affection she shared with them was of a different order from the intimacy she had known with him.

To make up for it, she threw herself even deeper into her work, regularly staying behind when the others had finished so as to complete a report that could easily have waited till the following day. As a result, she often felt exhausted when she got home. But when she went to bed she found it difficult to sleep: her mind raced and she missed Joe's warm body beside her.

She remembered the sleeping tablets Fiona had given her and searched in her bedside drawer till she found them. She took one with a glass of water and immediately fell into the deepest sleep she had enjoyed for weeks. When she woke the following morning, she felt thoroughly refreshed and bursting with renewed vigour.

**

She slipped into the habit of taking a tablet each night before she went to bed. The peace and relaxation that the tablets gave was like balm to her weary body and frazzled nerves. But the day came when all the tablets were gone.

She rang Fiona and asked if she could provide some more.

'Are you having trouble sleeping?' her friend asked.

'Not every night,' Ellie lied. 'But I've a lot on my plate right now and I need to be on top of my game. I find when I take a tablet I have more energy in the morning.'

They agreed to meet for lunch the next day at a pub near Ellie's office. When Fiona sat down, she took a box of tablets out of her bag. 'This is the last batch I can give you,' she said. 'I'm breaking the rules by doing this. Your GP should prescribe your medication.'

'Thank you,' Ellie said, placing the box in her handbag. 'I won't trouble you again. I may not use them but it's good to know they're there just in case.'

'You never had this problem before,' Fiona said. 'You were always an excellent sleeper.'

'That was before Joe died.'

Fiona nodded. 'Are things busy at work?'

'Manic.'

'Maybe you should slow down a little.'

'No.' Ellie laughed. 'I'm well able to handle it. I enjoy my job. I like being busy. It keeps my mind occupied.'

'How are you coping with Joe gone?'

Ellie sighed. 'It's lonely, of course. I think of him all the time. But I have you and Mags and Caroline. And I have my children. Everyone has been marvellous. But I miss him terribly.'

'I think you should have a chat with your GP,' Fiona said. 'Tell her what you've just told me.'

'Surely you can't be serious. A bout of sleeplessness doesn't warrant a visit to the doctor. She has much more urgent cases to deal with. There are people with life-threatening illnesses.'

'Just do as I say,' Fiona said firmly.

***

But Ellie hadn't been entirely truthful with her friend. While she tried to keep up a brave front, inside she was feeling very low. And it was getting worse. Some mornings she would wake as if from a bad dream and the depression would hang over her all day. She told herself it would pass. It was just a matter of pulling herself together.

Meanwhile, Christmas intervened. Ellie wasn't looking forward to it. It would be the first Christmas since they were married that Joe wouldn't be there, sitting at the head of the table with a party hat on, pulling crackers with the children and carving the turkey.

As if she had anticipated this, Dee suggested that they

should all have Christmas lunch at her house in Raheny. Ellie was glad to accept the invitation and to relinquish the stress of preparation and cooking. It turned out to be a very jolly occasion.

There was a fire blazing in the hearth and a tree twinkling in a corner of the room. The family sat around a large table and ate a lovely meal, exchanged presents and afterwards watched television together. When it was all over, Ellie was sorry to leave and go back to her silent house.

Early in January, after the new-year festivities, she returned to work. Mallory and O'Keefe had now entered an intense period as the publication of the government's annual financial statement approached. It outlined the economic plans for the coming year and afterwards clients clamoured for guidance about how they should invest their funds.

Normally, Ellie remained in the background, preparing her economic reports, but now some clients demanded to talk to her directly. It was a very busy time: everyone was under intense pressure and Ellie felt it more than most. There were days when she was irritable and tense, and returned home feeling nervous and exhausted.

Since her talk with Fiona, she had tried to cut down on her use of the tablets, but as the financial statement approached, she found herself relying on them more and more, sometimes taking two to make sure she got a good night's sleep and was ready to face the rigours of the following day.

To add to the stress, Joe's birthday was drawing near and with it came a flood of memories. It had always been a happy occasion. Ellie had made sure to buy him a nice present and a card, and Joe had always insisted on taking her to one of his favourite restaurants to celebrate. This year there would be no presents and no celebration. She would have dinner alone. She was dreading it.

When the day arrived, Ellie was up early. She showered and got dressed, ate toast and scrambled eggs, then set off for work. But as she drove along the busy city roads, a knot was tightening in her stomach.

Once she arrived, she sat in the parking bay for a few minutes while she did some breathing exercises in an effort to calm herself. Then she got out, locked the car and strode purposefully into the office.

It was half past eight and already the phone on her desk was ringing. She sat down and picked it up. One of their best customers was on the line, anxious to talk about a report she had prepared. She took him through it line by line while she tried to answer his questions.

'There's a lot of money riding on this,' the man explained. 'If I make the wrong call I'll be in big trouble.'

'I understand. But we can only offer advice based on the available evidence. We can't predict what the government is going to do, Mr Jones.'

'So what am I supposed to do?'

'I can't tell you that. You must make your own decision. I have set out the government's borrowing requirements and I have also included world and European growth forecasts and financial predictions from the European Central Bank and the Bank of England. These are all based on published statistics.'

'And what if you're wrong?'

Ellie was determined to remain calm, but the tension was rising. 'Wrong about what?'

'The statistics you've included in this report.'

'I'm not wrong. I've just explained that the statistics are all published figures.'

'And what happens if I make the wrong investment decision?'

'You don't have to invest right now, Mr Jones. If you want to be absolutely safe you could postpone your decision till after the financial statement has been published. Then you'll know exactly what you're dealing with.'

'And so will everyone else. The whole point of consulting you is to get ahead of my competitors. I don't know what I'm paying you for,' the man said, terminating the call.

Ellie sighed. What did Mr Jones think she was? An astrologer? But she had scarcely gathered her breath when the phone rang again and another nervous investor was on the line.

It continued like that for the next few hours, non-stop interrogation from clients anxious for any scrap of reassurance, all of them edgy and some more excited than others. Ellie's head was aching.

It reached a climax just before lunchtime when she was subjected to a twenty-minute tirade from an angry stockbroker called Sam Arnold. He was another of their most important clients and always aggressive. As he fulminated and argued with her, Ellie felt herself struggling for breath, as if a strait-jacket had been fastened around her chest.

A thought occurred to her. Why was she allowing him to abuse her like this? She didn't have to take it. Meanwhile, her head felt as if it was about to explode. 'I'm sorry, Mr Arnold, I have to go now.'

'I haven't finished talking,' he snapped. 'You still haven't explained—'

Ellie could take no more. She reached out and turned off the phone, terminating Sam Arnold's call in mid-sentence. Immediately, she felt shocked at what she had done. To cut off a client like that was totally unprofessional. She had never done it before. She stared at the phone in horror, waiting for it to ring again so she could apologise. But it remained silent. She glanced at her hands. They were trembling. And then she felt her chest heave. Next moment, her head had sunk onto the desk and she was weeping uncontrollably.

Chapter Nineteen

She became aware of a stunned silence all around her. Her colleagues had stopped working and were staring at her in embarrassment. The silence continued till a woman approached and put her arms around Ellie's shoulders.

It was Barbara Scales, Hugh O'Leary's secretary. 'Come with me,' she said gently. She gave Ellie a tissue to wipe her eyes while she guided her towards the Ladies. Inside, she locked the door, sat her down and poured a glass of water. 'Drink that,' she said soothingly. 'Just try to relax. Take a deep breath.'

Ellie did as she was told.

'Don't try to talk, just slow down. Everything is going to be all right.'

It was quiet in there, away from the clamour of the main office. Ellie felt the tension begin to ebb and the piercing headache recede. At last, she stood up, bathed her eyes in the washbasin, then dried them with a towel.

'Here,' Barbara said, producing a hairbrush. 'Tidy yourself up. Are you feeling better?'

Ellie nodded. 'I don't know what came over me. I made a complete fool of myself.'

'Don't worry about it. Now, if you're ready, Mr O'Leary would like to see you in his office.'

***

Hugh O'Leary's tall, elegant figure was seated behind a large executive desk. Barbara followed her in, closed the door, then sat down at her own desk and busied herself with some paperwork. Ellie's hands were trembling again. 'I'm terribly sorry,' she said, and felt the tears starting once more.

Hugh O'Leary tore a handful of tissues from a box and gave them to her. Ellie blew her nose and took a deep breath.

'What brought it on?' he asked.

She told him of the confrontation with Sam Arnold. 'He was bullying me and I couldn't take any more. I'm afraid I snapped and cut him off. I feel thoroughly ashamed of myself.'

'I'm not surprised,' O'Leary said. 'Arnold's a tyrant. It's a wonder no one's cut him off before.'

'But he may cancel his account.'

'Let him. In fact, I may just fire him. I don't care for clients who think they can abuse the staff, particularly the women. I've noticed that he rarely treats the men like that.' He smiled gently. 'I blame myself for this. You've been under extreme pressure recently, with Joe's sudden death and everything. I shouldn't have allowed you to come back so soon.'

'But I wanted to.'

'Nevertheless, you've suffered a trauma. You need time to

get over it. I think you should take indefinite leave, Ellie, and see your doctor.'

She stared at him. This was terrible. Never in her entire career had she been told to stay away from work.

'I want you to recover and get your strength back. You haven't looked well for some time. Why don't you go home and take it easy for a while? You'll continue to be paid your salary.'

'But what will people say?'

'Who cares what they say? If anyone asks, tell them you're on compassionate leave. The main thing is that you get better so you can come back and be a fully productive member of the team again. Is there someone at home with you?'

'My daughter.'

'Where is your car?'

'In the car park.'

'I'll get someone to drive you home.'

She began to protest, but Hugh O'Leary was firm. 'I'd never forgive myself if you were involved in an accident. Now, give me the keys, Ellie. And I don't want to see you in the office again till you're fully recovered. Do you understand?'

'Yes.'

He stood up to indicate that the interview was over.

***

As soon as she got home, she went into the kitchen and made a cup of tea. She was still in shock and now it was compounded by shame. She had let herself down in front of the staff. She was older than the others and a senior executive. She was supposed to show leadership. Instead she had broken down, like a babbling idiot.

And she had been put on indefinite leave. How had she

allowed that to happen? She sat staring at the silent room as she tried to get her thoughts in order. She had to speak to someone she could trust. She picked up the phone and called Fiona. 'I need to talk to you.'

'What's happened?'

'I had an incident in work today. I've been sent home on compassionate leave and told to see my doctor.'

'Incident? What sort of incident?'

'I cut off a client and broke down in front of everyone.'

There was a momentary pause.

'Are you at home now?'

'Yes.'

'I'm on duty but I'll be free shortly. I'll come out to the house and you can tell me all about it. Don't go anywhere in the meantime. Okay?'

'Okay,' Ellie agreed.

She looked at her watch and saw it was almost two o'clock. She should eat some lunch but her appetite had gone. Instead, she turned on the television and stared at the screen till at last she heard the sound of a car pulling into the drive. When she opened the door, Fiona was standing on the step with a worried frown.

'Come in,' Ellie said. 'Would you like some tea?'

'That would be very welcome.'

They sat on the sofa in the living room. 'Why don't you just start at the beginning and tell me exactly what happened?' Fiona said.

Ellie recounted the incident with Sam Arnold and the later interview with Hugh O'Leary. 'There's something else I haven't told anyone. Today is Joe's birthday and I'd been dreading it. I've been tense all morning.'

Fiona was nodding sympathetically. 'So how do you feel now?'

'Pretty depressed. I feel ashamed. I don't know what the younger members of staff must be thinking.'

'Are you still having difficulty sleeping?'

'Yes. I miss Joe lying beside me. I even dream about him.'

'How about the sleeping tablets?'

'I'm still using them.'

'Alcohol?'

Ellie looked up sharply.

'Don't get excited,' Fiona said. 'I'm simply trying to get a fix on how you are.'

'I haven't taken to the bottle, if that's what you're implying.'

'What about food? Are you eating normally?'

'Most of the time.'

Fiona finished her questioning and sat up straight. 'Right. For what it's worth, I think the incident with the stockbroker was just a symptom of something much deeper. Hugh O'Leary is right. You came back to work too soon. And you *do* need to see a doctor.'

'But I wanted to be busy. I wanted to work because it would distract me. I thought it would stop me thinking about Joe all the time.'

'But you have to go through a process of grieving, Ellie. You can't avoid it. And Joe's death came right out of the blue. That must have caused a lot of shock. You could be suffering from post-traumatic stress.'

'So what should I do?'

'I think you should see a colleague of mine. Her name is Christine Palmer. She's a bereavement counsellor. She might be able to help.'

'What would it involve?'

'She'll talk to you and help you to unwind. She's very experienced. Do you want me to make an appointment?'

Ellie paused. What harm can it do? she thought. I've got nothing to lose. 'Okay,' she said.

***

The appointment was for the following Monday at ten o'clock in Christine Palmer's clinic in Ranelagh. Ellie arrived ten minutes early, feeling nervous.

Christine Palmer was a small, friendly woman in her early forties. 'So you're Fiona's friend,' she said.

'Yes,' Ellie said.

'Please sit down.' She pointed to a comfortable chair beside her desk, drew out a seat for herself and smiled. 'You've been feeling tense and depressed since your husband's death?'

'That's right. He died suddenly in London from a heart attack. It was a terrible shock.'

'Tell me more about him. Where did you meet him?'

'In a bar.'

'What attracted you to him?'

Ellie's thoughts went flying back to that evening in Neary's pub all those years before. 'He was handsome, well dressed, perfect manners and very generous. He paid for my drinks although I didn't even know him. That impressed me.'

'Why didn't I meet a man like that?' the counsellor joked, and despite her nervousness, Ellie found herself smiling.

As the conversation went on, she began to relax. Ms Palmer continued to probe, enquiring about their courtship, Joe's career and their wedding. She had a pad on the table in front of her and occasionally she wrote something down.

But the questioning was gentle and Ellie never felt she was being interrogated. Before she knew it, the hour was up. Christine Palmer opened her diary. 'Same time next week. Does that suit?'

'Yes,' Ellie said.

***

At their next session, the counsellor asked about the family and Joe's qualities as a husband and father. 'Was he a good provider?'

'Very,' Ellie responded. 'We were never short of money. Of course, I was working too. We both had well-paid jobs.'

'What about the children? How did they relate to him?'

'They adored him.'

'Did he take an interest in their education?'

'Yes, indeed. Even though he had a very busy job, he always made time for them. When they were small he used to sit with them and go over their homework. Working on a newspaper, he could get tickets to sporting events and concerts and he would take the children with him. They loved that. When they got older, he would advise them about possible careers. They admired their father and always looked up to him.'

'What about you? Did you have a happy married life?'

'Oh, yes, but we had our ups and downs, like most married couples. He was a journalist. It's a very disruptive profession.'

'How do you mean?'

'It isn't a nine-to-five job. Joe could be sent off somewhere at a moment's notice. That's why he was in London. Often he might leave for work at ten o'clock in the morning and I mightn't see him again till midnight.'

'How did you react to that?'

'He had warned me before we got married so I was expecting it. But Joe compensated when he had time off. I told you he was very generous. We ate in lovely restaurants and he used to buy me wonderful presents. And any spare time he had, he spent with me and the children.'

'He seems to have been a remarkable man,' Christine Palmer observed.

'He certainly was. He was the most remarkable man I ever met. That's why I married him.'

**

When the third session came around, Ellie was surprised to find she was looking forward to it. Christine Palmer had a knack of putting her at ease. And she took comfort from talking so honestly about her husband.

'When did you realise you were in love with him?'

'Oh, that's easy. I can remember it exactly. Joe had to go down to Marbella to interview a contact and he took me with him. Have you ever been there?'

'Never.'

'It's a beautiful place and we had a wonderful time. It was May and the sun shone all day long and everywhere you looked there were flowers in bloom.'

'It sounds idyllic.'

'It was. It was on that trip that I knew I was in love. We went to Marbella again for our honeymoon.'

'Were there any things about Joe that you didn't like?' the counsellor asked.

Ellie thought of their early days together, living in the apartment in Monkstown. 'When we got married we lived in this fabulous apartment. Joe had been living alone and he was rather untidy. That irritated me so I had to housetrain him.' She smiled. 'But he soon fell into line.'

'Anything else?'

She paused, then shook her head. 'I can't think of anything. Most of the time, we got along extremely well.'

'Did you ever have disagreements?'

'There were differences of opinion sometimes but nothing major. We were both plain-speaking people. We didn't believe in bottling up grievances till they turned into resentments. When we had big decisions to make, we usually talked them over. Joe supported me when I wanted to leave my job to look after the children, and later when they were older and I wanted to go back to work.'

Christine Palmer was nodding. 'Jaw-jaw is always better than war-war. It's the best policy.'

**

One day, towards the end of a session, Christine Palmer surprised her. 'Tell me how you learned of his death.'

Ellie felt a shock run through her as that terrible day came rushing into her head. The tears welled in her eyes. 'Do I have to?'

'I think it would be better for you to confront it. But if you prefer, we can leave it for another session.'

Ellie wiped her eyes and took a deep breath. 'No, I'll talk about it now. Joe had gone to London at short notice. It was supposed to be a short trip so I thought nothing of it. When I got home from work, his editor, Tom Matthews, was waiting for me outside our house. The hotel had called to say Joe had suffered a heart attack.'

She stopped as the words choked in her throat and now

she was weeping. The counsellor waited patiently till she had composed herself and was ready to continue.

'It was the worst moment of my life. I thought my world had come to an end.'

'Go on.'

Ellie trawled through the memories of that day, the house filling with people, the whispered words of sympathy, the sad faces, the cards, the flowers and then the funeral. When she had finished, she felt exhausted.

'That's enough for today,' Christine Palmer said.

***

At the next session, they returned to the subject, but this time Ellie felt more relaxed about discussing it. When it was over she felt as if she had let go of an enormous burden.

Christine Palmer congratulated her. 'You've been extremely brave,' she said. 'I know it's been hard but now you've got it all out.'

The entire course took eight weeks and when it was over, Ellie felt much better. She was sleeping again and her energy was back. Most important, the gloom and depression that had weighed her down had lifted.

***

At the final session, Christine Palmer took her hand. 'Ellie, I must say that Joe Plunkett seems to have been a wonderful husband. Any woman would have been proud of him.'

'Thank you.'

'But we should know that nothing lasts for ever. Now, I think it's time for you to move on. That doesn't mean you should forget Joe. You still have those wonderful memories.

But you must come to terms with what has happened, difficult as that might be.'

'Am I ready to go back to work?'

'Not quite. You've been through a very harrowing time. I think you should treat yourself to a nice holiday. Why don't you go somewhere you and Joe were happy? Indeed, I have the perfect place. Why don't you go to Marbella?'

***

When Ellie got home, she rang Fiona. 'Christine has suggested I take a holiday in Marbella.'

'And how do you feel about that?'

'I'm a little unsure.'

'Well, Christine is the expert so I'd be inclined to take her advice. In fact, I have an idea. If you're worried about going on your own, why don't you invite Mags to go with you? The Easter break is coming up and she'll be off school.'

'You're a genius,' Ellie said. She rang Mags at once.

'My counsellor has suggested I take a holiday in Marbella. I wondered if you'd like to come with me. I'd be happy to pick up the costs.'

'Would I!' Mags replied. 'I'd bite your arm off for an offer like that. When do we go?'

'As soon as I can organise the tickets.'

Chapter Twenty

Ellie set to work at once. By now, she was fired up by the idea and anxious to visit the Costa del Sol again. But because it was Easter, lots of people had had the same idea. As a result, flights were hard to come by and so was accommodation. But she was determined and eventually managed to get two seats to Málaga via London. However, when she tried to book a room in Hotel Majestic, where she had been twice before, she was told it was full. It took some time surfing the internet before she finally got a double room in an establishment called the Alhambra. It was smaller than the Majestic but closer to the centre of the town. They booked for five nights.

Once those essentials were taken care of, she was able to concentrate on preparing for the trip. This was half the pleasure.

Mags, who had never been to Spain before, wanted to know what to pack.

'My advice is to bring as little as possible. Just take some light clothes for the daytime and a couple of dresses for the evening. It's all very casual down there. No one expects you to get dressed up. Oh, and bring a swimsuit and a good book. I've checked the weather forecast. It's going to be warm. We'll spend plenty of time in the sun.'

Finally, she told the children. Their reaction was unanimous. They thought it was a brilliant idea. They were aware, of course, of the pain she had suffered after their father's death and wanted to encourage her.

'When are you going?' Jack asked.

'On Easter Monday. I couldn't get a direct flight so we're flying to London first, then on to Spain. But we're coming back straight to Dublin.'

'What time have you got to be at the airport?'

'Ten o'clock.'

'I'll drive you.'

'Thank you, Jack. That's much appreciated.'

He shrugged. '*De nada.*'

Ellie couldn't help a smile. 'So you're speaking Spanish now?'

'*Poco, poco,*' he replied.

***

At last, the departure day arrived. They had agreed that Mags would come to Ellie's home in Clontarf and travel to the airport with Jack and her. She turned up in a buzz of excitement, having read up about Marbella on the internet. They got into Jack's car and set off.

There was little traffic on the roads and they made the journey in plenty of time. Jack carried their luggage from the car and gave Ellie a hug as he was leaving. 'Go off and have a great time, Mum. We're all rooting for you. It's time you got a break.'

Ellie had a lump in her throat as he kissed her goodbye. Then they loaded their luggage onto a trolley and set off through Security.

The flight to London left on time, but they had a rush to change terminals at Heathrow airport before they boarded the Málaga flight. There was a roar of engines as the aircraft took off and the land disappeared from view. When the stewardess came round with the trolley, they purchased two glasses of champagne. Ellie sat back in her seat and gave a contented sigh. 'How do you feel?' she asked her friend.

'Like a giddy schoolgirl on her first holiday abroad,' Mags replied.

'Me too. Something tells me we're going to enjoy this trip.'

***

It was late afternoon when they arrived in Málaga but the sun was still strong. A board above the terminal exit gave the temperature at 17 degrees centigrade, which was a big advance on the nine degrees they had left behind in Dublin. Once they were outside, they made straight for the taxi rank and gave their destination. Five minutes later, they were on the motorway.

The resorts flashed by, Benalmadena, Fuengirola, Calahonda, till at last they reached Elviria and the outskirts of Marbella. Soon after, the taxi pulled into a driveway with a large sign announcing Hotel Alhambra and deposited them at the front door.

A porter appeared to take their cases while Ellie paid the driver. They stood for a moment to take in their surroundings.

The Alhambra appeared to be an old hotel that had been refurbished. There was a lawn in front, and to the side they could see the sun sparkling on the blue water of the swimming pool. They followed the porter to the registration desk.

The room they were given lacked some of the luxury she had enjoyed at the Majestic. It had two single beds, an en-suite bathroom and a television but there was no fridge or writing desk, and instead of a terrace, there was a large window with the curtains drawn. But Ellie wasn't in a mood to complain. She was happy to be there and felt lucky to get the room at such short notice.

'So what do we do now?' Mags asked, once they had unpacked.

Ellie had half a mind to go for a swim, but she sensed that her friend was anxious to get out and explore their surroundings. The pool could wait till tomorrow. She checked the time and found it was half past five. 'Are you hungry?'

'Not really.' They had eaten a snack on the plane.

'Why don't I show you the town and later we can find somewhere to eat?'

'Perfect.'

It took half an hour to get showered and changed into light, casual clothes. Outside, the air was warm. The shops were open again, after the siesta, and there were lots of people on the streets. After walking for fifteen minutes, they caught the tang of sea air. They rounded a corner and were on the Paseo Maritimo.

A rush of memories came flooding back. Ellie had walked this promenade so many times with Joe on the previous occasions she had been there. She felt a catch in her throat and her eyes misted. Then she recalled what Christine Palmer had told her. She would always have the wonderful memories of her dead husband but she had to move on. That was the reason she was there.

She pasted a smile onto her face, took Mags's arm and joined the crowds that were surging along the Paseo. They wandered for more than an hour, stopping occasionally to watch the buskers and the street entertainers. Mags got out her phone and began taking photos. She was fascinated, swept away by the intoxicating atmosphere of the music, the laughter, the lights and the evening air. Eventually, they came to the end of the promenade and decided it was time to eat. They found a pleasant restaurant nearby, went in and sat down.

'What do you want to eat?' Ellie picked up the menu.

'I don't think I could manage a big meal. Besides, I'd like to get a good night's sleep.'

'I agree. In fact, I know the very thing.'

She summoned the waiter and ordered tortilla for them both – a potato and onion omelette, served with salad and a basket of bread. To accompany the snack, they drank glasses of red wine.

When they returned to Hotel Alhambra it was almost ten o'clock and the lights of the bar were on. From inside, they could hear someone singing 'The Fields of Athenry'. On the way past, they glanced in and saw a group of men drinking at the counter. The man who was singing waved to them as they went by.

In their room, they undressed, washed and slid into their beds, tired after all the travelling. Outside the window, a big moon was casting light into the room. Ten minutes later, they were asleep.

***

Ellie woke at ten past eight to find Mags still fast asleep. She took a pair of shorts and a T-shirt from the wardrobe and went into the bathroom to put on her swimsuit. Then she put her clothes and a towel into a bag, slipped on a dressing gown and tiptoed quietly from the room so as not to wake her friend.

Downstairs, the hotel was coming awake. The cleaners were mopping the floors, and from the dining room she could smell breakfast cooking. She made her way to the side of the hotel where she had glimpsed the pool the previous afternoon. By now, the sun was higher in the sky and the air was warming. As she approached, she was surprised to see a man stepping out of the shower.

'Good morning,' he said cheerfully, in an unmistakably Irish accent. 'Best time of the day for a swim. The water's really refreshing.'

He was middle-aged, fair-haired, with a strong athletic build. And his face was familiar. Suddenly, she recognised him: he was the man who had been singing in the bar the previous night.

'Have you just arrived?' he asked, as he started to dry himself.

'No, we came yesterday.'

'And may I ask where you're from?'

'Dublin.'

'The same as myself.' He held out his hand for Ellie to shake. 'My name is Mick Flynn. I'm here on a golfing trip with some of my friends. We come down at this time every year.'

'I'm Ellie Plunkett.'

'I'm pleased to meet you, Ellie. You'll enjoy it here. The staff are marvellous. We have a sing-song every night in the bar, if you and your husband would care to join us.'

'My husband isn't here. I'm with a woman friend.'

He winked. 'That's even better. You're both welcome. Have a good day now, Ellie, and mind you don't get burned. That sun is very strong.' He finished drying himself, pulled on a dressing gown and walked away. Ellie was glad to see him go so she could get into the pool and have her swim.

Back in their room, she found Mags up, dressed and anxious to have breakfast. 'What are the plans for today?' Mags asked.

'I'd like to unwind by the pool. Later we can go into town and find somewhere nice to have dinner.'

'That sounds ideal.'

'Incidentally, those guys who were singing in the bar last night? They're Irish golfers.'

'Really?' Mags looked surprised. 'How do you know that?'

Ellie tapped her nose and grinned. 'I wasn't married to a reporter for all those years without picking up a few tips.'

Mags was shaking her head. 'Irish golfers, indeed? The bloody Irish are everywhere. We travel all this distance and we still can't escape them.'

***

The dining room had a large breakfast menu, including bacon and eggs, cereals and fruit. The two women contented themselves with coffee and golden croissants smeared with honey. They finished with slices of melon. Once they had eaten, they made their way out to the pool.

It was deserted, apart from a young couple reading the papers in the shade. A pile of loungers was stacked in a corner. They selected two, spread out their towels and applied some sun cream. Then they took out their novels and settled down to read.

It was peaceful, the only sound the occasional drone of the bees around the flowers. As the morning progressed, the sun grew stronger and more people arrived. After a while, Ellie decided to have another swim and Mags agreed to join her. Then they stretched out once more on the loungers until one o'clock, when they began to feel peckish. They repaired once more to the dining room where they had a light lunch.

By now, they had decided they'd had enough sunbathing and found a shaded part of the garden where they continued to read. Ellie sighed. It was so pleasant to sit out there and relax. Gradually, her eyelids began to droop and the book slipped from her fingers. A few minutes later, she was fast asleep.

She came awake with Mags shaking her shoulder. For a split second, she thought she was back home in Clontarf but when she sat up and looked around she recognised the garden. 'What happened?' she asked, rubbing her eyes.

'You dozed off,' Mags replied. 'You've been asleep for an hour and a half.'

'What time is it?'

'Ten past five. I thought I'd better wake you. I want to get out and see some more of the town while it's still bright.'

'Sure,' Ellie said, getting up. 'Let's go to our room and get changed.'

***

By six o'clock they were ready to set off. Above them, the sun had begun its descent. 'What would you like to see?' Ellie asked, as they turned into a street outside the hotel.

'You tell me. You've been here before.'

'Okay! Why don't we take a look at Plaza de Los Naranjos, otherwise known as Orange Square? I think you'll like it. It's the old part of town, with fountains, cobbled streets and plenty of quaint little shops. And there are lots of nice restaurants in that area.'

Half an hour later, they arrived at the Casco Historico, Marbella's historic quarter, where Ellie had been on her first trip. It was a maze of narrow alleys filled with boutiques, hanging baskets of flowers and little squares dominated by ancient churches. They browsed for a while amid tourists busily taking photos but saw nothing they wanted to buy. At last, they turned their attention to finding a suitable restaurant.

There were plenty to choose from. After checking menus they found a place they liked the look of in a street off the main square. They were promptly shown to a table.

'What would you like to drink?' the waiter asked, in very good English.

They chose a bottle of chilled white wine and gave their order for food. The waiter returned promptly with the wine and a basket of freshly baked bread. Ellie poured and raised the glass to her lips. She sat back in her chair and closed her eyes. Coming back to Marbella had been the right decision. Already she could feel the benefits.

The waiter was back with their first courses, a crispy chicken salad for Mags and smoked salmon for Ellie. Mags followed her salad with roast lamb and Ellie had a plump fillet of sea bass grilled with garlic. The dishes were garnished with broccoli, carrots, peppers and sautéed potatoes.

As they ate, the vacant tables began to fill up till they were all taken. The buzz of conversation swelled around them in several languages. By the time the waiter arrived with the dessert menu, they were so full they had to decline but accepted his offer of liqueurs.

By now the setting sun was casting a red glow across the evening sky. The lights came on and music spilled out from a bar further along the street. The crowds of tourists increased. It was time to pay. Ellie took out her purse but Mags insisted she put it away. 'You paid for my flight and accommodation. The least you can let me do is buy you dinner.'

The bill came to forty-five euros, which they both agreed was remarkably good value for such an excellent meal. Mags left fifty euros in the dish and they set off again through the busy streets, taking their time to savour the lively carnival atmosphere that was now abroad.

It was half past nine when they got back to the Alhambra and too early to go to bed. Mags suggested they stop off at the hotel bar and have a nightcap. They had just bought their drinks when Ellie spotted the golfers at the end of the room and remembered they would be having their sing-song.

The golfers had also spotted them. The fair-haired man she had met at the swimming pool detached himself from his friends and began to make his way towards them. Ellie tried to remember his name. It was Mick something. Mick Flynn – that was it. He approached with his hand outstretched.

'So you're Ellie's beautiful friend,' he said to Mags. 'She's already told me about you.'

Ellie watched Mags struggle not to laugh as she made the introduction. 'This is Mags Bannon. Mags, this is Mick Flynn, the handsome swimmer I met this morning. He's from Dublin.'

This time it was Mick who laughed. 'She's a bit of a comedian, isn't she?' he said to Mags. 'How are you ladies enjoying your trip?'

'So far, so good,' Mags replied. 'We've just been out to dinner.'

'Anywhere nice?'

She produced the card the waiter had given them and Mick studied it. 'Restaurante Lopez? That's near Orange Square, isn't it? I think I've been there. Did you have a nice meal?'

'Excellent.'

'We're spoiled for choice, aren't we?' he continued. 'There are so many good places it's hard to go wrong. Now, we're about to start singing. Why don't you come and join us?'

Ellie exchanged a glance with Mags, who shrugged. If they refused, it might appear rude. 'We can't stay long,' Ellie said. 'We need our beauty sleep.'

'No, you don't. You're beautiful enough already. Now, let me help you with your drinks.'

He carried their glasses from the counter to where his friends were waiting and quickly introduced them. 'Can you ladies sing?' he enquired.

'Only in the shower,' Ellie replied, to a gale of laughter.

***

The singing session turned out to be much more fun than they had expected. Mick Flynn acted as master of ceremonies and called each of his friends in turn. The songs were well-known favourites with choruses that everyone could join in with, and some of the golfers had excellent voices.

The session never got rowdy and none of the other guests in the bar seemed to mind. Indeed, a group of British holidaymakers joined them at one stage and contributed to the merriment. As a result, Ellie and Mags thoroughly enjoyed themselves and stayed much longer than they had planned. It was midnight when they left and went up in the lift to their room.

'I think Mick Flynn has a thing about you,' Mags said, as they were undressing for bed.

'Don't be daft,' Ellie retorted. 'He was just being friendly.'

'I'm not so sure. He never took his eyes off you. I notice things like that.'

***

The holiday quickly settled into a pleasant routine. Because they only had five days, they decided to forgo any sightseeing trips. Each morning, the two friends woke at seven o'clock as the sun was coming up. Ellie put on her swimsuit, wrapped herself in a dressing gown and went down to the pool, where she enjoyed a vigorous swim. Afterwards, she joined Mags in the dining room and together they had breakfast.

Then it was out to the garden where they spent the next few hours sunbathing and Ellie had another swim. Around one o'clock they had a light lunch in the dining room or at a nearby bar then returned to the garden. In the evening, they dressed up and went out for dinner. When they got back, they dropped into the bar for a nightcap with Mick Flynn and his golfing friends.

The time passed quickly and suddenly the holiday was drawing to a close. On the last day, they went into the centre of Marbella and did some shopping for gifts. That night they went back to Restaurante Lopez.

But when they returned to the hotel they got a surprise. They called into the bar, expecting to have a farewell drink with Mick Flynn and his friends, but found it deserted. When they asked the barman, he told them they had left to go home to Ireland.

**

In the morning Ellie and Mags were up early and packed their cases. Ellie went down to the reception desk and settled the bill, then joined Mags for breakfast. At nine o'clock a taxi came to transport them to the airport for the flight to Dublin, which left at midday.

As the plane roared along the runway and took off, Ellie turned to the window and watched the landscape of Spain receding below them. She felt a twinge of sorrow. She always felt sad to leave Spain.

Chapter Twenty-one

When she got home, everyone commented on how well she looked. She certainly felt good. The holiday had been a tonic: it had revived her spirits and restored her confidence. Now, she couldn't wait to return to work.

First, though, she made an appointment to see Christine Palmer. They sat in her office in Ranelagh and drank tea.

'How do you feel?'

'Fantastic. The break in Marbella was a marvellous idea.'

'The depression has gone?'

'Completely.'

'And you've got your energy back?'

'Yes.'

'What about sleeping?'

'Like a baby.'

'So, you've accepted Joe's death and now you want to move on?'

'Yes. I want to go back to work.'

'Well, I don't see why you shouldn't,' the counsellor said. 'The routine will be good for you.'

***

Later, Ellie rang Fiona to tell her.

'Congratulations,' her friend said. 'That's great news. Now, take a word of advice. Don't start acting like Superwoman. Pace yourself. Ease yourself in.'

'Yes, Doctor,' Ellie said.

She was exhilarated at the prospect of returning to Mallory and O'Keefe and meeting her colleagues again. She had lost touch with them since she had been away. In preparation, she took her business suits out of the wardrobe and brought them to the dry cleaner. She went to the salon and had her hair styled. Then she rang Hugh O'Leary. She'd been gone for ten weeks and she knew he'd be pleased to have her back. But instead of Hugh, it was his secretary, Barbara Scales, who answered.

'Ellie,' she said. 'It's great to hear from you. How are you keeping?'

'I'm good, Barbara. I'm fully recovered.'

'Well done. That's excellent news.'

'I'm feeling really well and looking forward to getting back to work. Is Hugh there? I'd like to speak to him.'

'He's in Berlin for a few days, attending a conference.'

'When will he be back?'

'This weekend.'

'Would you ask him to call me whenever he's free?'

'Of course. I'm delighted for you, Ellie. I really am.'

While she waited for Hugh's call, Ellie busied herself with small chores. She got out the mower and cut the grass. She weeded the flowerbeds and fed them some fertiliser. She paid a visit to Joe's parents, who were going through their own grieving process. She went online and scanned the financial news sites to keep abreast of developments.

A week went past and Hugh O'Leary didn't ring. Ellie began to feel uneasy. It dawned on her that, since the calls he had made to her during the first month of her leave, he hadn't been in touch for two months.

When that thought crossed her mind, she quickly dismissed it. He was a busy man and the world didn't stop just because Ellie Plunkett had been unwell. She had to be patient. He would contact her in due course. But when a second week had passed, and he still hadn't called, she became concerned.

Barbara Scales was a super-efficient secretary so Hugh O'Leary would certainly have been told about her request to return to work. He must have forgotten or ... A worse possibility crashed into her mind. He was deliberately ignoring her.

That idea set off a panic. What should she do? She could ring again and remind him, but that might be counter-productive. It might make her seem anxious or, worse, neurotic. But if she did nothing, it would appear that she didn't care. Now she had a dilemma.

She waited for a few more days, growing very uneasy. A new thought had entered her head. She was the chief analyst at Mallory and O'Keefe, one of the most senior executives in the company. What did it say about her professional standing that she was being forced to hang around for more than a fortnight, waiting for her phone call to be answered?

That decided her. She took out her mobile and rang him. He answered at once.

'Hello, Hugh. It's Ellie. I called two weeks ago to say I was ready to return to work and I haven't heard from you.'

Immediately he was apologising. 'I know, I know. I have Barbara's message right here in front of me on my desk. I'm sorry, Ellie. Things have been hectic in here recently. When are you free to have lunch?'

They agreed to meet at the Tour d'Argent restaurant on Baggot Street at one o'clock the following day. Ellie was relieved that things were now moving forward. She knew the restaurant well. It had been one of Joe's favourite haunts.

She made sure to get there before Hugh and was pleased when the waiter showed her to a table at the back of the room where they would have privacy to talk. She sipped a glass of iced water while she waited. Bang on one o'clock she saw his tall figure striding in to join her. He bent to kiss her cheek, then sat down across from her. She saw his eyes examine her carefully.

'It's good to see you again, Ellie.'

'You too. I want to begin by thanking you for your support, Hugh. You were right, of course. I should have taken more time to grieve after Joe's death. I understand that now.'

'There's no need to thank me. You weren't thinking straight. You had just received the biggest shock of your life. Now you want to come back to work?'

'Yes.'

He placed his palms together as if in prayer. 'I've given this matter some consideration, Ellie. Before I can agree to you returning, I want you to see the company doctor.'

She sat back in surprise. 'But I've been seeing a bereavement counsellor and she says I'm fit to return. Besides, I'm feeling fine. I'm sleeping well. I'm—'

He cut her short. 'You're a valued member of staff, Ellie, and naturally I want to see you get back to full health. This is for your own good. Besides, it's company policy. I thought you knew that.'

'But ... but ...'

'You're not listening to me. I want you to see the company doctor. If he says you're ready to come back then there is no problem.'

She sat back in defeat. 'So what do I do?'

'I'll ask Barbara to arrange an appointment. She'll ring and confirm it with you. In the meantime, I must ask you to be patient. Once I've got the doctor's report I'll contact you again.'

She felt crushed. But she sensed there was no point in arguing. Hugh O'Leary had obviously made up his mind. 'Whatever you say, Hugh.'

'Good. Now, where has that damned waiter gone? I'm starving.'

**

It wasn't a long lunch. They had finished by two o'clock. Hugh paid the bill and they parted at the door. The sun had come out and some people were sipping drinks at outside tables. For a moment, Ellie was reminded of what she had left behind in Marbella.

But the meeting had upset her and she was angry as she made her way back to the car. She decided to ring Fiona.

'I've just had lunch with Hugh O'Leary. Before I can return to work, he wants me to be examined by the company doctor.'

'Have you got a problem with that?' Fiona enquired.

'Damned right I do. It's totally unnecessary. There's nothing wrong with me. Christine Palmer said I was ready to come back.'

'All right, calm down. He's being cautious, that's all.

Employment law has been tightened up considerably in recent years. I suspect he just wants to make sure that everything is watertight before you come back.'

'I don't understand. What on earth are you talking about?'

'For God's sake, do I have to spell it out for you? He doesn't want to be blamed if you have another meltdown.'

Ellie caught her breath. 'Really, Fiona, you of all people, I thought I could rely on you for support.'

'And so you can, but in this case, I think Hugh O'Leary is right. Why don't you just go along with it? You'll get a clean bill of health and be back to your old routine in a couple of weeks.'

'Thanks for nothing,' she said bitterly.

**

By the time she got home to Clontarf, she had calmed down a little, although her confidence was shaken. She had foolishly expected to sail back into work. She had believed that Hugh O'Leary would be so pleased he would roll out the red carpet for her. Now she saw she had been naive. His long delay in returning her phone call should have warned her.

Barbara Scales rang later to say that an appointment had been made with the company doctor for tomorrow morning at nine o'clock. Since her cholesterol levels would be checked, she was to fast from midnight. Ellie thanked her. She sat staring at the television screen for a couple of hours, then decided to go to bed: she'd have an early night.

She was up at half past seven and at the doctor's surgery for ten to nine. He was a thin, serious-faced man, who began by taking a blood sample, sounding her chest, checking her weight and blood pressure. Then he proceeded to ask a series of questions about her diet, exercise, sleeping pattern, alcohol consumption and family medical history, while he scribbled notes on a pad.

He finished by asking about Joe's sudden death and the counselling she had received from Christine Palmer. 'So how do you feel now?'

'Perfectly fit.'

'You work in a very stressful occupation, Mrs Plunkett. Have you any reservations about returning?'

'None whatsoever. I'm looking forward to going back.'

'And your counsellor is of the same opinion?'

'Yes. She said I was ready to return.'

The doctor stood up and shook her hand. 'I should have the results of the blood tests in a couple of days. Your weight and blood pressure are fine. You appear to be healthy. My report will be with Mr O'Leary within the next few days.'

Ellie left the surgery feeling ravenous. She hadn't eaten since the previous evening. She went to a nearby café, threw caution to the winds and treated herself to a full Irish breakfast.

***

Hugh O'Leary called a few days later, after he had received the doctor's report. She already knew what it contained because she had received a copy that morning in the post. It said she was perfectly healthy and ready to resume work. The news had pleased her immensely.

'I've got the report,' he began. 'I suppose you have too?'

'Yes.'

'You've been given the all-clear. That's excellent news, Ellie.'

'Thank you. When can I start?'

'Whenever you like. Is tomorrow all right?'

'Tomorrow will be fine.'

'There's something else. I don't think it's a good idea to throw you in at the deep end right away. It might be better if you eased yourself back in. I'm thinking of a shorter working day, say nine to two. When you feel comfortable, you can resume your full duties again.'

Ellie was taken aback. 'Is that really necessary? The medical report has cleared me, and I'm anxious to get back to my job.'

But his voice was firm. 'Nevertheless, you've been gone for quite a while. It will take time to readjust. Now, why don't you come in a little earlier tomorrow, let's say eight o'clock, so that you're already in position when the others arrive? It will save any embarrassment.'

Ellie gasped. But before she could respond, she heard O'Leary's phone switch off. *Embarrassment*, she thought. *So that's what I've become.* She was angry again. She didn't believe his story about easing back into work. Something had changed at Mallory and O'Keefe. Before, she had been treated with dignity and respect. Now she was being treated like a doormat.

She thought of the two weeks she had been forced to wait for Hugh O'Leary to return her phone call, then being sent to see the company doctor and now this insult. She felt the resentment boil up. She needed to talk to someone, but not Fiona. She would get no sympathy there.

She thought of Mags. She would listen and give good advice. Besides, she was active in the teachers' union and had been its representative for her school. She might have come across situations like this before. She waited for an hour to make sure she would be home, then dialled her number.

Mags answered at once. 'Hi, Ellie, back at work yet?'

'I'm starting tomorrow.'

'That's good. How long have you been gone? Two months?'

'Almost three.'

'Is it that long? You must be dying to get your bum back on that seat.'

'That's why I'm ringing, Mags. I've run into a problem and I need to talk to someone sensible. So I thought of you.'

'Is it bad?'

'It could be.'

'Well, in that case, I'd better come over right away. Are you at home?'

'Yes.'

'Sit tight. I'll be with you in twenty minutes.'

As soon as she'd ended the call, she felt better. Immediately, she set about preparing for Mags's visit. She arranged two comfortable chairs in the living room with a table between them and laid out little dishes of nuts and crackers. Then she went out to the garage and chose a good bottle of Rioja from her small wine store. It was her favourite wine and always revived happy memories of Spain. She was about to uncork the bottle when something made her stop.

It might not be a good idea to drink just now. The conversation with Mags was very important and she needed to give it her full attention. Afterwards, when they had finished talking, she might treat herself to a glass. She brought the bottle into the house and put it on the sideboard just as the doorbell rang.

Mags was on the doorstep, smiling. 'It's so good to see you,' she declared, as they greeted each other in a flurry of hugs and kisses. Ellie took her coat and led her into the living room.

'Why don't you tell me what's going on?' Mags began.

Ellie recounted the various obstacles she had met and how

Hugh O'Leary had practically ordered her to work a shorter week. 'I thought they'd be delighted to have me back. I'm the firm's chief analyst, that's a key position, but Hugh O'Leary's not exactly popping the champagne corks at the news.'

'What do you think is going on?'

'I'm not sure. Fiona says he's being cautious in case I have another meltdown but that's not going to happen. Sometimes I wonder if they want me back at all.'

'Mmm,' Mags said. 'Fiona could be right. But on the other hand, it sounds like he has been rather heavy-handed. There is another scenario but you're not going to like it.'

'Tell me.'

'You're getting on a bit, just like the rest of us. We're all going to be fifty this year.'

'Go on.'

'For the period you were out on leave, someone else was doing your job, probably some bright young spark, eager for promotion. Has it occurred to you that Hugh O'Leary might be planning to replace you?'

Ellie's face went pale. 'Never.'

'It would explain his reluctance to let you come back.'

'He can't do that, can he?'

'He can do whatever he likes. He's the boss. But it depends how he goes about it. It's illegal to discriminate against someone on the grounds of age or gender. So you have rights too.'

'What do you suggest I do?'

'First thing is to avoid a confrontation. If my suspicion is right, you don't want to give him any grounds for taking action against you. So don't react, just remain calm, and do whatever he says. But make sure to keep a diary. Take notes of conversations, dates, times, anything you think is relevant. You might need the information later.'

Ellie sighed and sat back in her chair. 'I never dreamed it was anything like that,' she said. 'I've been with the company for over twenty years, practically from the beginning.'

'Look,' Mags said, placing a comforting hand on her friend's shoulder, 'this is pure speculation. It may never happen. But there's no harm in preparing for all eventualities.'

Ellie nodded. Her anger was gone. Now, it had been replaced by fear. 'I think I'll have a glass of wine,' she said.

Chapter Twenty-two

That night, she couldn't sleep. Until now, she had considered her position at Mallory and O'Keefe to be unassailable. She was one of the longest-serving staff members with a proven record for turning out high-quality reports. She was easy to work with and popular with her colleagues. She had always believed she was indispensable. It had never crossed her mind that her job could be under threat.

But that incident at work had changed everything. If only it hadn't happened. If only she hadn't reacted to that pompous bully, Sam Arnold. If only she had held herself together and allowed him to rant till he was out of breath. But she had been under too much pressure. She was tired. And it had been Joe's birthday.

Now, though, she had been warned and would be on her guard. Mags had given her good advice. Whatever Hugh O'Leary might do, this time she would not react. She would remain calm. She would be courteous, punctual and efficient. She would be the perfect employee, the sort of person that no one in their right mind would ever dream of replacing. And she would keep her diary.

Finally she drifted off. But a couple of hours later, the clanging alarm clock shook her awake again. She jumped out of bed, showered, dressed, ate a quick breakfast and was driving into the early-morning traffic by half past seven.

When she arrived at the office, she found a handful of early birds had got in before her. They came up to her, shook hands and seemed genuinely pleased to see her back.

'Like a coffee?' one of the juniors asked. 'I'm going down to the deli.'

'Sure,' she replied. 'A latte, please. Here, let me give you the money.'

But he waved it away. 'It's on me.' He grinned. 'Welcome-back present.'

She sat down at her desk. Someone had swept it clean in preparation for her return. She took a deep breath and savoured the experience. It was good to be there. She switched on her laptop and began scanning the financial papers. As the staff drifted in, they approached and said how glad they were to see her.

At half past eight, Barbara Scales came out of her office with a bundle of economic documents. She smiled sweetly as she placed them on Ellie's desk. 'Hugh's asked me to give you these. It's great to see you again, Ellie. You're looking really good.'

'Thank you, Barbara.'

'My pleasure.' She smiled again, then walked back across the floor. Before long the phones were ringing and the buzz in the office reached its usual pitch. Another busy day had started at Mallory and O'Keefe.

When lunchtime arrived, Ellie sent the messenger boy out for a sandwich and ate it at her desk. She continued working till two o'clock when she closed her laptop, stood up and left, as agreed with Hugh O'Leary. Her first day back could not have gone more smoothly.

As the days slipped past, Ellie began to adjust to her new routine. Hugh O'Leary went out of his way to welcome her and publicly compliment her on her work. When the weekly planning conference arrived, she took her place among the other senior staff and joined in the discussion. Gradually, she began to relax and feel at home. It was as if she had never been away. The only thing that was different was her shorter working day.

But she soon discovered that this had advantages. Now she had all this free time to enjoy the glorious weather, which had arrived with the advent of summer. She rediscovered the joys of reading a good novel, listening to some music or just sitting in the garden letting the sun warm her face while the birds chattered in the trees.

She drove out to Howth and went for walks along the cliffs. She called in on the children. She made several trips to the cinema, something she hadn't done for ages. She had lunch with Caroline one afternoon and listened while she related the ups and downs of another problematic relationship.

As the conversation continued, she remembered something she had meant to ask Caroline after Joe had died. This was her opportunity. 'I've always wondered how Joe got my name and phone number all those years ago when he rang and asked me out on our first date. It was you, wasn't it? You told him all about me. He even knew I was an economist.'

Caroline blushed. 'Yes,' she confessed. 'He was very

insistent. He said he just had to talk to you. So in the end I told him. I didn't think there was any harm. As it turned out, I did you a favour, didn't I?'

Ellie smiled. 'Yes,' she said. 'You certainly did.'

She began to revive the idea of having a celebration for their fiftieth and decided to talk to Mags first. If she got her on board, the others would surely follow. She arranged to see her in town one afternoon when they had both finished work. They met in the foyer of the Gresham Hotel.

'How are things going with the job?' Mags said, once they were seated in a quiet corner with tea and scones.

'Much better than I expected,' Ellie confessed. 'Everyone's been lovely. Nobody's mentioned that day when I put the phone down on Sam Arnold and burst into tears. Indeed, Hugh O'Leary has been so kind that sometimes I wonder if I might have been a bit paranoid about him.'

'Let's hope it stays that way,' Mags said. 'And what about the children? How are they?'

'All fine, I'm glad to say. I think we might have another wedding on our hands before too long.'

'Really?' Mags leaned forward to pour the tea.

'I've been told nothing officially but I have a suspicion that Jack and Mollie might make an announcement one of these days. I have a sixth sense about these things. I remember deciding that you were about to marry Peter before you declared it.'

'Get away.'

'It's true. I remember the occasion well. It was at the first dinner party we gave in Joe's apartment.'

'And what led you to that conclusion?'

'Your general demeanour. When you saw the kitchen you

gasped and said it was exactly what you wanted. I remember thinking, Mags is planning a place of her own.'

Her friend laughed. 'And you were right. I'd already decided that Peter was the man for me. I just had to get him to realise it too.'

'And before long you were walking down the aisle.'

'Yes,' Mags said wistfully, then straightened up. 'Now, tell me what exactly you have in mind for this birthday celebration.'

Ellie buttered a scone and took a bite. 'Fifty is a milestone in any woman's life and I thought we should mark it in some way. We could have dinner in a good restaurant and spend the evening reminiscing. We might even bring some old photographs.'

'And take some new ones,' Mags said, warming to the idea.

'Exactly. I always enjoy the occasions when the four of us get together.'

'Well, I'm certainly up for it,' Mags announced. 'And I expect Fiona will agree too. However, you might have a problem getting Caroline to come on board. You know she has a thing about birthdays. She prefers not to be reminded.'

'I had lunch with her recently,' Ellie said.

'And?'

'It's the same old story. We spent most of the time talking about her latest beau, some businessman called Freddie Hawthorne. He's entirely smitten, apparently, sends her bouquets of roses, waits for her at the theatre door and phones her first thing in the morning and last thing at night.'

'He sounds great.'

'Caroline doesn't think so. She says he's too clingy.'

'Oh, for God's sake!' Mags groaned. 'What exactly does she want?'

'Drama. Caroline isn't happy unless there's turmoil and break-ups and tearful reunions and undying professions of love. She needs excitement in her relationships. I don't think she'll ever meet a man she can marry.'

'I'm afraid you might be right,' Mags agreed.

***

Ellie set to work on the scheme at once. First, she went on a reconnaissance mission to check out several potential venues. She finally hit on the Avondale Hotel, which was close by in Clontarf. It was a small hotel with a cosy restaurant offering an extensive menu at modest prices. It had just the right air of privacy and intimacy. Ellie knew they would be able to relax there without being disturbed by noisy diners.

By now, Fiona had also agreed to come on board, which left Caroline. But when Ellie approached her, she was adamant: 'You know how much I hate birthdays. I can't see the point of them, except to remind us that we're getting closer to the grave.'

'Oh, Caroline, don't be so ghoulish.'

'Well, it's perfectly true. I think everyone would be much happier if birthdays were abolished altogether.'

'Fiona and Mags are coming. It's going to be a great evening. Fiona has unearthed some old photographs of us when we were living at the flat in Blackrock. It will be great fun remembering those happy times together.'

'Thanks for inviting me, but I'm afraid I'll have to decline. I have my own memories and some of them aren't so happy.'

'But it won't be the same without you,' Ellie protested. 'You were a key member of our club.'

'Now you're trying to butter me up.'

'Not at all. I'd just like you to come because you mean so much to us all.'

'Let me think about it,' Caroline said reluctantly.

While she waited, Ellie went ahead and booked the restaurant for a Saturday night in two weeks' time, saying there would be three diners and possibly a fourth. The restaurant manager assured her it wouldn't be a problem. They would simply add another place.

As the date approached, she found herself getting excited. She searched her own photo albums and came across pictures of the girls at various college functions and parties. She marvelled at how young and innocent they looked, and how old-fashioned their clothes, hairstyles and makeup now appeared. And she thought of how happy they had been as their lives lay waiting before them, filled with golden promise.

The day before the dinner, she got the awaited call from Caroline.

'Is there still time?' she asked.

'Of course. For you there will always be time.'

'Then I'll come. I've just had a flaming row with Freddie and I want to teach him a lesson. Besides, I feel a bit guilty. We really were something special, the four of us. It would be a shame if I didn't celebrate it.'

'Now you're talking sense,' Ellie said.

* * *

On the night of their celebration, they gathered in Ellie's house beforehand and drank champagne while they congratulated each other on their choice of outfits and hairstyles. Having finally agreed to come, Caroline was in fine party mood, regaling the group with titbits of salacious theatrical gossip that had everyone in shrieks of laughter. She was clearly intent on enjoying herself.

Ellie had arranged a taxi to transport them the short distance to the restaurant. Just as they were about to leave, Alice appeared. She insisted on forming them into a group and taking their photograph. She turned her phone around to reveal her handiwork.

'Definitely another for the album,' Mags opined.

The evening was a sparkling success. There were only a handful of other diners in the restaurant so they had it practically to themselves. Once they were seated at a corner table, the conversation began again and soon they were chatting and laughing hilariously as they shared stories and recounted old memories. Meanwhile, the waiter quietly got on with his task of serving them a superb dinner.

It was one o'clock when the party finally broke up. By now, everyone was tiddly and Caroline was slurring her words. Ellie said she could stay overnight at her house in Clontarf so the waiter ordered a taxi. When it arrived, they all piled in, Ellie pressing a generous tip into his hand.

As they approached Ellie's front door, Caroline suddenly wrapped her arms around her and kissed her cheek. 'What a night,' she declared. 'I haven't enjoyed myself so much for as long as I can remember. We must do it again next year.'

Chapter Twenty-three

By now, Ellie had got used to her new working environment. She was performing the same job as before but with less pressure and more free time. But she couldn't wait to resume full-time working. The firm's business was expanding and soon Hugh O'Leary would have to decide when she was ready to take up her normal duties. It was exasperating but there was nothing she could do.

By patient enquiry, she had discovered who had replaced her when she was out on compassionate leave. As Mags had guessed, it was someone younger: a thirty-two-year-old economics graduate called Alan Courtney.

He was a likeable young man, hard-working and industrious, and had recently got married. Ellie had sat on the interview panel that had hired him three years previously. Since her return to work, he had been extremely pleasant and deferential to her, always asking if she wanted anything when he made his morning trip to the deli. When she looked at him working, his head bent over his laptop, she didn't see anything to threaten her or make her feel nervous.

Once more, she wondered if she had allowed her imagination to run away with her. Perhaps Fiona had been right all along and Hugh was simply being cautious by sending her to the company doctor and placing her on shorter working hours. If he had allowed her to come back too soon, and she'd had another meltdown, he might indeed have been blamed. And, she thought grimly, it might have been the end of her career.

***

One morning, she received a call from Barbara Scales to say that Hugh wanted to see her in his office. She left her desk at once and went and knocked on his door. She found him leaning back in his executive chair with a smile. She noticed that Barbara had absented herself.

'Sit down,' her boss said pleasantly. 'How are you feeling?'

'Good.'

'No more ...?'

'No,' she said. 'I'm fine.'

'That's good news. I have to say I'm very pleased with your work and so are our clients. I've had several calls recently to say how accurate your economic forecasts have been. Congratulations, Ellie.'

'Thank you.'

'So, do you think you're ready to resume a normal working schedule?'

'Of course. I'm ready whenever you are.'

'In that case, you can start tomorrow. We'll extend your working day from nine till six.'

She felt a thrill of excitement. 'That's great, thank you.'

He smiled. 'Don't you think it's ironic that you're thanking me for extending your working day? Many employees would regard that as an imposition and denounce me as a slave-driver.'

'Not me. I enjoy my work. I take pride in it.'

'I know that, Ellie, and it brings me to another matter I want to discuss with you.'

She sat up straight.

'Recently, I've been giving some thought to reorganising the staff and bringing up some of the younger people. I've found a new role for you.'

The alarm returned. Here it was at last, the change Mags had warned her about. Hugh O'Leary was going to tell her she was being replaced. She forced herself to sit still while he continued.

'Instead of compiling general analysis reports, which are sent to all our clients, I'd like you to draw up reports specifically tailored to individual clients to meet their particular requirements.'

His eyes were studying her face but Ellie remained motionless.

'There's a growing demand for this service. Several of our key customers have enquired about it. And if we don't provide it, our competitors certainly will. I thought you would be ideally suited to this job, Ellie. You've got the qualifications and the experience.'

'Would my conditions of employment be altered?'

He dismissed her question with a wave of his hand. 'You don't have to be concerned on that front. If anything, your conditions will improve. You'll get a salary increase and you'll be free to work from home when you're not required in the office. And we'll upgrade your company car. So, what do you say?'

It sounded very tempting but she remembered Mags's advice to remain calm and not react. 'This is a surprise, Hugh. Do you mind if I take a few days to consider it? And would you also put it in writing for me?'

'Of course. I'll get Barbara to do it immediately. There is one more thing I have to stress, however. This conversation is confidential. I must ask you to keep the information to yourself.'

Ellie got up to leave, when something crossed her mind. 'Do you mind if I ask another question?'

'Not at all.'

'If I accept, who will fill my present position?'

'I have Alan Courtney in mind. He's young and sharp and has buckets of energy. And he has recently got married. He could use the salary increase.'

She went back to her desk and continued working. But she found it difficult to concentrate and couldn't wait for two o'clock to come so she could get away and write down what she could remember of the conversation. Despite Mags's warning, the development had caught her off guard.

The morning seemed to drag, but eventually it was time to leave. She tidied her desk, put on her coat and went down to the car. It took twenty-five minutes to get home. She went at once to the living room, sat down, took out a notepad and began writing. At five o'clock, when she was sure that Mags would be home from school, she called her.

'There's been a development at work,' she said.

'Oh! Tell me.'

'You were right in your suspicion. I had a discussion with Hugh O'Leary this morning. He wants to move me.'

'I hope you did what I told you?'

'Yes. I didn't react. I just let him talk, then asked for time to consider the situation. And I've got it all down on paper.'

'Good. Are you at home now?'

'Yes.'

'Okay. Let me take care of a few things and I'll be with you shortly.'

As she put the phone down, Ellie realised that she had broken her boss's instruction to keep the conversation confidential. But this matter was too important. She needed advice and, besides, she knew she could trust Mags not to tell anyone else.

While she waited, she poured a glass of wine and went outside to the garden to sit in the sun. By now, her mind was in a spin. The new job sounded like an improvement on her present situation. But she had to be aware of potential drawbacks. Once Alan Courtney had taken over her present position, it would be too late.

At last, she heard the sound of a car coming into the drive. She went back into the house as the doorbell sounded. Mags was standing on the step in a light summer dress with a cardigan thrown across her shoulders. They went into the living room.

'Can I offer you something to drink?'

'No, let's get right down to business.'

'So,' Ellie began. 'I was called into Hugh O'Leary's office this morning and he told me I could resume my normal working schedule from tomorrow.'

'That sounds like progress.'

'It is, but then he dropped his big surprise into my lap.'

She told Mags about the new job, glancing occasionally at her notes even though she had the details off by heart. When she had finished she waited for Mags's reaction.

'I must say it sounds pretty reasonable. You're getting more money, a better car and you can work from home. How do you feel about it?'

'I know it sounds attractive but I'm worried in case it's a trap. Once I leave my present job, I can never get it back. And he did say he was doing it because he wants to move up some of the younger people. He particularly mentioned Alan Courtney's youth and energy.'

'But that's not necessarily a bad thing,' Mags replied. 'Young people may lack experience but they do have more energy. And they need to be given their chance. Besides, Hugh O'Leary has to take account of the overall situation. Perhaps he's worried that Alan Courtney might look elsewhere if he thinks his chances of promotion are being restricted.'

'So you think I should take it?'

'That's for you to decide. But on the basis of what you've told me, I don't think you have any grounds for saying you're being discriminated against.'

'And if I refuse?'

'He could make life difficult for you. You know that, Ellie. When does he expect a response?'

'In a few days.'

Mags got up to leave. At the front door, she stopped and looked into Ellie's face. 'If you want to talk again just pick up the phone. But, remember, there are lots of people who would give their right arm for an opportunity like this.' She paused. 'You know, Ellie, as we get older, we become settled and many of us don't welcome change because it's disruptive and we don't like that. Are you sure that's not what's really bothering you?'

***

Over the next few days, Ellie thought hard about what her friend had said. Perhaps she *was* afraid of change. She had grown comfortable in her present job. Perhaps the time had arrived to accept the new challenge.

It wasn't a major change. She would be doing what she had always done, drawing up reports based on her analysis of economic and financial data. The only difference was that she would be dealing with individual clients. And there were the benefits to consider: a bigger salary, a better car and the chance to work from home. She might grow to like it.

The letter came from Hugh O'Leary setting out the terms of her new position. She read it carefully but already she was making up her mind. She waited another couple of days and then she went to see him in his office. 'I've made my decision.'

'Yes?' he asked.

'I've decided to accept. When do you want me to start?'

He smiled, stood up and shook her hand. 'You've made the right call, Ellie. I promise you won't regret it. Now, why don't we keep this under our hats for the present? I have a few more staff changes to make. It would be best if I announce them all at the same time.'

She left his office feeling quite light-hearted. But she didn't have long to dwell on the situation. In quick succession, two announcements came and banished all other thoughts from her mind. First, Jack declared that he was marrying Mollie. Then, two days later, Dee called to see her with Tony, and told her she was pregnant.

Chapter Twenty-four

J ack's announcement wasn't a big surprise but Ellie was still delighted. Jack was her first child and her only boy, and he had a special place in her heart.

His girlfriend, Mollie, was a clever young woman with a sunny personality and a pretty face beneath a mass of curly blonde hair. She worked as personal assistant to the manager of a big department store in Henry Street. She had been living with Jack for three years, which Ellie reckoned was plenty of time to get to know each other. From observation, she believed the pair were well matched and the marriage would be happy.

The really startling news was Dee's pregnancy. She had been married to Tony Mulhall for just a few years and they both had good jobs and busy lives in advertising. Ellie had always believed they would wait till they had consolidated their financial situation before starting a family.

She wondered if the pregnancy had been unplanned, like hers with Jack and Dee had been. But it didn't matter. She was about to become a grandmother, with all the special joys that would bring. From the moment she heard the news, she began looking forward to the birth with intense anticipation.

However, the immediate item on the agenda was Jack's wedding. It was scheduled for September, which was only a few months away and there was a lot of planning to do. Thankfully, most of the work would fall to the bride's family. Ellie remembered the frantic preparation that had gone into Dee's wedding and gave a quiet sigh of relief.

The first thing she must do was get to know Mollie's parents. She had often heard them mentioned in conversation but they had never met. She knew that Mollie's father, Jim Brennan, was a senior civil servant in the Department of Finance and her mother, Sally, ran a thriving fashion business selling women's clothes from a boutique in fashionable Dawson Street. They lived in Dalkey in south Dublin.

She decided to give a little dinner party to which she would invite the Brennans, Dee and Tony and, of course, Alice. When she put the suggestion to Jack and Mollie, they thought it was a wonderful idea, while Alice and Dee said they would pitch in and help her.

'Are you sure? I'm quite capable of doing it myself,' she said.

'We know that, Wonder Woman,' the girls replied. 'But there can be a lot of hassle with dinner parties and we want you to be able to relax and enjoy it too. We're going to help you whether you like it or not.'

'Okay.' Ellie laughed. 'In that case, you can roll up your sleeves.'

The Brennans accepted the invitation, and the date was fixed for the following Saturday evening at eight o'clock. Now Ellie had to plan the menu. Thankfully, there were no fussy eaters among the guests or anyone with food allergies. She sat down with Dee and Alice and got to work.

'The secret of dinner parties,' Dee began, with the air of an experienced hostess, 'is to keep the menu simple. Avoid anything that is complicated or takes too long to cook. Above all, don't experiment. Leave that to when you're cooking for yourself. Then if it's a disaster, you are the only person who is affected.'

Ellie stared at her in amazement. 'Where did you gain this culinary knowledge, might I ask?'

'I've been attending classes.'

'Good for you!' Ellie exclaimed.

After some discussion they agreed on a simple cucumber and sweet onion salad to accompany roast duck breasts with maple syrup, which Dee said would take about forty-five minutes to cook. This would be followed by pepper-crusted salmon with potatoes, carrots and broccoli, cooking time twenty-five minutes. And for dessert they would have lemon tart, which could be bought from any decent pastry shop.

'It will look good, taste fabulous and leave everyone feeling satisfied,' Dee declared. 'And before you ask me how I know, I've already served the same menu to some of my friends. Believe me, nothing can go wrong.'

'You heard that?' Ellie said to Alice. 'Nothing can go wrong. Now I've got a witness.'

***

Ellie left the shopping till Saturday morning since Dee had assured her that the preparation and cooking would take very little time. In the meantime, she tidied the house, not that it needed much cleaning since she and Alice were the only occupants and Alice spent much of her time with her college friends. But she wanted to create a good impression on her future in-laws. For good measure she went out and tidied the garden.

When Saturday arrived, she set off early for the supermarket with Alice to escape the weekend rush. It took very little time to gather together the ingredients she required. She also stopped off in the wine department and bought some extra supplies, adding a couple of liqueurs to her trolley.

They had barely returned home when her phone rang and Dee announced that she would drop by around five o'clock to give her a hand. This suited Ellie: it meant she could catch a little nap to charge up her batteries before preparing for the busy night ahead.

Not that it turned out to be particularly busy. By six o'clock, with her daughters' help, she had done all the preparation. The salad was made, the vegetables prepared and the lemon tart was waiting in the fridge to be sliced. She had actually bought two in case someone asked for a second helping. All that remained to be done was to cook the duck breasts, vegetables and salmon.

She left Alice watching television in the living room while she disappeared into the bathroom to have a shower and change into a party dress she had bought at a sale last summer. She examined herself in the mirror. She thought the dress fitted her perfectly and looked quite classy. She hoped Sally Brennan would think so too. She was in the fashion business and was sure to have a critical eye for clothes.

She had asked Jack and Mollie to get to the house for seven thirty so that they could make the introductions when the guests arrived. They were quickly followed by Dee and Tony.

When the doorbell rang at five past eight, a welcome party was waiting in the hall.

A middle-aged man with receding hair was standing on the doorstep dressed in a casual suit, shirt and tie. Beside him stood a small, thin woman with the same blonde hair as Mollie.

'Come in, come in,' Ellie cried, accepting the flowers that Sally Brennan offered, and ushered the guests into the living room where Mollie stepped forward to introduce her parents. Everyone shook hands.

'What can I get you to drink?' Ellie asked, when the formalities were completed.

'Nothing for me,' Sally replied, with a smile. 'I'm the driver tonight.'

'That's so that I can relax.' Jim Brennan grinned. 'I wouldn't object to a gin and tonic.'

Dee was already moving quickly to the drinks cabinet while everyone sat down.

'I hope you didn't have any trouble finding us?' Ellie asked.

'Not at all,' Sally replied. 'The directions were very good. And the traffic was light.' She made some complimentary remarks about the house and the furnishings. 'How long have you been living here?'

Ellie thought back to the summer's day when they had moved in and the housewarming party she had given soon after. It seemed like only yesterday. The children had been so small and now Jack had grown up and was getting married. Where had the time gone? 'Almost twenty years. Before that we lived in an apartment my husband owned in Monkstown.'

'Jack talks about him all the time. He has great affection for his father. He must have been a wonderful man.'

Ellie felt a lump rising in her throat but she quickly composed herself. 'He was that and more,' she replied.

The time came to serve the meal. They all trooped into the dining room and took their places round the big table while Alice and Dee disappeared into the kitchen and returned with the salad and the roast duck. Meanwhile Jack had opened some bottles of wine and was filling the glasses.

By now, the initial reserve had melted away and everyone was talking animatedly.

'Have you guys thought about where you're going to live when you get married?' Jim Brennan asked his daughter.

Mollie and Jack exchanged a glance.

'We thought we'd continue to rent in Sandymount for a while but we've started saving for a house,' Jack said.

'That's a wise move. House prices are stable right now but they can only go one way and that's up. The sooner you get your feet on the property ladder the better. Do you intend to buy in Sandymount?'

'We haven't decided. It's a nice area and handy for work,' Mollie replied, 'but prices are a bit on the high side.'

'That's because so many people want to live there. When the time comes, talk to me. I might be able to offer some advice.'

Ellie was anxious to discuss the wedding. 'You've got an awful lot of planning to do,' she said.

'I can vouch for that,' Dee added. 'There are the bridesmaids, the dresses, the reception and lots of other smaller things that you tend to forget about, like someone to sing at the service.'

'Tell me about it.' Sally Brennan sighed. 'But I have to confess that I'm actually enjoying it so far. And I must congratulate Mollie and Jack. They're very well organised. Mollie has all these lists made out, so it's a simple matter of ticking things off as they get done.'

'Well, if there is anything I can do to help, don't hesitate to ask,' Ellie said.

'We might take you up on that,' Mollie replied.

'Have you decided on your honeymoon destination?'

'We're thinking we might go to Thailand. It's a place we both want to visit.'

'Thailand,' Ellie mused wistfully. 'Joe and I went to Marbella and we thought it was the height of sophistication.'

'We went to Spain too,' Sally Brennan remarked, and everyone laughed.

The plates were cleared away and the salmon was served. Ellie was pleased to see them all tucking into the food. Hopefully it meant they were enjoying it, not just being polite. When the time arrived to deliver the lemon tart, there was a lively buzz of conversation around the table.

She felt herself relax as any fears she'd had for the success of the dinner disappeared. The Brennans were a warm, friendly couple who were clearly just as pleased as she was about the forthcoming marriage. It was after midnight when the party broke up. Jack and Mollie accepted the Brennans' offer of a lift to Sandymount and their party set off.

Soon after, Dee and Tony left for the short drive to Raheny. Only Alice and Ellie remained. Ellie walked into the kitchen expecting to find a pile of dirty dishes and pots and discovered the dishwasher chugging away. The room was spotless. She turned to her daughter. 'Who is responsible for this?' she asked.

'Dee and I. Surely you didn't think we'd leave it all for you to do.'

Ellie's heart filled with tenderness. She put her arms around her daughter and drew her close. 'Thank you,' she said. 'I've been blessed with wonderful children.'

***

After that, the marriage preparations seemed to move up a gear and there was a flurry of activity. A venue and cars had to be booked and a band hired, the wedding cake ordered, and a photographer engaged. Then there were the consultations with the priest who was going to conduct the marriage ceremony.

A lot of time seemed to be devoted to the design of Mollie's wedding dress and those of the bridesmaids. This was something that Sally Brennan got deeply immersed in since she had special expertise in fashion. Ellie's main contribution, apart from some small matters, was deciding which friends of the Plunkett family should be added to the guest list.

It was a minor nightmare studded with pitfalls. Since her own wedding she had been aware that some people could take offence if they weren't invited while others hated weddings and would prefer not to be asked at all. She had lengthy discussions with Jack and Mollie and eventually they managed to establish whom they should ask.

She wondered what she should give the young couple as a wedding present. She knew that lots of their friends would be giving household items for when they eventually set up home. But she wanted to do something special, something they would always remember. After turning it over in her mind, she rang Mollie one day at work. 'I've been thinking about your wedding present,' she said. 'Is there anything you would particularly like?'

'Oh, Ellie,' Mollie said. 'We've already received loads of stuff. You don't have to waste time worrying about that.'

'But it's important to me and I want to get it right. Are you still thinking of Thailand for your honeymoon?'

'Yes. Jack's been making enquiries.'

'Then let me pay for it.'

She heard a small gasp of surprise.

'That's far too much.'

'No, it's not. Jack is my only son and you are going to be my new daughter. Now, I have to insist on this. Book a good hotel in a good resort and send me the bill. And do the same with flights. Don't spare any expense. I'm going to pick up the tab. I want this to be a honeymoon you'll remember for the rest of your lives, just as mine was.'

Chapter Twenty-five

In the blink of an eye, the wedding day was upon them, all the planning and preparation, the hiccups, hitches and last-minute phone calls behind them. Ellie woke to a beautifully mild September morning, with the roses and geraniums opening and the sun already bathing the garden in golden light.

Ellie and Alice were travelling to the church with Dee and Tony, and she had arranged with Hugh O'Leary to take a couple of days' leave, having worked late to finish some urgent reports. Now she was free to enjoy Jack and Mollie's big day.

She threw back the duvet and went to the bathroom to have a shower. Then she put on a dressing gown and ran down to the kitchen, where she found Alice preparing scrambled eggs, toast and coffee. Jack had spent the night with his groomsmen in a hotel in Killiney to be closer to the church. Ellie had just finished eating when the phone rang and she heard Alice say, 'Hello, Jack, I'm glad you're up! How's it going over there? ... Great ... Okay. See you later.'

It was now twenty past nine. The wedding was at midday in Dalkey parish church and they needed to leave in plenty of time to get there, particularly as Alice was to be one of the bridesmaids. They would never be forgiven if they were late.

The phone rang again and this time Ellie answered. She pushed back her chair and stood up. 'That was Dee. She'll be here at half ten so you'd better get a move on. Leave the washing-up to me.'

'Okay,' Alice said, and departed.

Ellie cleared up the breakfast things, then went to her bedroom and began to get dressed. She had bought a new outfit for the occasion and had had her hair styled at the local hairdresser's. She slipped into the dress, bent her head closer to the mirror and began to apply some makeup. Then she examined herself. She thought she looked good, particularly for a woman in her fiftieth year.

When she was ready, she went and knocked on Alice's door. She had put on her bridesmaid's dress and was standing in her stockings, brushing her hair. 'Let me see you,' Ellie said, sitting down on the bed and appraising her daughter. 'You're ravishing. You'll draw a lot of attention, mark my words.'

Alice smiled, delighted at the praise. 'You really think so?'

'I wouldn't tell you so if I didn't. Perhaps the next time you wear a dress like that, it'll be on your own wedding day.'

Alice laughed. 'Don't hold your breath.'

'Can I help you with anything?' Ellie asked.

'Yes, you can do up my zip.'

Ellie quickly did so, then walked to the door. 'You've got twenty minutes. Don't hang about.'

She sat down and waited for Alice to finish dressing. Fifteen minutes later her daughter appeared, holding up the hem of her dress lest it snag on her shoes. 'So how do I look?' she asked.

'Like an angel. In fact I'm going to take a photograph to prove it.' She got out her phone, took several pictures, then showed them to Alice.

They heard Dee's car turn into the drive. 'Here's our lift. I think you'd better put a coat over your dress. You can leave it in the car when we get to the church. It's going to be a long day and it might turn cold later. Have you packed clothes to change into after the reception?'

'They're in a bag in my room.'

'I'll go and get it. Tell Dee I'm on my way.'

**

They piled into the back of the car while Dee took the front seat beside Tony, who was driving.

'You look lovely,' Dee said, turning her head to admire her sister. 'Are you excited?'

'I'm nervous,' Alice admitted.

'Just think how Mollie must feel.'

'Oh, Mollie will be fine. She's so together, she won't turn a hair. She'll enjoy every minute.'

'And why not? She's the main attraction.'

The morning rush had passed and they made quick progress across the river to the south side, then headed towards Dalkey. It was half past eleven when they reached the church and Tony found somewhere to park. By now, the early-morning promise had resulted in a beautiful sunny day.

Ellie took out her phone again and rang Jack. 'I'm just calling to put your mind at ease. We've arrived. Alice will wait at the church for the other bridesmaids.'

'They're about to leave,' Jack replied. 'And so are we.'

'How are you? Sleep okay? I hope you weren't up half the night carousing with your friends.'

'No, Mum, we were all in bed by midnight. Now, don't worry about me. I'm going to be fine.'

'Best of luck,' Ellie said. 'See you soon.' She switched off the phone and turned to Alice. 'Jack seems to be in good form – no sign of nerves with that boy. Now, let's get you inside.'

The church was already filling with wedding guests and the photographer was on standby outside ready to snap the bride as she arrived. Tony and Dee left to take their places with the groom's guests, while Ellie waited with Alice in the porch for the other bridesmaids. Five minutes later, Jack arrived with his entourage. Ellie watched proudly as he made his way down the aisle to wait for his bride.

Soon afterwards, the bridesmaids drove up to the front door in a limousine. This was Ellie's cue to leave Alice and take her seat. A few minutes later, Sally Brennan and her party slipped into their pew. She waved and smiled to Ellie. By now the church was packed and an expectant hush had descended as the minutes ticked away towards midday.

Suddenly there was a blast from the organ and all the heads turned to see Mollie make her way slowly down the aisle on her father's arm to where Jack was waiting to receive her. Jim Brennan paused and handed his daughter to his new son-in-law. Jack kissed his bride's cheek. The remainder of the bridal party took their places and the ceremony began.

**

The reception was held in a nearby hotel. Ellie made her way there with Dee and Tony where they were shepherded out to the garden and all the guests were assembled for a group photograph. Then there were more pictures of the bride and groom and family members. When that was over, they returned to the hotel lounge while the photographer concentrated on the immediate bridal party.

Several waiters were circulating with trays of champagne. Ellie reached for a glass and heard a voice at her shoulder. She turned to find Sally Brennan standing beside her, beaming. 'Weren't they magnificent?' she said. 'I don't think I've ever seen such a handsome couple. Jack looked so dashing. You must be very proud of him.'

'Not as proud as you must be of Mollie. She was absolutely stunning. And her dress was beautiful. Who designed it?'

'A friend in the fashion business.'

'Well, full marks. Mollie was radiant.'

'And they looked so happy,' Sally went on. 'Oh, I'm thrilled to bits that everything has gone so well.'

Ellie remembered the joy she had felt at Dee's wedding, and the excitement of her own at the parish church in Ballymount all those years ago. 'Enjoy every moment of it,' she said, raising her glass. 'May they have a long and happy life together.'

Sally returned the toast, then said she must leave to have her photograph taken again. Dee had appeared at Ellie's side. 'So far, so good,' she remarked. 'Do you know where we're seated?'

'There's a plan over there in the corner. I know I'm at the top table. *And* I've got to deliver a speech.'

'Can't you just rehash the one you gave at our wedding?' Tony said, with a grin. 'No one will notice. Wedding speeches always sound the same anyway.'

'I'm afraid not. I don't think that would do at all.'

A waiter was passing with a tray. Dee stopped him and selected a glass, which she passed to Ellie, then one more for Tony.

***

It was half past seven before the meal was over and the speeches were finished. The hotel staff started clearing space at the back of the room where a band began to play. People left their seats and got up to dance. This was Ellie's opportunity to escape. It had been a long, tiring day and now she was anxious to get home.

The bride and groom were staying overnight at the hotel and departing for their honeymoon in the morning. Ellie went to them and said farewell, then thanked the Brennans for their wonderful hospitality. Last she sought out Dee and Tony. They, too, were ready to leave because they had to be at work in the morning.

Outside, the evening had turned cold. She got into the back of the car and Tony turned on the heat.

'I'm afraid I'm not as fit as I used to be,' she confessed, as she leaned her head on the seat. 'I'm completely exhausted.'

'Join the club,' Tony replied. 'It was a great wedding but it went on too bloody long.'

It was almost nine o'clock when the car turned into Ellie's drive. She kissed her daughter and son-in-law and waved them goodbye. Then she opened the hall door and stepped into her house. By ten, she was tucked up in bed, fast asleep.

Chapter Twenty-six

Now that the wedding was successfully out of the way, Ellie was able to give all her attention to her daughter. Dee was twenty-two weeks pregnant. She was putting on weight and her bump advertised to any observant onlooker that a baby was on the way. She had broken the news to family and friends, and alerted her employers to her condition. Just as Ellie had done, she was planning to continue working for as long as possible before taking maternity leave.

By now she was making regular visits to her doctor and the baby clinic for check-ups. One day she told Ellie she had an appointment for an ultrasound scan, to check for any problems. It also showed the baby's sex. The radiographer would tell her whether it was a boy or a girl if she wanted to know. She couldn't decide. What did her mother think?

'That's entirely a matter for you. Some women like to know in advance so they can get used to the idea and think about names. Others prefer a surprise. The scan gives your doctor lots of information – like whether you're carrying twins.'

'Twins?' Dee caught her breath. 'I never thought about that.'

'There's no history of twins in the family.' Ellie laughed. 'But who can tell?'

Dee's scan confirmed that there was only one baby and it was progressing well. She had decided she didn't need to know its sex. She wanted the surprise. It was something to look forward to.

***

Ellie was enjoying her daughter's pregnancy. It was almost as if she was pregnant again herself. She recalled those early days at the apartment in Monkstown and the way she had been torn about returning to work. She hoped Dee wouldn't face similar doubts. Dee had said she planned to go back as soon as her maternity leave expired because they needed the money.

Ellie wondered if they were having financial difficulties. 'Are things tight for you money-wise?' she asked.

'Well, not exactly,' Dee replied. 'We can probably manage quite well on Tony's salary, especially when you factor in the cost of childcare if I go back to work. But we were hoping to have a little nest egg put together for the children's education before we started a family.'

So her guess had been right. The baby was unplanned. 'Don't think too far ahead,' Ellie advised. 'Sometimes these things have a way of resolving themselves. And before you make any big decisions, talk to me.'

***

Soon after Ellie and Dee had had that conversation, a problem at Mallory and O'Keefe caused a change in Ellie's working situation. Since taking over her new job, she had fallen into the habit of working at home for two or three days each week, which gave her more free time for her daughter.

Until one day Hugh O'Leary called to say that Alan Courtney was ill and would be out of action for a while. He needed Ellie to take over her former job again, which meant she would be working from the office.

'What's the matter with him?' she asked.

'I'm not quite sure. Recently, he's been coughing and wheezing quite a lot. It's best that he stays away till he recovers. I don't want everyone going down sick.'

Reluctantly, she resumed her old work pattern, which meant leaving home at half past eight each morning and not getting back till almost seven at night. Some evenings she was forced to bring work home with her because her clients still wanted her specialised reports. But Ellie always found time each day to ring her daughter.

There were weekends, too, when she was free and she looked forward to them. She drove down to Raheny on Saturday mornings and spent the day with Dee, helping with household chores and shopping. Tony had taken on the more robust tasks, like trimming the lawn and doing the laundry.

Dee had become friendly with a neighbour called Angie, who had two small children and regarded herself as something of an expert on child-rearing. Ellie would often find the pair of them at the kitchen table with mugs of tea while they discussed the pros and cons of bottle or breast feeding and the best way to get a good night's sleep once the baby had arrived.

Meanwhile, Jack and Mollie had returned from their honeymoon in Thailand with tales of the wonderful time they'd had. They called to see Dee regularly and Alice also helped. Together, they made sure she had plenty of support as her due date moved closer.

By now, Dee was in the last trimester of the pregnancy. She was quite heavy and was finding it uncomfortable to move around. Ellie broached the subject of leaving work early. 'Why don't you go two weeks before your due date?'

'I'd get bored sitting at home all day.'

'Nonsense, you've got Angie on hand. She'd be delighted to keep you company. And I'll come and see you each evening after work. The big thing is you'll be able to rest. You're going to need all your energy when the baby arrives.'

Dee took the advice, rang her boss and told her of her decision. Now when Ellie called, she found Dee sitting in an armchair watching television or reading.

***

She was at work one afternoon when she got the phone call she had long been expecting. 'I'm going into labour,' Dee gasped. 'The baby's coming.'

Ellie took a deep breath. 'Okay. Ring the hospital and tell them so they're expecting you. Have you got your bag packed?'

'It's been ready for weeks.'

'After you've called the hospital, ring Tony.'

'I've done that.'

'Good girl. You've got everything under control. I'll be with you shortly.'

She went immediately to Hugh O'Leary's office and told him what was happening.

'Of course you must go. I fully understand. Is there anything I can do?'

'I don't think so. I'll get back to work as soon as possible.'

'Don't worry about us for the time being. We'll muddle through. The main thing is your daughter. Now off you go. And good luck, Ellie.'

She raced to the car and started it. By now her nerves were in shreds. She used the car phone to call Dee again. 'Have you done as I said?'

'Yes. Tony's going to meet me at the hospital.'

'Okay, I'm on my way. I'll be with you in twenty minutes.'

The school rush was over and the roads were pretty clear. She resisted the urge to put her foot down. At last, she reached Raheny village and turned into Dee's road. A small knot of neighbours had gathered outside the house. Ellie parked the car and strode purposefully towards the front door.

One of the neighbours recognised her. 'She's fine,' the woman said. 'Angie's looking after her.'

'Thank you,' Ellie replied, and pushed open the door.

She found Dee stretched out on the sofa with Angie holding her hand and wiping the sweat off her face.

'Thank God, you're here,' Dee said. 'I'm afraid of the baby coming too soon.'

'Just try to relax,' Ellie said. 'Can you stand up?'

Dee lowered her feet to the floor and, with help from Angie and Ellie, she managed to stand.

'How regular are the contractions?'

'About every ten minutes.'

'Okay, let's get you into the car. Would you like a glass of water?'

Dee shook her head.

Ellie and Angie each took an arm and together they got Dee into the car and strapped her into the back seat. Ellie got in and started the engine. Then they set off. 'You'll be fine,' she said. 'Now, don't be worrying about anything.'

As they approached the city centre, the traffic got heavier. Ellie's heart began to pound but at last the hospital loomed into sight. She pulled into a parking bay and left the engine running while she rushed inside.

'My daughter's in labour,' she explained to the woman on the desk. 'I have her outside in my car. She needs a porter.'

'Right away,' the receptionist said, and reached for the phone. A couple of minutes later, a burly man appeared. Ellie followed him to the car and watched as he expertly transferred Dee to a wheelchair.

Satisfied that everything was under control, she drove to the car park, then returned to the hospital. This time, she was directed to the delivery suite. When she got there, she introduced herself to a nurse, who assured her that Mrs Mulhall was being looked after.

'May I see her?'

'Certainly.'

'What about the father? He'll be along soon.'

'He can see her but we prefer only one of you to stay for the birth. Too many people get in the way.'

'Of course,' Ellie said.

'So, if you'd like to come with me, Mrs Plunkett.'

She followed the nurse to a room where she found Dee dressed in a hospital gown and lying on a bed. She smiled when she saw Ellie and held out her hand.

'How are you feeling?'

'Not too bad – they're saying it shouldn't be long.'

'You're in expert hands. If the contractions get too severe, I'm sure they'll give you something.'

Dee closed her eyes as another contraction began. By the time it had faded and she opened her eyes again, Tony had arrived. He kissed his wife and held her other hand. 'How are you?' he whispered.

'I've been better.'

He brushed her hair back from her forehead.

'I'm going to leave,' Ellie said. 'They prefer just one relative at a time. And since Tony's the father, he should have the privilege. I'll wait outside.'

There was a machine in the waiting room delivering coffee in plastic cups. Ellie bought one, lowered herself into a chair and gave a sigh. She hated to see Dee in pain. She took out her phone and rang Alice, then Jack to tell them what was happening and promised to call again when she had more news.

She put her phone back into her bag and took a sip of the lukewarm coffee. The hours dragged by. Several people had joined her in the waiting room, all looking anxious as they waited for news.

After what had seemed like eternity, the door opened and a nurse looked in. 'Mrs Plunkett?'

Ellie immediately stood up. 'That's me.'

The nurse smiled. 'Your daughter has just given birth to a little girl, weighing seven pounds. Mother and baby are fine.'

Chapter Twenty-seven

Once she was home from the hospital, Dee enjoyed being the centre of attention, with friends sending presents and cards, cooing over the baby and saying how pretty she was. She liked being fussed over by Tony, too. But the novelty soon wore off and she was left with the hard work of baby-rearing. She quickly got used to changing nappies and being woken in the middle of the night by a crying child demanding to be fed.

Ellie spent as much time as she could with her daughter. By now, Alan Courtney had recovered and she had reverted to her old routine of working from home several days a week. Whenever she got a chance, she drove down to Raheny in the afternoon and took care of the baby so that Dee could have a nap.

The child still hadn't got a name and the time was approaching for the christening. Ellie was aware that this could be a touchy subject. Perhaps Tony wanted his mother recognised in some way. She skirted around the question on several occasions, then asked straight out: 'Have you decided what you're going to call her? The sooner she gets used to the sound of her own name, the better.'

'We discussed it just last night,' Dee replied.

'And?'

'I think it would be nice to include Tony's mother. As you know, her name is Ruth.'

'You're going to call the baby Ruth?' Ellie said, disappointed.

'Only as her second name. Her first name will be Josette, for Dad.'

'I like it,' Ellie said, brightening. 'It has a nice ring to it. That's a very good compromise. You would have made a great diplomat.'

***

Eventually, Dee's maternity leave ended and it was time for her to return to work. She had reached an agreement with Angie whereby her neighbour would look after the baby but, of course, she had to be paid. When she told Ellie what she had decided, she agreed it was a good arrangement.

Angie was a competent mother of her two children and there was the added benefit that Josette would have company. Ellie said she would have the baby at weekends if Dee needed to go shopping or if she and Tony wanted to go out some evening.

So, each morning at half past eight, Dee dropped little Josette at Angie's house, drove to her office in central Dublin, then picked her up again at six. At the beginning, she would ring Angie regularly to make sure that all was well with Josette, but gradually she got used to the arrangement. She missed the baby, though, and couldn't completely relax till she was back at home and had her in her arms again. She talked to other women in the same situation and they reassured her that, over time, everything would settle down.

***

Meanwhile, Ellie's working arrangements were about to change again. One day, Hugh O'Leary called her into his office and, after some small talk, said he had another proposition to put to her.

'Tell me.'

'How would you like to work from home on a permanent basis?'

'Why?'

He smiled. 'I need your desk. You're not using it a lot of the time and, as you can see, we're very crowded in here.'

'How would it work?'

'Simple. We can fax or email material to you and you can talk directly to the clients. We'll pay your phone and internet bills, of course. It'll spare you the hassle of commuting – and we'll have a win-win situation all round.'

The arrangement appealed to Ellie since it meant she would have more time to spend with Dee. But she also had doubts and it was some time before she became aware of the full implications.

Gradually, more of her duties passed to Alan Courtney. She was no longer invited to the weekly meetings of senior staff where major company decisions were made. Eventually she was shocked to discover that she had been pushed out of the loop.

She was upset and resentful. But before she could do anything about it, something else occurred to claim her attention. A crisis erupted involving Dee and the baby.

***

Dee had taken a call at work that threw her into a panic. Angie had rung to say that Josette was sick. She had started vomiting and was running a temperature.

'Oh, my God! How bad is she?'

'I'm not sure,' Angie said, 'so I'm taking her to Dr Armstrong. She'll probably give her something to bring her temperature down.'

'I'm coming,' Dee said. 'I'll see you at the surgery in half an hour.' She got into her car and set off, her heart hammering. This was any mother's nightmare: her child was ill and she wasn't there. When she got to the doctor's surgery, she found Angie in the packed waiting room with Josette and her own two children.

She took the baby in her arms and held her close. Josette lay still and appeared to be sleeping. 'Has she vomited any more?'

'Not since I called you.'

She placed her hand gently on Josette's hot forehead. 'Tell me what you think, Angie. Is she going to be all right?'

By now, Angie was clearly frightened. 'I don't know.'

'Has either of yours been throwing up?'

'No.'

Just then the doctor's secretary put her head around the door and called Angie's name. They got up and followed her into the surgery.

Dr Armstrong was a pleasant young woman with a reassuring manner. She looked from Angie to Dee. 'Who is the mother?'

'I am,' Dee replied. 'Angie's my neighbour. She was looking after the baby while I was at work.'

'And what's the problem?'

Angie explained about the vomiting and the temperature.

'Any diarrhoea?'

'Yes,' Angie replied. 'She had a messy nappy this morning.'

'Anything since?'

Angie shook her head.

Dr Armstrong asked Dee to undress Josette, which she did. Then the doctor examined her and took her temperature. 'The poor little thing has gastroenteritis.'

Dee felt her heart jump. 'Is it serious?'

'Lots of children get it at one time or another. Take her home and keep her warm. Give her plenty of drinks. That's very important. She's dehydrated. It should clear up within seven days.'

The doctor switched her attention to Angie's children. 'Are these yours?'

Angie nodded.

'I'd better examine them too.'

She gave them a quick inspection and declared them well. 'You'll have to keep them away from the baby. They can't be together or they may get infected too.' The doctor turned back to Dee. 'If she doesn't improve by the end of the week, contact me and I'll prescribe something for her. Hopefully, she won't need it.'

Dee drove Angie home and carried on to her own house. As soon as she got inside, she went straight to the kitchen, made Josette a bottle and coaxed her to drink it. Then she put her in her cot and made sure she was warm. Once that was done, she rang her boss, told her what had happened and said she would have to take some time off work. Finally, she rang Ellie. 'I'm at home,' Dee explained. 'I got a terrible fright this morning.'

'What happened?'

She explained about Josette and the visit to Dr Armstrong.

'Don't be too upset,' Ellie said. 'Gastroenteritis is quite common.'

'So the doctor said, but you're missing the point.'

'Which is?'

'I wasn't there when my child got sick. That's my place. I'm her mother. Instead Angie had to take care of her.'

'Don't blame yourself,' Ellie said. 'It's not your fault.'

'So whose fault is it?'

Ellie sensed that the conversation was getting tense. 'How is she now?'

'She's sleeping.'

'Right, I'll come and see you. We can have a good chat.'

***

It was two o'clock when she got to Raheny. She found Dee waiting anxiously with the baby in her arms.

'Any change?' Ellie asked.

'Her temperature's returning to normal.'

'Good. Has there been any more vomiting or diarrhoea?'

'She had another messy nappy but no vomiting.'

'Is she feeding all right?'

Dee nodded.

'And you're getting her to drink?'

'Yes. I'm doing everything the doctor said.'

'She'll be okay,' Ellie said soothingly. 'Babies are always picking up infections. It's part of growing up.'

'I was thinking about that,' Dee said. 'Maybe she got it from Angie's kids.'

'I thought the doctor told you they were clear.'

'Maybe they were carriers.'

'You can't know that for sure.'

'I'm not blaming Angie. I'm just saying it's a possibility.'

'Listen,' Ellie said firmly, 'I understand that you're worried. Any mother would feel the same. But you can't wrap Josette in cotton wool. I never heard of a single child that didn't get sick from time to time.'

'I just feel so guilty that I wasn't there.'

'That's ridiculous. You were at work. You can't be everywhere.'

'I can be at home looking after her. That's where I should have been.'

Ellie stayed with Dee till Tony returned from work at seven o'clock. Then she went home. But she couldn't help feeling uneasy.

Over the coming days, little Josette recovered, just as Dr Armstrong had predicted. Dee returned the baby to Angie's care and went back to work. But the following weekend, Ellie had another call from her daughter to say that she wanted to talk. She sounded unhappy. Ellie got into her car and drove again to Raheny.

When she arrived, the baby was sleeping in her cot. Dee went into the kitchen and made tea. Then the two women sat down to talk.

'Where's Tony?' Ellie asked.

'He's playing golf with some of his pals.'

'So, what's on your mind?'

Dee took a deep breath. 'I'm giving up my job,' she said.

Ellie stared at her. 'Are you sure you want to do that? I assume you've looked into all the consequences.'

'Yes. Money's going to be tight. We'll only have one salary

coming in. We'll have to forget about the nest egg we were planning. And I'll have to give up the car. But we're lucky. Many families are living on social welfare.'

'How will it affect your career?'

'I can pick it up again later. I've got a good CV.'

'It's a big step to take,' Ellie said.

'I know, but I've never been happy leaving Josette with Angie. I think about her all the time when I'm at work. I worry that she's okay. And I can't wait to get home to her. It means I don't give my full attention to my job. I've got the worst of both worlds.'

'Does Tony agree with you?'

'He always agrees with me,' Dee said. 'But it doesn't mean he's happy about it.'

'Have you said anything to your boss?'

'Not yet.'

'Okay. Don't do anything till I talk to you again. Maybe we can find another solution.'

'Like what?'

'I don't know yet. I need to think about it.'

***

She drove home, downcast. She felt sorry for Dee. She was under so much pressure when she should be enjoying her baby. Besides, she didn't share her daughter's optimism that she would pick up her career again when she decided to go back to work. Advertising was a very competitive industry. There were always bright young people waiting to slip into your shoes.

When she got home she had a shower and changed her clothes. She made a snack and a mug of hot chocolate, then sat in the living room, staring out at the garden. A plan was taking shape in her head.

The following morning, she rang Dee again. This time, she sounded much more cheerful.

'How's Josette?'

'She's fine, thank God.'

'Excellent. I was thinking of calling to see you. Will you be free to talk?'

'Of course, Mum. I'm always glad to talk to you.'

'I'm on my way.'

***

'Would you like a cup of tea?' Dee asked, when Ellie arrived.

'No, thanks. I shan't stay long. I've been thinking about what you said to me. I don't want you to do something you might regret.'

'Please, Mum, we've already had this conversation. My mind is made up.'

'Just listen to me for a minute. If we could find some other baby-minding arrangement, might you change your mind?'

Dee gave her a strange look. 'What do you mean?'

'Would it make any difference if I looked after her?'

Chapter Twenty-eight

Dee stared at her. '*You* look after her? What on earth are you talking about? You're working all day.'

'I could change that ... I might be able to persuade the company to come to an arrangement.'

'An arrangement? What sort of arrangement?'

'I might persuade them to let me go.'

'Mum, that's crazy. You've got a well-paid job. You enjoy it and you're good at it. You can't just end your career like this.'

'Let me be the judge of that.'

'But it doesn't make sense.'

'I said *I* would decide. Now, you haven't answered my question. If I was available to take care of Josette, would you change your mind?'

Dee gave a deep sigh. 'I'd certainly be a lot happier,' she conceded. 'But are you aware of what's involved? Looking after a new baby is no stroll in the park.'

'I know all about that. I raised three of you, didn't I?' Ellie said. 'Now, before I go ahead with the idea, I need to be absolutely sure that you'll agree to me minding her.'

'Of course. I couldn't think of anyone more suitable.'

'And you wouldn't leave your job?'

'No. But who knows what might happen in the future?'

'Let the future take care of itself,' Ellie said. 'Meanwhile, I have to talk to my boss. I'll let you know how I get on.'

She left Dee and drove home. What had come to her as a crazy notion was now becoming a real possibility. She had worked for Mallory and O'Keefe for a large slice of her life. She still had lots of energy but her career with the company had reached a plateau. Hugh O'Leary had told her that he wanted to bring on some of the younger staff. She had to face the truth. She would never again be a key player at Mallory and O'Keefe.

She was a little sad, but there was a positive side too. She was fifty. Hopefully, she had many years of productive life ahead of her, some of which she would spend with her little granddaughter.

When she got home, she sat down at the kitchen table with a pocket calculator and began to do some sums. She had a healthy investment portfolio, which was earning good returns. The bulk of the mortgage on her home had been paid off. In addition she had the insurance the *Gazette* had paid out when Joe died. However things turned out, she would be comfortable.

Tomorrow she would sit down with Hugh O'Leary and make her pitch. She had a hunch he would agree. He might even welcome her proposal. With the money the firm would save from her salary, he would be able to hire a couple of thirty-year-olds who would work round the clock to please him.

That night she slept well, and the following morning she

got out of bed feeling much better than she had for several days. She had breakfast, then rang Hugh's office and spoke to Barbara Scales.

'When Hugh gets a moment, would you tell him I'd like to speak to him privately in his office about a matter of mutual concern?'

'Of course, Ellie.'

She really is the perfect secretary, Ellie thought, as she put down the phone. She never asks questions, never gets ruffled, never loses her poise. Even if an earthquake shook the building Barbara would go on smiling.

Twenty minutes later the phone rang. 'Hugh will be available to see you at midday,' the secretary said.

Ellie glanced at her watch. It was now ten o'clock. 'That's perfect, Barbara. Tell him to expect me.'

She began to get ready. She brushed her hair and put on some makeup, changed into a white blouse and her best business suit. Then she made a cup of tea, sat down at the kitchen table with a pen and notepad and began to prepare her pitch.

***

Hugh O'Leary was smiling when Ellie entered at exactly twelve o'clock. Barbara Scales excused herself and left them alone. Hugh shook her hand and pointed to a chair. 'So, Ellie, what can I do for you?'

She had decided not to waste time but to get straight to the point. 'How would you respond if I asked for an early-retirement package?'

She had caught him by surprise. He flinched, then quickly composed himself. 'Are you unhappy?' he asked. 'I'd no idea.'

She had made up her mind not to dwell on the resentment she felt about the way she had been edged aside. It would serve no useful purpose.

'I've had a very satisfying career with Mallory and O'Keefe. This is a personal matter, Hugh. I've reached a stage in my life where I want to spend more time with my family.'

He relaxed. 'That's perfectly understandable.'

He had turned on his computer and was scanning her personnel file as he calculated how much a retirement package might cost the company and what benefits would accrue to Mallory and O'Keefe as a result.

'This is an unusual request,' he said. 'I don't think we've ever made an early-retirement offer before. But let me state at the beginning that I have no issue in principle with you leaving early.'

Good, Ellie thought.

'I'll be sorry to lose you, of course. You've always been a great team player and we'll miss you. As for the terms of any package we might be able to agree, I'll have to talk to the accountants before I make an offer.'

'I understand.'

'I'll get back to you as soon as possible.'

'Thanks, Hugh.'

'In the meantime, let's keep this strictly between ourselves, shall we?'

'Of course.'

It had been a short interview but Ellie left the office with a good feeling. At least he hadn't turned her down flat. Now it was a matter of waiting to see what terms he would offer.

It was two weeks before he came back to her and she was facing him once more in his office.

'Before we begin, let me say this is the best offer we can make. I'm not here to negotiate with you on the terms. This is the maximum the company can afford.'

'Go on.'

He had a folder before him. He opened it and passed a sheet of paper across the table. 'In addition to a lump-sum payment of €130,000, we can offer you an immediate pension of fifty thousand per annum or a deferred pension of seventy thousand, which would commence at normal retirement age.'

It was less than she had hoped for but it was still quite generous. 'Whichever pension option I choose, I'll still get the lump sum, is that right?'

'Yes.'

'I need time to make up my mind, Hugh.'

'That's fine. Let me know if the terms are acceptable and we can agree a departure date.'

As soon as she got home, she rang an old friend of Joe's, who worked as an actuary, and put the terms to him. He took down her details and said he would have to make some calculations. Half an hour later, he rang her back. 'All in all, it's not a bad offer,' he said. 'They could have given a bit more but you're the one who wants to go early. The terms are always better when a company is trying to persuade employees to leave.'

'So you think I should take it?'

'That's a matter for you to decide, Ellie. But if I was in your shoes, I wouldn't turn it down.'

'Should I take the immediate or the deferred pension?'

'Oh, the immediate option. I don't wish to sound pessimistic but you might not live to be sixty-five.'

Ellie chuckled. 'Thank you,' she said.

He had confirmed her growing conviction, but she still had

a few more calls to make. In quick succession, she rang her friends and told them about the retirement package. They all agreed that she'd be crazy not to accept it.

'If someone made me an offer like that,' Caroline said, 'I'd bite their hand off. Then I'd go and live in Paris where people still believe in romance.'

Ellie waited another two days before calling her boss. 'I'm happy to accept your generous offer, Hugh.'

'Excellent. I'm glad we see eye to eye, Ellie. I believe people should always part on good terms in situations like this.'

'I do too.'

'Have you thought about a departure date?'

'As soon as possible.'

'How about two weeks? That should give the payroll department ample time to get everything in order.'

'Two weeks is perfect.'

'I'll ask Barbara to give you a letter to that effect. In the meantime, just carry on as usual.'

***

On the day of her departure, she met Hugh O'Leary for lunch at the Shelbourne Hotel. Afterwards there was to be a presentation in the office. Over lunch, O'Leary asked her what she planned for the future.

'I'm going to be busy, Hugh. I'll be looking after my little granddaughter but I'm going to enjoy it.'

'You're right. Children grow up so quickly. It's one of my biggest regrets that I didn't spend more time with my own kids. And you should go travelling, visit all the places you've never got to see. That's what I would do.'

Back at the office, her colleagues seemed genuinely sad

that she was leaving and crowded round to shake her hand and wish her well. She was moved by these expressions of goodwill but her mind was firmly made up. She knew she was doing the right thing.

The time approached for the farewell presentation. Hugh stood beside Barbara and called Ellie forward. He proceeded to make a short speech, saying what a wonderful colleague she had been and what dedicated service she had given to the company over the years. He declared that he spoke for everyone when he said she would be sorely missed. He wound up by presenting her with a gold bracelet and a card signed by the staff.

Ellie responded by saying how much she had enjoyed her time at Mallory and O'Keefe and that she would remember them all with fondness. She ended by inviting everyone to join her in the local pub for a farewell drink.

She stayed for several hours, then left in a taxi to go home to Clontarf. She felt optimistic about the future. One phase of her life had come to an end but another was about to begin.

Chapter Twenty-nine

The following morning at eight thirty Ellie began her new role. Dee left little Josette with her before travelling on to work. With her, she brought a bag containing baby wipes, nappies, Josette's bottles and various other items. A few evenings before, Tony had dropped off a travelling cot, a collapsible playpen, blankets, picture books and toys. Ellie was ready to begin.

'I'll pick her up at half six,' Dee said. 'If anything crops up in the meantime and you need to call me, don't hesitate.'

'Stop fussing,' Ellie said. 'Nothing's going to crop up. Now, go into the office and concentrate on your work. She'll be here in one piece when you get back.'

At the front door, Dee paused. 'You don't know how grateful I am, Mum. Tony is delighted with this arrangement. He never wanted me to leave work.'

'You don't need to thank me,' Ellie said. 'I'm going to enjoy it. If I wasn't, I'd never have offered.'

The new plan had required some delicate diplomacy with

Angie. Dee didn't want to tell her neighbour that she was uneasy about leaving Josette in her care in case Angie was offended. Instead she said that Ellie had taken early retirement and had begged to take care of her little granddaughter. The story was partly true and seemed to appease Angie.

At a year old, Josette was starting to crawl and was now eating solid food. She was an energetic child and quite inquisitive so Ellie had to keep a constant eye on her as she scooted around the house, exploring her new surroundings, pulling open doors and cupboards in search of interesting objects to play with.

She was also cutting her first teeth so she was sometimes whingey and dribbling. At the end of the first day, when Dee called to pick the baby up, Ellie was exhausted. When they had gone, she ran a bath and soaked in it for half an hour before pouring a glass of wine and preparing her evening meal.

As the week went by, she began to get a handle on the situation. She cleared out one of the bedrooms, put up some bright posters and turned it into a nursery with Josette's toys and cot. She also established a routine. She played with the baby till midday, reading to her and singing nursery rhymes. Then she fed her and put her down for a nap. Now she could relax till three o'clock when Josette woke again.

Demanding as this work was, Ellie didn't see it as a chore. It was a labour of love. She was caring for her granddaughter, watching over her as she grew and developed. And she was helping her daughter. She knew the situation wouldn't last for ever. Eventually Josette would go to nursery school. And somewhere in the future, she felt sure that Dee's financial situation would improve and she would devote herself full-time to the child. In the meantime, Ellie would savour every precious moment.

At weekends, Ellie began to miss the baby's presence around the house. The days seemed empty and she waited impatiently for Monday morning to arrive when the doorbell would ring and the baby's eyes light up with pleasure at the sight of her grandmother's face.

***

The second anniversary of Joe's death was approaching. The previous year, she had arranged with the parish priest to have an anniversary mass said in his memory. Many of his former friends and colleagues from the newspaper industry had turned up and the church was full. She wondered if she should do it again this year.

As she tossed the matter over in her mind, she realised with a jolt that she had had practically no contact with the *Gazette* since her husband's funeral. Some of his colleagues had stayed in touch but not the senior executives. The editor had never called. And Joe's immediate boss, Tom Matthews, who had broken the terrible news to her that awful day, hadn't rung to see how she was coping. She began to wonder why.

She knew that the newspaper industry was a frantic business that never stood still but it hurt her to think that they could forget her husband so easily. He had been the paper's star reporter, working tirelessly to break stories, travelling all over the country and abroad, clocking up long hours. Indeed, he had died in the service of the *Gazette*.

But it was no good thinking bitter thoughts. She should remember the good times. Joe had lived a full life and had enjoyed every hectic minute. He had loved his job and all the excitement it brought. But it had killed him. She should remember that too. And so should Tom Matthews and the senior executives at the *Gazette*, who seemed to have forgotten him so quickly.

She put the subject out of her mind and concentrated on her granddaughter. In the end, she decided not to have another mass. The family would remember Joe in their own private way. But the matter refused to go away and, in quiet moments, her mind kept returning to it. Another issue began to gnaw at her. No one had ever given her a clear explanation for Joe's death. She had been told how he died but she had never been given any details.

She had a vague recollection of Tom Matthews's personal assistant, Paula O'Brien, saying that he had been working in his room at the Excelsior Hotel in Knightsbridge when he collapsed. And that when they'd got the doctor, it had been too late. But at the time she had been in a state of shock and confusion.

Now questions began to present themselves. Who had alerted the hotel staff? How had they known Joe was unwell? Did he ring to tell them? Was he alone at the time? Or was someone with him? The questions refused to go away and she finally decided to seek some answers.

***

One afternoon when she had put Josette down for her nap, she rang Tom Matthews. It was a few minutes before she heard his voice on the line. 'Ellie,' he began, 'it's good to hear from you. How have you been keeping?'

'I'm well,' she said.

'And the family?'

'Everyone is fine. I have a little granddaughter now. I'm looking after her.'

'Are you not working?'

'I've left my job. I was offered an early-retirement package.'

'I wish someone would do that for me.' He laughed.

'I've been thinking about Joe's death,' she went on. 'His anniversary is approaching.'

'Is it really? My God, it seems like only yesterday that he went.'

'It's almost two years.'

'We miss him dreadfully. No one will ever fill Joe's shoes. How exactly can I help you?'

'I'd like to find out exactly what happened to him.'

There was a slight pause.

'He had a massive heart attack, Ellie. I thought you knew that. It's on the medical certificate.'

'I'd like more details. I was told he was working in his room when it happened, and by the time the doctor arrived, he was dead. But who informed the hotel management? How did they know to send for the doctor?'

'I suppose it was a cleaner or someone like that.'

'Did the hotel say so?'

'I assumed that was what happened.' Tom Matthews sounded uneasy now. 'Why are you so curious, Ellie?'

'Wouldn't you be curious if your loved one died suddenly in a London hotel room? Wouldn't you want all the information?'

'I suppose I would. Look, it was a dreadful shock for you, but would it not be better if you simply accepted what happened and moved on? You're only causing yourself more grief, Ellie.'

'I need to get to the bottom of this.'

'Well, I'm afraid I can't help you. I've told you all I know.'

Ellie ended the call, dissatisfied. Tom Matthews had been evasive and unhelpful. Indeed, he had sounded as if he was trying to hide something. If there was something they were covering up, she wanted to know about it. But how should she go about finding out the truth?

She decided to skip Tom Matthews and go directly to the hotel. It was a matter of minutes to find the number for Reception. She dialled and heard it ring.

'Excelsior Hotel, Knightsbridge,' a foreign-sounding voice said.

'Hello,' Ellie began. 'My name is Mrs Plunkett. I'm calling you from Dublin.'

'Do you want to book a room, Mrs Plunkett?'

'No. I'm enquiring about the death of my husband, Mr Joseph Plunkett. He was an employee of the *Gazette* newspaper in Dublin. He died in your hotel two years ago.'

There was a short silence.

'Wait a moment, Mrs Plunkett. I'm transferring you to Security.'

There was a click and a fresh voice came on the line. 'How can I help you?'

Ellie repeated her story.

'I don't know anything about that,' the voice replied.

'Who am I speaking to?'

'My name is Tariq Nind. I am the security director.'

'Mr Nind, my husband died in the Excelsior Hotel two years ago. He had a heart attack. I'm trying to find out what happened exactly.'

'You must speak to the manager, madam. He is the only person with authority to discuss such matters.'

'What is his name?'

'Mr Parker.'

'Would you put me through to him, please?'

'I'm afraid not. You must make an appointment to see him. We cannot give information of this nature over the telephone.'

Ellie's heart sank. 'Then will you make an appointment for me?'

'You must speak with Mr Parker's secretary. If you hold the line, I will put you through to her.'

There was another pause and this time, Ellie found herself speaking to a polite Englishwoman. She told her story again.

'You say you are Mr Plunkett's widow?'

'That's correct.'

'I remember that incident,' the woman said. 'It was a terrible shock to us all.'

'I'm seeking more information,' Ellie repeated. 'The little I know I have learned second-hand. I want to find out exactly what happened. I've been told I must make an appointment with the manager, Mr Parker. Could you arrange that for me?'

'Just bear with me,' the woman said. There was a longer delay, then Ellie heard her voice again.

'Mr Parker will see you next Saturday at three p.m., Mrs Plunkett. Do you know where we are?'

'I'll find you.'

'And please bring your passport for identification.'

She was lightheaded with relief. Several times in the past ten minutes she had felt as if she was going round in circles. But now she had gained an interview with the manager. He would surely know all the facts.

She went online and quickly found a flight that would get her into London at eleven o'clock on Saturday and another to bring her back that evening. That should give her plenty of time. She used her credit card to pay for the ticket. Then she made a cup of tea, took out a sheet of paper and began writing down the questions she wanted to ask Mr Parker when she met him. She had just finished when a plaintive cry from the nursery notified her that Josette was awake.

***

She told no one of her plans and counted the days till Saturday arrived. She would travel light, with just a raincoat, her handbag and a briefcase containing a notebook and pen.

On Saturday morning, she was up early and on the road to the airport by eight thirty. The flight left on time, and fifty minutes later, the plane was coming in to land at Heathrow.

Once she had cleared Immigration, she bought some sterling, then made her way outside and caught a train to Paddington station, where she took a cab to her destination. The city looked majestic in the afternoon sunshine as she stepped from the cab in the middle of Knightsbridge at half past one.

She had ninety minutes to spare before her interview with Mr Parker. To pass the time, she went into a coffee shop and ordered tea and a pastry. The people sitting around her were mainly tourists with their maps and guidebooks spread out before them, discussing which attraction to see next. Ellie drank her tea and waited as the minutes ticked away.

At twenty to three, she paid her bill and left. The Excelsior was just up the street. She introduced herself at the reception desk and waited till a young man appeared to take her to Mr Parker's office on the second floor. She waited again until eventually the door opened and she was ushered inside.

Mr Parker was sitting behind a large desk. He was about

forty with an amiable face and a friendly manner. He got up, shook her hand and asked her to take a seat. 'You've come about your husband,' he began.

'Yes.'

'First, let me extend our deepest sympathy,' he said. 'This was a terrible event for us. But for you it was a tragedy. I'm so sorry.'

'Thank you. I've come to find out how my husband died. So far, I've only had second-hand information.'

'I have the report of the incident here,' Mr Parker said, placing his hand on a brown folder. 'What did you want to know?'

'How were you alerted to the fact that my husband was ill?'

'The young woman called the reception desk asking for assistance.'

Ellie stared at him. 'I don't understand. What young woman?'

'The young woman who was with him, his assistant, Ms Tobin.'

PART THREE
2012–2015

Chapter Thirty

Ellie's face turned pale with shock. 'Ms Tobin?' she said, incredulous. 'I don't know any Ms Tobin. My husband didn't have an assistant.'

'That was how she described herself,' the manager went on. 'I have it here in the report. Ms Emily Tobin. It's also how she signed the register. I have a photocopy. You can see for yourself.'

He pushed a piece of paper across the table to her. She read it with astonishment. 'Could there be a mistake?'

'Not in a matter as serious as this. In such circumstances we are very scrupulous. The police interviewed her and she confirmed that she was Mr Plunkett's assistant. She was the person who alerted us to the fact that he was ill. But by the time the doctor arrived your husband was dead.'

A terrible thought came rushing into Ellie's mind. 'Did she share his room?'

'She had her own room on the same floor.'

There was a pause while Mr Parker waited. 'Is there any other information you require, Mrs Plunkett?'

'I don't think so,' Ellie said. 'Thank you very much for your help.'

'It's my privilege,' the manager replied. 'Once more, let me extend our sympathy on your sad bereavement. If we can assist you again, please don't hesitate to call.'

He took a business card from a tray and gave it to her.

**

Ellie left the hotel in shock. She struggled to digest the information she had been given. Joe had been with a woman when he died. It seemed incredible but the manager had shown her the photocopy of the register. Who was Emily Tobin? Joe had never mentioned her. She had always believed he had travelled to London alone. And why had the woman pretended to be his assistant?

A host of dark thoughts flooded into her mind. When she looked at her hand, she saw it was trembling. She had to sit down somewhere and compose herself. There was a little park nearby. She went there and sat on a bench while she struggled to come to terms with the dreadful information. More questions kept popping up. Did Tom Matthews know about Emily Tobin? Was that why he had been so coy when she spoke to him? Had he been covering up for Joe?

She clung desperately to the hope that there might be some innocent explanation. The alternative was too terrible to face. Slowly a plan began to form. As soon as she got back to Dublin she must question Tom Matthews again. Meanwhile, she would tell no one of what she had learned.

She watched a young mother playing with her children on the grass. They were carefree and happy. The scene brought back memories of earlier, better times and tears welled in her eyes. She got up, walked out of the park and went back to the airport.

***

Somehow she managed to get through Sunday. On Monday, once she had put Josette down for her nap, she rang Tom Matthews again. This time, his PA, Paula O'Brien, answered.

'Tom's in a meeting,' she explained.

'When will he be free?'

'I don't know. Can I help you?'

'Thanks, Paula, but I must talk to Tom. Will you tell him I called?'

'Of course. I'll make sure he knows.'

She waited till the evening, but his call never came.

The following day, she rang again and found herself once more speaking to Paula O'Brien.

'I told him you were looking for him,' she said.

'Well, he hasn't contacted me. Would you tell him this matter is urgent? I *must* speak to him.'

By now she was convinced that Tom was avoiding her. She made up her mind. If he didn't return her call soon, she would go into the *Gazette* office and confront him.

The next morning, as she was playing with Josette, the phone rang and it was him.

'You were looking for me?' he began.

'Just hold the line. I have a baby in my arms.'

She deposited Josette in her playpen then picked up the phone again. 'I want to talk some more about Joe's death.'

'Ellie, I've already told you everything I can. What more can I do?' He sounded irritable.

'You can tell me what you know about Emily Tobin.'

There was a silence on the line. Then she heard Tom

Matthews cough. When he spoke again, his voice was more subdued. 'Where did you pick up her name?'

'From the manager of the Excelsior Hotel, a Mr Parker. I know she was with Joe when he died. She alerted the hotel staff that he was ill. Now I want to know what she was doing there and why you kept this information from me.'

'Calm down. I can explain.'

'It'd better be good,' Ellie said. 'You were Joe's boss. You would have authorised his travel arrangements. You must have known all about her.'

There was a pause and she heard him give a long sigh. 'You'd better come in and see me, Ellie. When would suit?'

They arranged to meet at seven thirty that evening. By half past six, she was ready. Dee arrived soon after to pick up the baby and Ellie set off.

When she reached the newspaper's offices, Tom Matthews was waiting for her. Once she was seated, he locked the door and told the switchboard he wasn't to be disturbed. Then he stared at her. He looked like a cornered animal. 'I'm sorry about this, Ellie. I want to apologise.'

'So you knew all along. Why did you conceal it?'

'If you must know the truth, I didn't want to upset you. I didn't see what good it would do if you knew.'

'But these dirty little secrets have a habit of coming out, don't they? Tell me about her.'

He paused. 'Are you sure you want to hear this?'

'Yes, and this time you'd better not hide anything.'

'Do you know how attractive Joe was to women, Ellie?'

'I should do. I married him.'

'But did you know how they threw themselves at him and

teased him? He was a magnet for them. He was like a footballer or a rock star. He wore those sharp suits, he was rarely off the television, he was witty and entertaining. Women were always coming on to him, and not just young women but older ones too.'

She closed her eyes. She'd had no idea about this and every word Tom Matthews spoke was like a dagger in her heart. Yet she wanted to hear more. She wanted to hear every sordid detail.

'Joe always resisted them. I never saw him once succumb to temptation. He was always faithful to you, Ellie.'

'Tell me how it happened,' she said.

'Emily Tobin came to the *Gazette* about three years ago, straight out of university with a degree in journalism. She was twenty years of age. Someone who knew the editor got her a placement. She had no experience of working on a newspaper. She didn't know how to write a news story, never mind how to find one. And then I had a brainwave. I decided to team her with Joe.

'I thought the way for her to learn was to work with a veteran journalist, not just any reporter but the very best in the business. You know how Joe would go to the ends of the earth to get an exclusive story? You know how he could corner a contact in a pub and coax the details out of him over pints of beer?'

Ellie remembered only too well. She recalled the nights when Joe had disappeared and the days when he'd gone missing, then returned with a boyish grin and another lead story for the *Gazette*. He had warned her about it before they'd got married. 'Go on.'

'It was a big mistake but I didn't see it at the time. Right from the start, Emily Tobin idolised him. She hung on his every word. She followed him around like a puppy. Anything Joe told her, she took as gospel. It was clear that she was besotted with him. By the time I realised, it was too late.

'I think Joe enjoyed having an attractive young woman like Emily trotting after him all the time. He was a middle-aged man and here was this twenty-year-old fawning over him. It was a boost to his ego. I know some of the other reporters were jealous. Joe had a contact in the drugs trade in London who was prepared to talk to him. He came to me and said he wanted to bring Emily with him.

'At first I said no, it was out of the question. I said if word ever got out there would be hell to pay. But Joe insisted. He said it would be good experience for her. He said there was no question of anything improper. Emily would have her own room. In the end I agreed.'

'Where is she now?'

'Why do you want to know?'

'I'd like to confront her. I'd like to ask her what she thought she was doing at a hotel in London with my husband.'

'She's gone, Ellie. The day after Joe's funeral, she came to me and said she was resigning. She had an offer of a job in Manchester.'

'Why did you object when he first proposed taking her to London?'

'Because of the expense and because I could see the dangers.'

'Yet you gave him permission in the end.'

'He told me there would be nothing improper.'

'If there was nothing improper why didn't he tell me? I was

his wife. If everything was above board, why did he have to hide it from me?'

Tom Matthews sighed. 'Only Joe could answer that.'

'So you believed him when he said it was innocent?'

'Yes, I did. Joe could be infuriating at times. But he never lied to me. When he told me there was nothing improper, I believed him. I'm quite sure if he had wanted an affair, Emily would have been happy to oblige. But I don't believe it ever happened. He was faithful to you, Ellie.'

'How can you say that? You don't know what took place between them.'

'No, I don't. I have to take what he said on trust. Why don't you do that too?'

***

By the time Ellie got home to Clontarf, it was ten o'clock. She felt bitter, bruised and weary from the shock of what she had learned. In bed, she lay in the dark room, staring at the headlights of the cars passing by on the road outside while thoughts of Joe's trip to London coursed through her mind.

She didn't share Tom Matthews's belief that nothing improper had taken place. And, besides, how could she know that he wasn't telling her what he thought she wanted to hear just to soften the blow? And salve his own guilty conscience? If she hadn't been so persistent, the whole affair would never have come to light. Why should she trust Tom Matthews now?

Just as she was drifting off to sleep, another thought came into her head. On that dreadful day when Joe had died, she remembered thinking how major events in her life had come in threes. Now the second had arrived. She wondered what the third might be.

She fell into a fitful sleep, and when she woke in the morning, the sun was shining. But it did nothing to lift her spirits. Her heart was still tortured with grief. And the bitter burden of doubt still weighed heavily on her mind.

Chapter Thirty-one

When Dee called at eight thirty to leave Josette, Ellie forced a smile to her face and pretended to be cheerful. But the thought of the long day ahead filled her with dread. She sat with the baby, sang nursery songs and tried to teach her to clap her hands. She tickled her and Josette giggled. In normal times, this would have been enough to brighten Ellie up but not today. The idea of her husband with another woman made her feel sick.

Overnight more dark thoughts had come to her mind. She remembered how Joe had taken her to Marbella and put the cost on his expenses claim. Was the visit to London the only time he had taken Emily Tobin away with him? He was forever darting around the country to talk to people. Had he brought her with him before? And, if so, how often? Was little Miss Tobin an isolated case or had there been other women she didn't even know about?

Suddenly it occurred to her that there were lots of things she didn't know about Joe's working life. She had rarely asked questions. She just assumed that when he left for the office each morning he was going into the *Gazette* to do his day's work. She didn't know whom he met, whom he had lunch with, whom he went drinking with after he'd finished. She had placed blind trust in him and that was why she was so hurt.

She had loved him practically from the moment they had met. She thought of how they had spent their lives together: the births of their children, the little illnesses and accidents, the wedding anniversaries, the exam achievements and the children's first jobs.

Thinking like this made her so angry that she decided to take the photograph albums from the cabinet in the living room and destroy every single picture of Joe. She put Josette into her cot and started for the living room, but just as she reached the door, her phone rang.

It was Dee. 'I'm leaving work early today. I'll pick up Josette in half an hour.'

'What's happened?'

'I'm not feeling good. I've been sick several times this morning.'

A thought jumped into her head. 'You're not pregnant again?'

'No. Just something I ate. It's a stomach bug. My boss has told me to take the rest of the day off.'

'Are you well enough to look after Josette?'

'Of course. I just need to be close to a bathroom. So you can get her ready. I'll be with you soon.'

***

It was two o'clock when Dee called at the house. Ellie helped her get the baby into the car and watched them drive away.

252

She was sorry to see them leave. Looking after Josette had provided some distraction. Now she was left alone with the terrible thoughts that were running through her mind. She decided to go for a walk. She changed into runners and jogging pants and set off along the seafront.

It was good walking weather and the promenade was crowded with cyclists and strollers. As she walked, she tried to deal with her anger. She was dying to talk to someone. That was what she always did. When she was feeling low, she would ring Caroline or Mags or Fiona and spill her heart out. But this time it was impossible. No one must know, not even her closest friends.

It was going to be hard to keep the pain bottled up inside her. She had to stay busy. She must find things to do. She must tire herself out so that when she got into bed at night she would fall fast asleep. She knew that over time most bad feelings faded and grew dim. She had to believe that this would happen again.

She walked for hours till she reached Sutton Cross. She went into a coffee shop and ordered tea and a pastry. By now, her joints were aching. Good, she thought. That's exactly what I need. She sat for an hour, watching the people strolling by, then paid the bill, stood up and began walking back to Clontarf.

By the time she got home, it was seven o'clock. She rang Dee to see how she was and was told she was feeling much better.

'So you'll be leaving Josette with me tomorrow as usual?'

'Yes, this is only a twenty-four-hour thing. I should be right as rain in the morning.'

'Good. I'll see you then.'

It was time for supper but she wasn't hungry. She made a

mushroom omelette and forced herself to eat it with a glass of wine. She watched television till ten o'clock, then got ready for bed.

But once she was under the duvet, the angry thoughts came rushing back, and it was several hours before she finally fell asleep.

***

By the end of the week, Ellie was exhausted. She had no appetite and was only managing three or four hours' sleep at night. Her plan to tire herself out by constant activity was not working. Instead, it was making her feel worse.

On Friday evening when Dee called to collect the baby, she remarked upon it. 'Are you feeling okay, Mum?'

'Why?'

'You're not looking well. You look like you need a good rest. Is Josette too much for you? I know she can be a handful at her age.'

'It's got nothing to do with Josette,' she said.

'I could ask Angie to mind her for a few days to give you a break.'

'No, no,' Ellie protested. How could she tell Dee that caring for the baby was the only thing keeping her sane? 'I haven't been sleeping very well.'

'Is something bothering you?'

'Just the usual stuff that life tosses up.'

'Do you want to talk about it? Talking is very therapeutic.'

'Thanks, Dee, but I don't see how burdening you with my problems is going to help either of us. I'll get over it.'

'Well, you know where to find me if you change your mind,' her daughter said.

Alice had gone to stay with some friends and now she faced the whole weekend alone. She had to get out of the house. Every room, every corner held memories of Joe Plunkett. She needed crowds of people that she could get lost in. On Saturday morning she got up early, walked to the DART station and took the train into town.

There was a festival going on and the city was packed with visitors and tourists. She walked along O'Connell Street, then turned at the quays and crossed the Halfpenny Bridge into Temple Bar. There were more crowds, young people with backpacks, lovers holding hands and buskers at every corner. It reminded her of somewhere. It came in a flash. It reminded her of the Paseo Maritimo in Marbella, the sun shining on the ocean, the aroma of food wafting out from every little bar.

But those memories brought Joe back once more so she quickly dismissed them and tried to think of other things as she made her way up Grafton Street to St Stephen's Green. She strolled in the shady park till she found an empty seat and sat down. Her strategy wasn't working. Already the angry thoughts were crowding in again. What if I'm going mad? she thought. Her head dropped into her hands.

Dee's words came floating back into her mind. *Talking is very therapeutic.* Her daughter was right. She needed to share her feelings with someone. Despite her vow of silence, she needed to overcome the secrecy and shame and talk to one of her friends.

But which one should she choose? Fiona or Mags would be best. Mags was more down-to-earth but Fiona was a doctor and had medical knowledge. She might know how to deal with this. She rummaged in her bag till she found her phone and pressed in the number.

Chapter Thirty-two

'Is this urgent?' Fiona asked, when Ellie said she wanted to talk.

This time, she wasn't going to lie. 'It's desperate. If I don't talk to someone, I think I'll go crazy.'

'Where are you now?'

'I'm in Stephen's Green.'

'Can you get back to your house?'

'Yes.'

'Go there and I'll be with you in an hour.'

'Okay.'

She ended the call. Already, she was feeling better.

**

She had barely got into the house when she heard Fiona's car crunch on the gravel of the drive. She hurried to the door and found her friend standing on the step.

'Thank God you could come,' she said, hugging her, then bringing her into the living room. 'Would you like some tea?'

'I'll make it,' Fiona said. 'You go and sit down.' She went off to the kitchen and came back a few minutes later with the teapot and cups. 'You don't look good,' she remarked, as she began to pour.

'I feel dreadful. I haven't been sleeping. I'm barely eating. I'm just about holding myself together.'

'Tell me what it is,' Fiona said soothingly.

'You must never breathe a word of this. Promise me.'

'I promise.'

Ellie was trembling and suddenly she was weeping. 'I've just discovered that when Joe died he had a young woman with him.'

Fiona sat still. 'Go on,' she said gently.

Ellie wiped her eyes. Slowly, she began to describe her doubts about Joe's death, her failure to get a satisfactory explanation from Tom Matthews at the *Gazette* and her trip to the Excelsior Hotel in London.

'The manager told me Joe had brought a woman with him, someone called Emily Tobin. I was in total shock. When I got home, I went to see his boss, Tom Matthews. This time, he told me the whole story. Joe told him nothing improper was going on but I feel devastated.'

Fiona reached out and held her hand. 'How long were they working together?'

'I don't know for sure. Tom Matthews said she idolised Joe. She hung on his every word and he was flattered by her attention. I just can't come to terms with it. And I have this terrible anger. It's like a rage that's eating me up. What am I going to do?'

Fiona sat up straight. 'You should see Christine Palmer again. She helped you the last time, remember.'

'But she's a bereavement counsellor.'

'This is a sort of bereavement too. I think talking to her would do you good. Would you like me to make an appointment for you?'

'Okay.' Ellie nodded.

'In the meantime, I'm going to prescribe some medication to help you sleep. Now I have to go home, Ellie. We're expecting some guests for dinner. But if you want to talk again, just pick up the phone. Don't suffer this alone. There are people who will help you. And, rest assured, this information stays with me.'

Before they parted, she took Ellie in her arms. 'I know it seems as if your life has come to an end. But that feeling will pass and, in time, the world will seem a happy place again. Do you believe me?'

Tears welled again. 'I have to,' Ellie said.

***

Fiona arranged the appointment for eleven o'clock on Monday morning. Ellie rang Dee and told her she was seeing a doctor and Dee arranged for Angie to look after Josette.

Christine Palmer was waiting in her office when Ellie arrived and pointed to the comfortable chair she had sat in on previous visits. 'Tell me exactly how you feel.'

Ellie gave a deep sigh. 'I can't sleep. I can't eat. I have this terrible black depression hanging over me all day long. And an angry rage that I never knew I possessed.'

'Talk about it. Take your time. Discuss your feelings. Don't hold anything back.'

Slowly Ellie began to recount the story while the counsellor took notes. She was still talking when the session drew to a close an hour later.

'How do you feel now?' the counsellor asked.

Ellie shrugged.

'You're going through what is known as the trauma phase. You're shocked and your emotions are raw. You're suffering grief and loss and resentment. But, hopefully, it will pass.'

'When?'

'It will take time.'

As the sessions progressed, Ellie began to notice an improvement. Simply having Christine Palmer listen while she poured out her feelings was a relief.

At one session Christine asked Ellie what she knew about Emily Tobin.

'I never met her. I've been told that she was twenty years old and attractive. I understand she idolised my husband. She followed him around like a puppy.'

The counsellor nodded and folded her hands together in her lap. 'Ellie, I have to be blunt with you. Your rage and your unhappiness are real. But I have to suggest that they may be misplaced. You have no evidence that your husband was unfaithful with Emily Tobin.'

Ellie gasped. 'But they spent time together in that hotel.'

'They had separate rooms.'

'That doesn't mean a thing. And he kept it hidden from me. If it was above board, why didn't he tell me?'

'Because he was afraid you'd misunderstand.'

'Now you're defending him,' Ellie said angrily.

'I'm trying to help you. Joe was in his early fifties, wasn't he?'

'Yes.'

'Let me explain something to you. Men of that age sometimes find the attention of a younger woman reassuring.

It's a psychological thing. It makes them feel young and attractive. But it doesn't necessarily mean they go on to have affairs.'

***

The sessions were coming to an end. Talking with the counsellor had helped Ellie enormously. She was even beginning to accept the possibility that Joe's relationship with Emily Tobin might not have been what she'd thought.

On the last day, Christine said, 'I think I've taken you as far as I can. How do you feel now?'

'An awful lot better,' Ellie admitted.

'But you still have feelings of anger and resentment?'

'Yes.'

'Do you understand that you will never be entirely free till you can let go of those feelings?'

'And how do I do that?'

'By forgiving your husband. Letting go is the key to your recovery. By forgiving him, you can draw a line under this. So he had this awestruck young woman chasing after him and it turned his head. He took her with him to London without telling you, which wasn't very clever. Why don't you give him the benefit of the doubt? Instead of regarding him as a horrible man who did a terrible thing to you, why don't you look on him as a foolish man who did a stupid thing?'

Ellie went home with mixed feelings. She was going to miss the sessions with Christine. She had been a good listener and talking to her had helped enormously. The dark cloud was finally lifting. And just then something else turned up to dominate her thoughts.

Chapter Thirty-three

One morning, her phone rang and an excited Mags was on the line. 'You're never going to believe this.'

'Believe what?'

'Caroline is getting married.'

'What?' Ellie said. 'Is this a joke?'

'No, I've just been talking to her. She's marrying that wealthy businessman she's been seeing.'

'Freddie Hawthorne?'

'That's him.'

'She told me he was too clingy.'

'She must have changed her mind. Or perhaps she decided he was the last bus and, if she didn't hop on board, it would leave the station without her.'

'I'm absolutely amazed,' Ellie said.

'Well, prepare yourself for a phone call. She's ringing around to tell everyone. Pretend to be surprised when you hear about it.'

'I don't have to pretend. I *am* surprised. In fact, I'm flabbergasted.'

As soon as she had ended the call, her phone rang again.

'Hello, darling,' Caroline began. 'As my dearest friend, I want you to be among the first to know my wonderful tidings.'

'Yes?'

'I've finally decided to end my solitary existence. I've agreed to marry Freddie.'

'Oh, Caroline,' Ellie gushed, 'I'm thrilled for you. That's great news. When did this happen?'

'Just last night. You know he's been pursuing me for ages, declaring undying love and promising me the sun, moon and stars; well, he finally wore me down. So I've accepted. We're going out to choose the engagement ring this afternoon.'

'I'm sure you'll be very happy. Freddie's obviously devoted to you and he's interested in the theatre so you'll have lots in common. And, from what you've told me, he's quite well off.'

'He's loaded, darling. He's in the antiques business and has inherited this marvellous house in Foxrock. Not that mere cash was a consideration in my decision, you understand. But money is always important in these matters, don't you think?'

'Of course.'

'One can be poor and happy. But having a healthy bank balance makes it so much easier.'

'I couldn't agree more. So when is this great event taking place?'

'As soon as it can be arranged. Now that I've made up my mind, I don't see any point in hanging around. And poor Freddie is positively straining at the leash. The wedding will take place in Paris. You know how I love that city. It's so romantic. Naturally, I want you, Fiona and Mags to be my bridesmaids. And don't even think of expense. Freddie will pay for it all.'

Ellie gasped. 'I'd be delighted to be your bridesmaid. It sounds wonderful. Oh, Caroline, I don't know what to say.'

'Well, I've kept you all waiting a long time. But now I'm about to make it up to you. I'll be in touch. Just keep your diary free for the next few weeks. There's so much to arrange. *Byeeee!*'

Ellie felt light-headed. She was happy for her friend, who had been so unlucky in love, but the news was so completely unexpected that she was still struggling to take it in. She had to go into the kitchen and make a cup of tea.

***

The next time she saw Dee, she told her the news. 'I'm giving you notice. I won't be able to look after Josette for a while. I've been invited to a wedding in Paris.'

'Good for you. Who's getting married?'

'My friend Caroline. I'm to be her bridesmaid, along with Mags and Fiona.'

'You're kidding. She took her time about it, didn't she? How old is she?'

'The same age as me. She's had lots of men in her life but she never met the right one till now.'

'And who is the lucky fella?'

'He's a wealthy antiques dealer called Freddie Hawthorne.'

'Well, it goes to prove that it's never too late. When is the wedding?'

'That's still to be arranged.'

'Don't be worrying about Josette. When the date's fixed, just let me know and I'll ask Angie to look after her. You never take a break, Mum. In fact, I was worried about you for a while. But I'm glad to say you're looking an awful lot better.'

'Thank you.'

'So just go to Paris and enjoy yourself.'

***

Next there was an invitation to meet Freddie Hawthorne for dinner.

'He's dying to be introduced to you all,' Caroline said. 'He's so excited that he's behaving like a schoolboy on the last day of term. I think he expected me to turn him down and now he can't believe his good fortune.'

'And it is good fortune,' Ellie said. 'I hope he appreciates the fantastic bargain he's getting.'

'Thank you – you're so kind.'

'Where are we meeting him?'

'In Buck's Bistro on Stephen's Green, tomorrow night at eight o'clock. He's booked a private room. I do hope you all like him.'

'Oh, I'm sure we will, Caroline. You always had exquisite taste in men.'

'It's a pity none of them stayed around for long.'

'That's their loss.'

'Oh, get away,' Caroline said.

The three friends decided to meet in advance and arrive at the restaurant together. At seven o'clock they congregated at Doheny and Nesbitt's pub in Baggot Street, which was only a ten-minute walk from Buck's Bistro.

'I must say this announcement has swept me completely off my feet,' Fiona declared. 'I never thought I'd see Caroline walk down the aisle. I thought she was temperamentally unsuited to marriage.'

'Me too,' the others chorused.

'She's gone out with so many men that I've lost count,' Fiona continued. 'And it always ended in tears.'

'The problem was she chose badly,' Mags added. 'And she rushed in without stopping to consider. Most of her boyfriends would never have made good husbands. I think she was lucky to escape.'

'She thought she was living in a movie,' Ellie said. 'It was all high drama with Caroline. She was never a little bit in love. It had to be all or nothing.'

'Well, let's hope she's found the right man this time,' Fiona said. 'At least, she'll never have to worry where her next meal is coming from. From what I hear, Freddie Hawthorne is rolling in dosh.'

'There is that point in his favour,' the others agreed, and finished their drinks.

The restaurant was an up-market establishment furnished and decorated in the modern style. It was filling up when they arrived at five minutes to eight. They found Freddie and Caroline seated at a table in a back room. He was a small, plump man in the early sixties with a tiny moustache and thin hair brushed across his forehead in a vain attempt to disguise his encroaching baldness.

He got up at once, took each of the friends by the hand and gently kissed their fingers while Caroline made the introductions. Then he bowed politely and they all sat down.

'I'm so pleased to meet you all at last,' Freddie said. 'Caroline is forever singing your praises. She says she's been blessed to have such faithful friends.'

'We think the same about her,' Ellie said. 'Caroline has always been very dear to us. Our friendship goes back over thirty years. We all met on our first week at university.'

'I'll echo those sentiments,' Fiona said. 'You've chosen wisely, Freddie. Caroline is going to make you a wonderful wife.'

'*Pleeease!*' Caroline laughed. 'We're here to enjoy ourselves. You'll have me weeping in a moment. Now, Freddie, why don't you be a dear and make yourself useful by pouring some champagne?'

A bottle of Krug Clos du Mesnil was resting in an ice bucket on the table. Freddie rose, expertly extracted the cork, then filled the glasses and passed them around. 'Your good health,' he said, and they sipped. Ellie coughed as the bubbles tickled the back of her throat.

'I have another toast,' Fiona said, getting to her feet. 'To the bride and groom.'

This time, everyone stood up. The second sip from Ellie's glass went down more smoothly. I'm going to enjoy this evening, she thought.

Within minutes, two waiters arrived to take their orders. There were starters of oysters, salmon and caviar and main courses of venison, beef, tuna and roast duck, with several varieties of salad. One glance at the menu told Ellie that this dinner was going to cost a small fortune. By now, Freddie had ordered a second bottle of champagne and was already topping up their glasses.

The women admired Caroline's engagement ring. It was a large diamond on a gold band surrounded by a cluster of smaller bead-set diamonds. It was beautiful and must have been very expensive. Ellie wondered if it was an antique.

The meal arrived and they began to eat. Each forkful exploded in Ellie's mouth in a burst of flavour. She could never recall eating more delicious food. Even Joe at his most generous had never matched this. Meanwhile, Freddie was keeping everyone entertained with humorous anecdotes while Caroline alternately teased and bullied him. It was clear to Ellie who was going to be the boss in their marriage.

'You're all on your own surrounded by four women,' Caroline said. 'Don't you feel intimidated?'

'Not at all.' Freddie grinned. 'I enjoy the company of women. I grew up surrounded by female cousins. I find women much more sympathetic than men and far shrewder. I have two women working for me in my business and they have a keener eye for a good antique than any man I know.'

'Where are you going to live when you get married?' Mags asked.

'We haven't made up our minds,' Caroline replied. 'Freddie has this amazing house in Foxrock. But it might be a teeny bit too big. I'm thinking of all the upkeep and the gardens. How do you feel, darling?'

Freddie shrugged his shoulders. 'I don't mind where I live as long as it's comfortable and I don't have rowdy drunks keeping me awake at night. Why don't you decide? You're going to be the mistress, after all.'

'He also has an apartment in Ballsbridge,' Caroline went on. 'It's quite cosy and closer to town. Maybe we'll live there.' She flung her hand into the air in a grand dramatic gesture. 'Oh dear, what was it Mae West said? "So many houses, so little time"?'

The conversation moved on to their honeymoon plans and Caroline grew even more animated. Ellie wondered if perhaps the champagne had gone to her head.

'I'm very keen on California. I thought we could fly to San Francisco and make our way along the coast to LA. It's been my lifetime ambition to visit Hollywood. I'm absolutely dying to sample all that glamour. We could have dinner on Sunset Boulevard. God knows who I might meet.'

'It sounds marvellous. Why don't you do that?' Fiona asked.

'Freddie doesn't like the sun. He wants to go to some dreary antiques fair in Vienna.'

She scowled, and Mags exchanged a glance with Ellie. There was little doubt in her mind where the honeymoon would finish up.

The dinner came to an end. Freddie paid the bill and gave the waiters a generous tip. 'How are you getting home?' he asked Ellie.

'There's a taxi rank along the street.'

'I'll order one to take you,' he announced, and summoned the waiters again.

'But we all live in different parts of town,' someone said.

'It doesn't matter. I won't have you lovely ladies queuing for taxis at this time of night. The driver can drop you off one after another. I'll make sure he's well looked after.'

The taxi arrived and they said goodbye. As it drove away, Ellie leaned against the thick upholstery. It had been a wonderful night. A smile crossed her lips as a thought crept into her head. Tonight had been the first time she had laughed since she had learned about Joe and Emily Tobin.

Chapter Thirty-four

After the introductory dinner, everything slowed down for a while. Several weeks went past before Ellie received a call one morning from Caroline to say she had found a beautiful little church in Montmartre where the priest had agreed to conduct the marriage service. Due to French legal requirements, though, they would first have to undergo a civil ceremony in Ireland. This would take at least three months to arrange. 'Isn't that a downer?' she said.

'It's not too long,' Ellie replied. 'Some people spend much longer planning their weddings. Nine months or a year isn't unusual.'

'But they're mostly youngsters with their whole lives before them. Every day that passes I move a step closer to the grave.'

'Oh, Caroline.' Ellie sighed. 'You're not *that* old. You're a young woman in mid-life. You've still got many years ahead of you.'

'I like that phrase,' Caroline said approvingly. '"Young woman in mid-life". I must remember it.'

'Anyway, there's nothing to stop you pressing ahead with the other arrangements. There are a lot of things to organise. I speak from experience. I've gone through this twice.'

'Sometimes I wish I'd chosen Las Vegas,' Caroline murmured dreamily. 'You can get married over there in less than twenty-four hours.'

***

A few weeks later, Ellie had another call from Caroline to say that she had found the perfect couturier, Nancy McStay, to design her wedding dresses and the bridesmaids' outfits. She suggested they should all get together so they could be measured. The following evening Ellie drove into town and went to meet her friends.

The couturier's salon was situated in an alley off Temple Bar. As soon as Ellie stepped inside the door she saw that Caroline had struck gold. The dresses on display were among the most elegant she had ever seen. There were so many beautiful gowns in the shop that it took Caroline a long time to decide. But after much deliberation, she finally settled for a pleated ballgown with a sequin cluster sash and satin ribbon.

'What do you think?' she asked the others, turning sideways so they could all get a good look at her. 'Is it me? Does it do me justice?'

'It certainly does,' Mags assured her. 'It's perfect.'

The others were nodding in agreement. 'It has your name on it,' Fiona said. 'It looks amazing.'

'Okay,' Caroline said to Nancy. 'I'll take it.'

The couturier gave a tight little smile. 'Madam has chosen well. You will look like a queen.'

After that, choosing the bridesmaids' dresses was much

easier. They simply asked Nancy McStay to provide something that would match Caroline's dress, and after showing them some illustrations and taking their measurements, she assured them the dresses would be ready in a few weeks.

It was only when they were out on the street that Ellie raised the question of cost.

'Don't worry about it,' Caroline replied loftily. 'I've already discussed it with her. Anyway, I told you that Freddie would take care of everything. Now why don't we go for a drink?'

'How many guests will there be?' Fiona asked, once they were all seated at a table in a nearby bar.

'This is going to be the smallest wedding you've ever attended,' Caroline said. 'Freddie has no immediate family so his best man will be an old school friend called Percy Somers who is also in the antiques trade. On my side, there's my mother and my sister, Joyce. But my mother is eighty-three and says she's too frail to travel to Paris so that leaves Joyce and her husband, Alex. Altogether there'll be eight of us.'

'And the civil ceremony?'

'That will be even smaller, just me, Freddie, Percy and my mother. You guys are invited too, of course, but I don't expect you to turn up unless you want to. The real wedding will be in Paris.'

'No friends from the theatre world?'

Caroline shook her head. 'Are you kidding? They'd turn it into a jamboree to get their pictures into the papers. Freddie and I have decided we want a quiet ceremony. I'm too old for all that razzmatazz.'

Times have certainly changed, Ellie thought. Once, Caroline would have killed for the chance of some good publicity.

'And what about Paris?' Mags asked.

'Paris is where we relax. Freddie is booking us all into the Hôtel Colonnade for a week before we fly off on our honeymoon. The Colonnade is *the* place to stay. It's wall-to-wall luxury. We're going to have a ball, darlings.'

'Have you decided where to go for your honeymoon?' Fiona wanted to know.

Caroline gave her a triumphant glance. 'I've got Freddie to agree on California. I can't wait to have a cocktail at the bar of Hemingway's Lounge in LA.'

***

Before long, the bridesmaids had been summoned several times to have fittings and adjustments made. When the dresses were finally ready, and Ellie was standing before the mirror in Nancy McStay's salon, she smiled at herself with satisfaction.

Everyone agreed that the dresses were dazzling, and Caroline's most of all. She looked stunning in the elegant dress that Nancy had produced. When she stood before the altar at the church in Montmartre she would be every inch the radiant bride.

Now events picked up speed. In quick succession, the wedding ring was purchased, the flights were arranged and the accommodation booked at the hotel. The priest in Montmartre had phoned to say that everything was in place for the wedding in his church. All that remained was to have the civil ceremony.

It was held on a Saturday afternoon. Ellie decided to ignore Caroline's advice and go along. The best man, Percy Somers, turned out to be a strapping sixty-year-old with the look of a former rugby player, while Caroline's mother was a frail old lady with a walking frame.

The five of them stood together before the registrar while he conducted the ceremony, asked them to sign some documents, pronounced Caroline and Freddie husband and wife, and then it was all over. They went for afternoon tea in Buswells Hotel, where Caroline's mother sat beside Ellie and insisted on telling her all about her arthritis.

It was several years since Ellie had visited Paris to attend an economic conference but she had never forgotten the experience. She knew it to be a city steeped in history with a reputation for good food and beautiful scenery, not to mention the romance that Caroline kept going on about. The previous trip had been short and there had been little time for sightseeing. Since she was now going to be staying there for a week, she decided to refresh her memory. She went to the local library, borrowed some books, then logged on to the internet to find out more.

What she read fired her imagination. She saw pictures of the Eiffel Tower, the cathedral of Notre Dame and the narrow, winding streets of Montmartre where the wedding would be held. She couldn't wait to get there.

She had alerted Dee, who had arranged for Angie to have Josette. Now all she had to do was pack her case. It was September, and her research on Paris told her that the weather would be dry with temperatures around 17 degrees centigrade. Just to be on the safe side, she packed a warm jacket for the evenings and a light raincoat.

Mollie and Jack had agreed to drive her to the airport where the others were waiting in the departure lounge. They found Freddie in ebullient mood, dressed smartly in a neat business suit and tie. When Ellie stole a glance at Caroline, she thought she looked a little nervous. She's waited so long for this, she thought. Let's hope she isn't going to panic at the last fence. However, Freddie soon lightened the atmosphere with his banter, introducing them to Percy Somers, Caroline's sister, Joyce, and her husband, Alex. Then they were walking to the gate: their flight was boarding.

**

The flight took just under two hours and before long they were descending over Paris. Once they had collected their luggage, they went to the taxi rank, climbed into cabs and set off.

As they approached the city, Ellie saw the Eiffel Tower towering magnificently above the skyline. When they were approaching the Louvre museum, in the centre of Paris, they were caught up in the crush of traffic, but their drivers negotiated their way skilfully through the ranks of honking cars. Eventually they pulled up outside the hotel and they all got out.

Uniformed porters were waiting to collect their luggage. Freddie paid the drivers and the group followed them inside to the reception desk. Inside, Ellie gazed around in wonder. The Colonnade was easily the grandest hotel she had ever set foot in. Everywhere she looked, she saw elegant women and well-dressed men, sumptuous carpets, luxurious furniture, dazzling chandeliers. She glanced at the others and saw they were similarly impressed, especially Caroline, who looked as if she had just wandered onto the set of a Hollywood movie.

They were quickly registered and given their room keys. Ellie had a double room with Mags while Caroline was with Freddie, and Joyce with Alex. Fiona and Percy had rooms of their own.

'So,' said Freddie, once the registration process was finished, 'it's now half past two. I suggest we all go and take a little rest. There's a swimming pool and a spa for anyone who's interested and also a sun lounge. If anyone is peckish, just lift the phone in your room and order something to eat. I've been assured that the staff speak perfect English. I've reserved a table for dinner at eight o'clock tonight. Why don't we meet again at half past seven for cocktails?'

This was agreed and they set off for their respective accommodation. A handsome young porter fell in beside Ellie and Mags, carried their cases to the lift and deposited them outside the door of their suite. Ellie hunted in her purse for money to tip him but Mags beat her to it. She pressed some cash into his hand. He thanked them and bowed politely.

The suite was a smaller version of the grand lobby downstairs. It contained two comfortable sofas, a writing desk, a large television, a drinks cabinet and two beds with the coverlets turned down. There was a sparkling en-suite bathroom and, outside, an elegant terrace. Ellie walked across the room, opened the sliding glass door and stepped out. She could see the spires and rooftops of Paris stretching into the distance. 'We've got some time to kill. What would you like to do?' she asked her friend.

'I don't really mind.'

'Why don't we take a walk? Oh, Mags, this is the most exciting city in Europe, let's go out and explore it.'

They left the suite and went down to the lobby with the city maps they had been given at the reception desk. Once they were outside, they were drawn towards the river Seine and the imposing Eiffel Tower. Already, Ellie could feel the magic of the city taking hold of her.

They passed restaurants and bars, with the patrons sitting outside in the sun, talking or reading newspapers while they sipped their drinks. They stopped at little patisseries to peer into their windows, and ancient book stores, their interiors crammed with dusty volumes. As they approached the river, they saw pleasure cruisers ploughing up and down, packed with tourists.

They were on the Left Bank of the Seine and many of the attractions they wanted to see were on the other side of the river. At Notre Dame, they crossed over. A queue of people was waiting to get into the cathedral so they decided to leave it for another day. Instead they began strolling in the direction of the Champs-Elysées. They had both brought their phones and began taking pictures. On the way, they passed the Pompidou Centre and the Louvre, and continued walking until they reached the majestic Arc de Triomphe.

By now they were tired. When they checked the time, they discovered they had been walking for over two hours. They found a little café, ordered cakes and a welcome cup of coffee, then decided to take the Métro back to their hotel. It was six o'clock when they reached their suite. Mags took a shower while Ellie unpacked her case. Then she, too, showered and they decided to unwind in the hotel's garden till it was time to meet the others for dinner.

The garden was practically deserted. Ellie sat back and opened the novel she had brought. In the distance, they could hear the muffled sounds of the city. She gave a sigh of satisfaction and stretched her face to the sun. 'Isn't this the life?' she said.

***

By the time half past seven approached, both women were hungry. They had been up early and, apart from a snack on the plane and the cake near the Arc de Triomphe, they'd had nothing since breakfast. They got dressed, tidied their hair and made their way down to the cocktail bar. Freddie and Caroline were already there with Percy. They were soon joined by the others.

'What did you get up to today?' Freddie enquired, after Ellie and Mags had been served with glasses of wine.

'We went sightseeing,' Mags replied. 'We walked as far as the Arc de Triomphe.'

'Enjoy it?'

'Indeed we did. I could spend the whole week exploring Paris.'

'Paris has a charm entirely its own. I can think of few cities to compare. I admire your stamina. I'm afraid I lay down on the bed to relax and didn't wake till half past six.'

It came time to take their seats at the table Freddie had reserved in the dining room. Ellie was wondering what the food was going to be like. If it matched the splendour of the hotel, it would be a meal to remember.

They had barely sat down when the head waiter swooped to present them with leather-bound menus. 'The special tonight is lobster thermidor,' he announced in perfect English. It was a dish Ellie had often heard about but had never sampled. 'I can also recommend the sole meunière and the beef. The Cassoulet Hôtel Colonnade is also excellent.'

He left them to study the menu, and when Ellie looked up, the wine waiter was at Freddie's side. Freddie gave the list a casual glance and ordered bottles of Bordeaux and Chardonnay with some Vichy water.

The first course arrived. It was an interesting salad of leaves, nuts and little spears of broccoli. At the same time, several baskets of rolls had been placed before them. Next they ate seafood soup, thick with clams and prawns. Then the main courses appeared. Ellie had chosen the lobster thermidor: delicious chunks of lobster in a creamy sauce. It tasted divine.

After the dessert, coffee arrived, and Ellie glanced at her watch. They had been eating for almost three hours and it had been the best dinner she had ever had.

Throughout the meal, there had been a buzz of conversation around the table. Percy had emerged as a character in the same league as Freddie and regaled the company with hilarious stories about his business experiences.

'On one occasion I was summoned to the home of this deceased army colonel down in County Wicklow. His widow was an elderly lady who lived alone. The house turned out to be a rambling mansion with no central heating. It was freezing and I couldn't imagine how the old dear survived in it without getting hypothermia.

'I discovered that the house had been in her husband's family for generations. Now she had decided to sell it and buy a small flat in Dublin to be near some of her friends. She said she wanted me to clear out the entire house and get rid of all the junk so that she could get in the decorators before she sold it. She asked me how much I would charge for the job.

'I tried to explain that this wasn't quite my line of business. I was an antiques dealer, not a rag-and-bone man. But she wouldn't take no for an answer, so reluctantly I agreed to take a look around. What I discovered completely bowled me over. The house was stuffed with valuable objects: paintings, ornaments, old coins and medals. There was even a couple of old masters. I persuaded her to let me sell the entire contents. It was one of the most successful auctions of my entire career. We made well over four million pounds.'

'And what was your commission?' someone asked.

'My usual five per cent,' Percy replied, to general laughter.

It was half past eleven by the time the party began to break up. Ellie went up to the suite with Mags. She barely had time to say goodnight before she was fast asleep.

Chapter Thirty-five

She was woken the next morning by birds chirping on the terrace outside. It was eight o'clock and Mags was still asleep. She walked quietly to the window, drew back the sliding door and stepped out onto the terrace. The sun was up and the city was bathed in a beautiful mellow light. Immediately, she wanted to be out again, exploring the grand boulevards and the little narrow streets.

She picked up the phone and asked for breakfast to be delivered to their suite, then had a shower and began to get dressed. Soon she heard a polite knock on the door and two waiters entered with trays of scrambled eggs and smoked salmon, a plate of croissants and jam and a steaming pot of coffee. They laid the table for two, with cutlery and china, then arranged the food precisely in the middle, and left the room noiselessly.

By now Mags was awake and the two women had breakfast while the sun climbed higher in the sky.

'I've been thinking,' Mags said. 'This trip must be costing

Freddie Hawthorne an absolute mint. The meal last night would have set him back several thousand euros alone, not to mention the cost of our stay here and the flights.'

'He seems happy to pay. Besides, he has no family and I don't suppose he's ever going to get married again.'

'Oh, please, God, no,' Ellie said, quickly. 'It's taken Caroline so long to find the right man that I'm sure she'll stick to him like glue. And Freddie seems devoted to her. She has him wrapped around her little finger already. I would bet good money this marriage will be a huge success.'

After breakfast, they rang home to let their families know they had arrived safely and were thoroughly enjoying themselves. Then they began to plan their day.

'I'm keen to get out again and do some more exploring,' Ellie said. 'What about you?'

'Good idea. We've only scratched the surface so far.'

'Why don't we ask Fiona to join us?'

'I'll give her a call.'

Fiona agreed immediately.

'Let's meet in the lobby in half an hour,' Ellie said. 'Make sure to bring your camera.'

***

This time, they decided to explore the city's Left Bank. They started again at the river and walked along the quays till the majestic spire of Notre Dame came once more into view. Then they turned onto the boulevard St Michel and kept walking till they reached the Luxembourg Gardens.

This was a green island of calm in the frantic city, and they were shielded from the noise of the traffic on the roads outside. They bought ice-creams and rested for a while on a bench while they watched little boys playing with their toy boats in the pond. Then they set off again towards the nearby Latin Quarter and the university of the Sorbonne.

They soon found themselves in a maze of winding streets packed with small bars and restaurants. They wandered around the district for an hour till they began to feel hungry and decided to find somewhere to eat.

'We're on holiday,' Fiona declared. 'Why don't we be adventurous and try something different?'

There was a Moroccan restaurant nearby. It was already filling up but they managed to find a table near the back. A young waiter soon appeared, gave them menus and took their order for wine. But they immediately encountered a problem. Fiona spoke some French but even she had difficulty interpreting the menus.

When the waiter returned, they sought his advice and, thankfully, he spoke English. After some discussion they agreed to let him choose the meal for them and sat back on the cushioned seats with a sense of achievement.

It turned out to be a culinary experience. First they were presented with a series of salads and a plate of pitta bread straight from the oven. This was followed by a large pan of couscous, a dish stuffed with chunks of lamb, courgettes, peppers, carrots and chick peas. They ladled the couscous onto their plates and started to eat. It was delicious.

By the time they had devoured the couscous they were already full, but more delicacies were still to come. They were now presented with a plate of pastries including mouth-watering coconut fudge cakes and pieces of deep-fried dough sprinkled with honey and sesame seeds. The meal was rounded off with cups of sweet mint tea. When the bill came it was a mere sixty euros. They paid, left a tip for the waiter and set off again.

This time, their journey took them in the direction of Montparnasse, made famous in the 1920s by artists and writers such as James Joyce, Pablo Picasso and Gertrude Stein. Here, they spent some time exploring the nearby cemetery, which included the graves of Samuel Beckett, Jean-Paul Sartre and Simone de Beauvoir. By now, it was almost four o'clock and time once more to take the Métro back to Hôtel Colonnade.

When they arrived, they found a note from Caroline and Freddie to say they had arranged a dinner that evening in a restaurant in the Place des Vosges for half past seven and would meet in the lobby at seven o'clock. Fiona and Mags said they were going to take a nap while Ellie headed off to the spa.

***

The rest of the week passed quickly with a series of outings. On one occasion the whole party set off to visit Notre Dame cathedral and on another day they joined the queue to get into the Louvre. But the three friends preferred more energetic pursuits. They went for long walks in the Bois de Boulogne, and spent a whole day exploring the Palace of Versailles, home of the ill-fated Marie Antoinette and Louis XVI. The weather remained dry, with sunny days and a gentle cooling breeze.

Before they knew it, the wedding was upon them, the highlight of the trip. Caroline and Freddie had already been to the church to talk to the priest and make sure that everything was in place. The ceremony was scheduled for one o'clock. From early morning, Caroline was in a tizzy of anticipation and could barely eat breakfast because of her excitement.

She had an appointment with the hotel hairdresser at ten,

then applied her makeup. The wedding gowns were taken out of their wrappings and the bride and her entourage got dressed.

Meanwhile, Freddie and Percy had slipped into their suits and were waiting patiently in the hotel lounge with Joyce and Alex. The bouquets had arrived and the taxis to take them to the church had been ordered for half past eleven. As the minutes ticked away, Percy began to get nervous and constantly checked his watch. Finally at a quarter to twelve, Caroline and the bridesmaids made their entry into the lobby.

Several hotel guests applauded as the party arrived. Alex, who had been appointed official photographer, got up at once and began taking pictures. Then they settled into the cabs and began the journey to Montmartre.

'We've cut it pretty close,' Fiona whispered to Ellie, as they sped across Paris. 'I hope we don't run into traffic.'

'If we're late, Caroline will have no one to blame but herself,' Ellie responded. 'I thought we'd never get her ready.'

At last, they reached Montmartre and began the slow ascent of the narrow, hilly streets. It was ten to one when they were finally deposited outside the church where the little priest was waiting at the door in his vestments. He shook hands with them all and went back inside. The taxis, which would take them afterwards to a nearby restaurant for lunch, departed with an assurance that they would return at two.

The party formed up and they entered the church. It was small and dark. Inside, candles flickered at the shrines to various saints, and a few elderly worshippers, attracted by the fuss, were already seated in pews near the front. The priest had positioned himself at the foot of the altar where Freddie was also standing to await the arrival of his bride.

The Love of Her Life

The bridesmaids straightened Caroline's dress and she began her stately progress down the main aisle, clutching her bouquet. An ancient organ began to creak out 'Ave Maria' as she arrived at the altar. Freddie took her hand and the service began.

It was a simple ceremony but very moving, and once or twice, Ellie found herself wiping a tear from her eye. When it was over, Caroline and Freddie thanked the priest and everyone exchanged kisses. Then they went outside where Alex was frantically taking more photographs.

By now, the cabs had returned. As they got in and sped off to the restaurant, a strange thought came into Ellie's mind. She was now the only one of the four friends who had no husband.

***

The lunch was another tribute to Freddie's exquisite taste. The service was polite and efficient. The wine flowed and the food was magnificent. Soon everyone was laughing and joking. Percy made a hilarious best man's speech, interrupted with witty remarks from the rest of the company. Ellie made a short contribution, expressing her delight that Caroline, of whom she had often despaired, had finally found a man she could love and admire. This brought a round of applause. Throughout it all, Caroline sat serene, with just a hint of a smile, like the movie star she had always aspired to be.

The lunch came to an end at four. Then it was back to the Colonnade to get changed and ready for the flight to Los Angeles at nine o'clock. This time, there were no delays and at six, the bride and groom appeared in the lobby with their cases. There were farewell kisses and hugs as they got into the waiting cab and sped away.

The guests were staying overnight and returning to Dublin in the morning. Ellie went up to her suite and lay down on the bed while Mags went off to buy some presents in the hotel shop. It had been a wonderful trip, and she was sorry it was coming to an end. She decided to take one last walk to stretch her legs and say goodbye to the place she had found so exciting.

She left a note for Mags to say she would be gone for a couple of hours, then slipped into casual clothes and set off. Her journey took her along the Seine to the place de la Concorde where the guillotine had once stood during the French Revolution. By now the streetlamps had come on and the vast square was bathed in light. Ellie sat down to rest, then began to walk back the way she had come. As she passed a little bar, she decided to go in and have a coffee.

A handful of people were standing at the counter and a few more sitting outside. The waiter came quickly and she gave her order for *café au lait*. She found a table, sat down and, while she waited, she picked up a newspaper and casually turned the pages. Gradually, she became aware that a man sitting alone across the room was observing her intently.

The coffee arrived and she set the newspaper aside. When she glanced from the corner of her eye, she saw that the man was still watching her. She felt uneasy. Then he got up and began walking towards her. He stopped when he got to her table. 'Excuse me, do you speak English?' he asked.

'Yes,' she replied, nervously.

'Forgive me for bothering you but I have a feeling we've met before.'

This time she looked directly at him. He was a fit-looking man of about fifty-five. His fine fair hair was brushed carefully across his forehead. And his face was definitely familiar.

'I'm Mick Flynn,' he said. 'We met in Marbella, Hotel Alhambra. You used to take a swim in the morning before breakfast. I was there with some friends on a golfing holiday.'

Now she remembered him. She relaxed immediately. 'You used to keep the guests awake at night with your sing-song in the bar.'

He laughed. 'Not at all, we always finished promptly at eleven o'clock.'

'I'm Ellie Plunkett,' she said, extending her hand.

He took it in his strong grasp. 'Imagine meeting you again in Paris, Ellie. What brings you here?'

'My best friend just got married. She left this evening on her honeymoon.'

'Are you staying on for a few days?'

'Unfortunately not. I'm going back to Dublin tomorrow.'

'That's a pity,' he said, looking disappointed. 'We might have been able to have dinner.'

'You're not here to play golf?' she asked.

'No. I'm simply enjoying a little break. I've always wanted to visit Paris, so when I saw a cheap offer, I decided to go for it.'

'Is your wife with you?'

He shook his head. 'I'm no longer married. We divorced.'

'I'm sorry to hear that.'

'There's no reason to be. It's all quite amicable. We married when we were far too young, then realised we weren't really suited to each other. My wife has married again. And you?'

Ellie lowered her eyes. 'My husband is dead.'

'Oh, that's sad. It must have been a hard blow.'

'It certainly was. It took me a long time to come to terms with it.' She was anxious to move away from talk of Joe so she quickly changed the subject. 'Are you still working?'

'No. I was in the motor trade, but when the recession struck I decided to retire and play more golf.' He smiled. 'What about you?'

'I did something similar. I worked for Mallory and O'Keefe, a firm of investment consultants. I was an economic analyst. After my husband died, I decided to leave early and spend more time with my family.'

'And did you make the right decision?'

'Undoubtedly.'

They talked for a few more minutes. Then Ellie said she had to go. Mick Flynn summoned the waiter and paid the bill. Outside, the air was cool and the night sky was filled with stars. He held out his hand once more. 'It's been great meeting you, Ellie. I've enjoyed our little talk. Maybe we'll meet again in Marbella some time.'

'Who knows?' she said, with a smile, and began to walk briskly back to her hotel.

Chapter Thirty-six

Mollie and Jack were waiting for her when she got to the arrivals lounge in Dublin airport the following morning. They threw their arms around her and held her tight. She had been sorry to leave Paris but now she was delighted to be home.

'This is a welcome I wasn't expecting.' She laughed.

'We missed you. So how did you get on? We're dying to hear all about the wedding,' Mollie exclaimed, as they walked out to the car park with Ellie's luggage after Mags and Fiona had departed.

'It was fantastic. I don't know where to begin. Let's just say that I've never attended anything to compare with it. It was red carpet all the way: champagne, the best food and Rolls-Royce accommodation in a top-class hotel. As for Paris, my mind is still reeling from all the wonderful sights I saw.'

She told them about the various places they had visited but Mollie was anxious to hear more about the wedding so she described the ceremony in the little church in Montmartre and the reception afterwards.

'It sounds like it cost a packet,' Jack remarked. 'I'm glad I wasn't picking up the tab.'

'Oh, Freddie Hawthorne isn't short of cash,' Ellie replied. 'He's a very successful antiques dealer.'

'Maybe I should have got into that racket,' Jack said, with a grin.

They dropped Ellie at her house, where she found a note from Alice welcoming her home and saying she was staying overnight with some friends but would be back the following day. There was some mail in the hall and the grass looked as if it needed a cut. Ellie decided to do it at once. She got out the strimmer and the mower and spent forty-five minutes trimming the edges and tidying the lawn. Then she went back inside, unpacked her case, had a bath and made herself a cup of tea.

That afternoon she decided to drop down to Raheny to visit Dee and little Josette. She was dying to see her granddaughter again, and in Paris, she had picked up a little French doll as a present for her. She rang in advance to say she was coming, then got into the car and drove the short distance to Dee's house. Josette's eyes sparkled when she saw her and she gurgled with delight when Ellie opened her bag and took out the present. 'Tell me how she got on without me,' Ellie said.

'She missed you at first but she soon settled down with Angie.'

'The little traitor,' Ellie joked. 'As soon as my back is turned, she's off with somebody else.'

Dee laughed. 'Did the wedding go smoothly? No last-minute hitches?'

'It went like clockwork. Here, let me show you some pictures.'

She got out her phone and the two women sat admiring the wedding party and their beautiful dresses while the baby played happily on the floor with her new doll.

'You look fantastic – the holiday's done you good,' Dee said. 'Did you have a lovely time?'

'I had a ball. I've never eaten so much rich food. I meant to weigh myself this morning. I wouldn't be surprised to discover that I've put on a few kilos.'

'That might not be a bad thing. I think you'd lost some weight recently. You're always running around.'

At that moment, Tony came in from the garden. 'So you're back from gay Paree,' he said, as he kissed her cheek. 'Meet any nice French gentlemen?'

'I should be so lucky,' Ellie replied. 'I've just been telling Dee what a great time we had. If you ever get an opportunity to go there grab it with both hands.'

They talked for a while, then Ellie left, saying she had some shopping to do.

Dee walked with her to the car. 'I'll leave Josette with you at the usual time on Monday morning, if that's okay,' she said.

'Of course! I'm looking forward to it.' She got into the driver's seat and started the engine. 'Is everything all right at work?' she asked, as she prepared to drive away.

'Why do you ask?'

'I just like to know that everyone is happy.'

'Well, you can relax. Work is going swimmingly. Tony and I are content as larks.'

'That's good to know. Enjoy the weekend. I'll see you on Monday.'

***

On Sunday morning, Mollie rang to invite Ellie and Alice to have lunch with them. 'It'll be nothing special, just a pot roast.'

'That's very kind,' Ellie said. 'What time?'

'One o'clock.'

'Perfect. I'll talk to Alice. I'm sure she'll agree.'

At a quarter past twelve, they set off with a couple of bottles of wine and some small souvenirs Ellie had picked up in Paris. As it was Sunday, the traffic was light and they made the journey in good time. The flat was small, just a kitchen and a couple of rooms in a house on the coast close to Sandymount village. But it had a view of the sea. When Mollie opened the door, the visitors were greeted with the rich aroma of cooking meat.

'I'm hungry already,' Ellie said, kissing her daughter-in-law and pressing the wine and the souvenirs into her hands.

They were ushered into the living room, where Jack was watching football on television. Mollie returned to the kitchen.

'Missing Paris yet?' Jack joked.

'I'm sure I'll get over it. Dublin has its qualities too. Sometimes we take them for granted.'

'Like what?'

'It's quiet here, more intimate, and we're close to the sea. The mountains are only a short drive away. The pace of life can be quite relaxed.'

'That may be changing,' Jack said.

Yes, Ellie thought. You could be right.

Jack disappeared to help Mollie with the lunch and ten minutes later, they were summoned to the kitchen where the roast had been set on a dish in the middle of the table. Steaming bowls of potatoes and vegetables accompanied it. They took their seats and Jack poured the wine.

'Who wants to serve?' Mollie asked.

'I will,' Alice said. 'I'm brushing up on my culinary skills.'

'Really?' Ellie remarked. 'I must remember that the next time I'm cooking Sunday lunch.'

They began to eat, and soon the conversation was flying around the table, jokes and anecdotes sparking laughter and comment. Ellie felt a mood of quiet satisfaction steal over her. She was so fortunate to have all her children around her. Alice would probably get married, Mollie and Jack would have a family, and there would be lots of grandchildren besides Josette. She had a full life to look forward to.

It was after five o'clock when she and Alice finally left. By now the afternoon traffic had increased and it was almost six o'clock when they arrived back in Clontarf. Alice promptly announced that she was going into town to meet some friends.

'Anyone in particular?' Ellie wondered.

'How do you mean?'

'They're not all girlfriends, surely. Have you no handsome young men among your acquaintances?'

'*Mother!*' Alice pouted.

'I know, I know,' Ellie said. 'It's none of my business. Just bring him home to meet me whenever you think the time is right.'

***

She was getting ready for bed when the phone rang. She picked it up and was surprised to hear Caroline on the line.

'Darling, it's me. I hope I'm not disturbing you. What time is it there?'

'Eleven o'clock.'

'My head's all over the place from jet-lag. I'm still trying to get used to all this travelling. It's three in the afternoon here in San Francisco, which means we must be eight hours behind you.'

'That sounds right. Anyway, you're not disturbing me in the least. How are you getting on?'

'We had a perfect flight. Of course we were travelling premium class. Every time I yawned a handsome young flight attendant appeared to ask if he could do anything for me.'

'And how is San Francisco?'

'Windy, but otherwise it's satisfactory. It's just like you see in the movies, all those hilly streets and cable cars and old Victorian houses and the Golden Gate Bridge. Freddie has us staying in this old-fashioned hotel near the bay. It's absolutely charming.'

'When are you travelling to Los Angeles?'

'Tomorrow. It's going to be the highlight of the trip. I can't wait to get there.'

'Are you flying?'

'No, we're taking the bus. We've been advised it's the best way to see the countryside. Besides, I've had my fill of planes for a while.'

'So you're enjoying your honeymoon?'

'Absolutely. Freddie is a perfect pet. He's always fussing over me. I should have met him years ago.'

Ellie found herself smiling. 'I want to thank you again for the wonderful time in Paris. I'll never forget it.'

'Oh, for God's sake!' Caroline exclaimed. 'You're my best friends. How could I get married and not have you all at my wedding? Tell the others I send my love. I'll ring you in a few days' time when we've settled into LA. Now I'd better go.

Freddie's hauling me off to have drinks with some long-lost American friend of his.'

***

A little later, when she was tucked up in bed, Ellie thought again about the conversation with Caroline. What she had said was so true. The four women had supported each other through all the ups and downs in their lives, the setbacks and the achievements. They had been there for her when Joe died. Friendship like theirs was such a blessed gift. Sometimes she wasn't sufficiently grateful for it.

Chapter Thirty-seven

Since her return from Paris, she had rediscovered her old zest for living. The depression that had dogged her since she'd learned about Joe's London trip had finally lifted. Now it was just a memory that she recalled occasionally with a shudder. The feelings of resentment and bitterness were receding with the passage of time. When she woke in the mornings, she felt good. When she went to bed at night, she drifted off at once and slept soundly.

She soon settled back into her familiar routine. She rang her friends most days, met them for coffee, tidied the house and garden, did her shopping and kept in close contact with her family. But mostly she took care of Josette. Dee dropped the child off each morning on her way into work and collected her again in the evening. It was a full life and Ellie enjoyed every moment.

Caroline came back from her honeymoon, bearing fantastic tales of the people she had met in LA. 'We were having dinner one night at this swish place on Rodeo Drive and who do you think was sitting at the next table?' she asked Ellie excitedly.

'Who?'

'Al Pacino! And when I told him I was an actor with the Gaiety Theatre in Dublin, he insisted on sending a bottle of bubbly to our table. Wasn't that sweet?'

'I'm very impressed.'

'He said he loved Dublin. It was his favourite city after Los Angeles. Of course he wasn't the only star I ran into. You can't go anywhere in that city without tripping over big-name personalities.'

'You're making me envious,' Ellie said.

'You know, I can't help thinking that the big mistake I made in my career was not locating there when I was younger. My life could have been completely different.'

'That's true. You wouldn't have met Freddie for one thing.'

'There is that to consider,' Caroline admitted. Then she brightened again. 'But I might have met some major film director. I could have had my name up in lights.'

'You wouldn't have liked it,' Ellie said. 'Life there is too fast and too brittle. I'm not sure that Hollywood is a very happy place.'

***

One evening when Dee called to pick up Josette, she said she had something to confide.

'Yes?' Ellie asked.

'Please keep this to yourself for a while. I don't want everyone to know just yet.'

'What is it, Dee?'

'I'm pregnant again.'

Ellie felt a thrill of pleasure. She was going to have another grandchild. She hugged her daughter.

'That's fantastic news. I'm so pleased for you. You and Tony must be over the moon.'

'Well, yes and no. Of course we'd love another baby but we weren't planning on having one quite so soon.'

'Sit down and I'll make tea,' Ellie said. She went into the kitchen and put on the kettle. She could sense what the problem was. Another baby was going to increase the financial pressure. She brought the tray into the living room and poured two cups. 'When did you find out?'

'I've suspected it for a while. But I only got confirmation today. I'm ten weeks.'

'You'll be fine,' Ellie said. 'The time will pass quickly and I'll be here to help you.'

'Of course I'll be fine. I love children. That's not what's bothering me. But how can I raise two babies and hold down a job at the same time? It's going to be extremely difficult, if not impossible.'

'I'm sure you'll work something out. Now, don't be worrying. Just concentrate on getting through the pregnancy.'

When Dee had gone, Ellie thought about the dilemma. She was happy looking after Josette – in fact, it was becoming easier as the child got older – but she couldn't handle two babies. And dividing them between different minders would raise all kinds of difficulties. Dee was right. It was going to cause a problem.

But a few days later, when she arrived with the baby, Dee's mood had changed. 'I had a good heart-to-heart with Tony last night,' she announced.

'And?'

'I'm going to give up my job when the baby arrives.'

Ellie had half expected this. 'Are you sure that's what you want?'

'Yes – in fact, I'm beginning to look forward to it. It's the obvious solution. You've been wonderful, Mum, but sometimes I feel a bit guilty dumping Josette on you.'

'You're not dumping her! You know I love taking care of the little dote. But what about the family finances? How are you going to manage?'

'We'll be fine. Anyway, it won't be for ever. In a few years, the children will be old enough for school and I can pick up my job again. I'll work something out with my boss.'

When Dee left, Ellie brought Josette into the nursery and placed her in the playpen. She watched as the child began to play with her toys. A feeling of loss crept over her. Happy moments like this one were coming to an end. She should make the most of them.

**

As the months slipped by, she watched Dee grow bigger as her due date approached. Dee had spoken to her boss, who had promised to find a job for her whenever she was ready to return. She now went around with a smile on her face, while Ellie waited for the moment when she would no longer have her granddaughter to mind.

As with her first pregnancy, Dee had decided to take her maternity leave after the baby was born. But, once again, Fate intervened. One morning, shortly before the baby was due, she rang Ellie to say she was feeling sick.

'Where's Tony?'

'He's gone to work.'

'Have you called Dr Armstrong?'

'I'm going to do that now.'

'I've got a better idea,' Ellie said. 'I'll take you to her. Just hang on. I'll be with you soon.'

She got into the car and drove to Dee's house. When she arrived, she found her daughter sitting in the kitchen looking pale and drawn. Ellie strapped little Josette into the back of the car and Dee got into the passenger seat beside her mother. When they arrived at the doctor's she was immediately ushered into the surgery while Ellie was asked to wait.

Fifteen minutes later, the door opened, and Dee emerged with Dr Armstrong.

'You'll have to take it easy for the next little while. But you're going to be fine. As soon as you feel the contractions starting, contact the hospital.'

They settled into the car once more for the drive back to Raheny.

'I'll have to ring the office and tell them I'm not coming in,' Dee said. 'And I'd better let Tony know.'

'I'll do that,' Ellie said. 'In fact, I've just had a brainwave. I should have thought of it sooner.'

'What?'

'You can come and stay with me. I've got plenty of room and all the time in the world to look after you.'

'Are you sure? What about Tony?'

'Tony will have to fend for himself. You heard what Dr Armstrong said. You have to take it easy.'

Dee and Josette were installed in a spare bedroom while Ellie cooked and fussed over them. Alice helped her mother, and Mollie and Jack popped over to visit. It was just like the old days when they all lived together. Tony called every evening after work and stayed for a few hours before going back to the silent house in Raheny.

The contractions began one afternoon about two weeks later. Immediately, Ellie swung into action. She rang the hospital, then Tony, got Dee and Josette into the car and set off. The medical staff were on standby when they arrived and Dee was whisked off at once to the delivery room. Soon after, Tony arrived, out of breath, and went straight in to his wife.

She didn't have long to wait. Forty-five minutes passed before the door opened and a nurse came out to see them. 'Are you Mrs Mulhall's mother?'

'Yes,' Ellie said, quickly.

'Your daughter has given birth to a little boy. Mother and baby are fine.'

***

Ellie had resigned herself to the fact that soon she would no longer be minding Josette, but for the first few months, Dee was so occupied with the new baby that Ellie continued to look after her granddaughter. She would drive down to Dee's house and pick up Josette, then drop her home again in the evening when Tony had returned from work.

Josette was now walking confidently and speaking short sentences. She enjoyed playing with her toys and loved getting out to the garden to see the flowers and the birds. She was beginning to ask questions, and developing her own personality. Ellie couldn't wait to see her each morning and hated parting with her at night.

The new baby was called Anthony and Josette was fascinated with him. She loved watching her mother changing his nappy and feeding him his bottle. She became so attached to her little brother that one morning when Ellie called to collect her she didn't want to leave.

'C'mon,' Ellie coaxed. 'I've got something nice for you at my house.'

'No,' Josette said. 'I want stay with Ant'ny.'

Dee laughed. 'I think she's slightly jealous. She's afraid of missing something. Why don't you take the day off? I'll be able to handle them both.'

'Are you quite sure?' Ellie said.

'Of course. I think they should spend more time together.'

Ellie left, feeling sad and disappointed.

After that, the gaps between Josette's visits to her grew longer until the little girl was spending only a couple of days each week with her grandmother. Then the visits stopped altogether. When Ellie returned to Clontarf, the house felt empty. There was no more childish laughter, no stories, no nursery rhymes. A new phase in her life was about to begin.

Suddenly she had time on her hands and no obvious way to fill it. She fell into the habit of meeting Fiona or Mags for lunch at weekends and visiting Caroline in the fancy apartment in Ballsbridge: she and Freddie had decided to live there until the Foxrock house was sold.

Caroline had taken to married life and was forever extolling the virtues of her new situation. 'This is the best thing that ever happened to me. I don't know why I waited so long.'

'You never found the right man,' Ellie responded.

'Well, I had plenty of offers but the time never seemed right. There was always something going on in my career. Now I can see that I should have done it sooner.'

'Everything happens for a reason,' Ellie said.

Caroline looked pensive. 'Do you think so? Maybe you're

right. By the way, do you mind if I ask? Do you miss Joe terribly?'

Ellie's chest tightened. This was a sensitive subject so she had to tread carefully. 'All the time,' she replied.

'Have you ever entertained the notion of another relationship? You're still a relatively young woman. And you're quite attractive, you know.'

Ellie smiled. 'Thanks for the compliment, but I'm not sure that would be a good idea.'

'Why not? There's a lot to be said for it. Don't you ever get lonely?'

Ellie glanced at her watch. This conversation was drifting into dangerous waters. 'My God,' she said. 'Is it that time already? I've got to go.'

'But you've just arrived.'

'I've got to meet Alice,' she said, grabbing her handbag and coat.

***

A few weeks later she was lunching with Fiona and told her about the conversation with Caroline.

'She does have a point, you know. You're only fifty-four. That's not old, not nowadays when some people are living into their eighties and nineties.'

'It seems ridiculous.'

'Why? We're not talking about a teenage love affair. This is about companionship. You're a widow, but that doesn't mean you have to withdraw from the world. You can have a relationship with a male friend. It might be the very thing you need. It might inject some fresh excitement into your life.'

When she got home, Ellie thought of what Fiona had said.

She had always given her good advice in the past. But where was she going to meet this male companion? She wasn't involved in any clubs or societies. She didn't go to parties. Since Joe's death her life had been centred entirely on her family.

Then one evening the phone rang, and when she answered, she heard a voice she didn't immediately recognise.

Chapter Thirty-eight

'Who is this?' she asked.

'Mick Flynn. I ran into you in Paris a while ago. You were attending your friend's wedding.'

She took a breath. 'How did you get my number?'

She heard him laugh. 'A little bit of detective work. You told me you used to work for a firm called Mallory and O'Keefe. So I rang them and pretended to be a relation who had to get in touch with you urgently. A very helpful lady gave me your details.'

'She's not supposed to do that,' Ellie said. 'You could have been a serial killer, for all she knew.'

'Then I wouldn't be speaking to you now. And I can put your mind at ease. I may have my faults but serial killing isn't one of them.'

It was Ellie's turn to laugh. 'So what do you want?'

'To see you again! What else? I thought we might have lunch sometime or maybe just meet for coffee. I enjoyed meeting you in Paris.'

'But we hardly know each other.'

'That's the point. I'd like to know you better.'

'I'm also very busy right now.'

'You can't be *that* busy. Lunch will only take a couple of hours. I can guarantee you'll enjoy it.'

She hesitated. 'You're quite assertive, Mr Flynn, aren't you?'

'You know what they say about faint hearts. And don't call me Mr Flynn. You're sounding like a police officer. My name is Mick.'

'Well, Mick, you've caught me by surprise. I need to think some more about this.'

'That's all right. I can ring again next week.'

'No, don't do that,' she said quickly. 'I have your number on my phone. I'll ring *you*.'

'Okay. I'll look forward to hearing from you. And don't leave it too long. I might have found someone else in the meantime.'

She heard him laugh again. There was a click and he was gone. Ellie shook her head. Amazing, she thought.

***

A few days later when she was having lunch with Mags, she mentioned the phone call.

'Is he the man who used to sing in the bar of Hotel Alhambra in Marbella?'

'That's right. He was with a bunch of guys on a golfing trip.'

'I remember him. He was quite attractive.'

'You think so?'

'Oh, yes, very masculine, strong build, fair hair and a good sense of humour. I said at the time he had a thing about you. So, now he rings out of the blue and wants to buy you lunch?'

'It's not quite out of the blue. I ran into him in Paris one evening.'

'You never told me that.'

'I didn't think it was important. It was the night before we came home. I'd gone for a walk and dropped into a little bar for a coffee. He recognised me and came over. We had a short chat and I left.'

'And now he's back again.'

'Yes. He says he'd like to know me better.'

'That sounds like Fate. What are you going to do?'

'I don't know. I thought you might advise me.'

'Well, I can think of several women who'd be delighted to get an offer like that. And you've got time on your hands now that you're no longer caring for your little granddaughter. I don't see any harm in meeting him.'

'I get the impression he might have more in mind than a simple lunch.'

'Oh, for God's sake, you don't need me to tell you what to do. You've been here many times before. Go along, have a nice lunch. Just play it by ear. If he bores you to death, you don't have to see him again. Although something tells me this guy isn't going to be boring.'

'I think you may be right,' Ellie said.

***

She waited a few more days before calling him.

'It's Ellie Plunkett,' she said, as casually as she could.

'Ellie! How are you?' He sounded delighted to hear her voice.

'I'm good. I've been considering your invitation.'

'And?'

'I've decided to come.'

'That's brilliant, Ellie. When would you like to meet?'

She paused, like a busy woman consulting her bulging appointments diary. 'I'm free on Thursday.'

'Excellent. I know a place you might like. It's called Marrakech.'

'What is it?'

'A little Moroccan restaurant in Dame Street.'

She remembered the delicious Moroccan meal they had enjoyed in Paris. 'That sounds nice. What time?'

'Is a quarter to one okay? You need to be early to get a good table.'

'I'll be there.'

'I'm really looking forward to seeing you again, Ellie. Thanks for agreeing to come.'

'My pleasure,' she said. She ended the call with a satisfied smile. She thought she had handled that quite well. Mick Flynn had sounded suitably grateful. Which was right and proper, she thought, since he was the one who was pursuing her.

***

In preparation for the lunch, she made an appointment with the hairdresser. Then she rifled her wardrobe for something suitable to wear. It was so long since she had embarked on a mission like this that she had almost forgotten the protocol. But one thing she was sure of: she had to look good.

She told no one about the meeting, not even Mags, who had encouraged her to go. Then, if it turned out to be a disaster, she would be spared the embarrassment of a post-mortem. On the other hand, if it went well, she would have something good to report. By midday on Thursday, she was ready to set off. She had showered, put on her best dress and applied a little makeup. When she examined herself in the bedroom mirror, she was pleased with what she saw.

She drove into town and left the car in an underground car park near St Stephen's Green. It was now half past twelve. She waited for ten minutes, then began to walk towards Dame Street. That was another thing she remembered. A lady should never arrive too early for lunch. It might be mistaken for desperation.

Mick Flynn was sitting at a table for two beside the window. When he saw her, his face lit up. He got to his feet and withdrew a chair for her to sit down.

'I'm sorry I'm late,' she said. 'The traffic was dreadful.'

'Forget it. I only got here a few minutes ago. Now, before we order, can I get you something to drink?'

'I'm driving,' she said. 'I'll stick to water.'

'That's very responsible. You don't mind if I have some wine? I'm taking the train.'

'Not at all. Where do you live?'

'Blackrock village. The DART stops almost outside my door.'

'That's a coincidence,' Ellie remarked. 'I used to live there when I first came to Dublin as a student. We had a flat near the sea.'

'I'll bet you had a ball.'

'We sure did. I have very happy memories of that time.'

'I like Blackrock,' he continued. 'It's quiet and it's not too far from the city.'

The waiter arrived with menus and Mick ordered a glass of red wine. 'Have you ever eaten Moroccan food before?' he asked.

'We had a wonderful meal in a Moroccan restaurant in

Paris when we were there. It was on the Left Bank near the Sorbonne.'

'What did you have?'

'Couscous.'

'So why don't we order it again?'

'Good idea,' she said, and Mick waved for the waiter's attention.

By now, she was at ease and enjoying herself. The meal arrived and Mick ordered another glass of wine. 'So you worked as an economic analyst. That's a very weighty subject. All that stuff about exchange rate mechanisms and fiscal adjustments.'

She looked up from her plate. 'Don't tell me you're an economist too?'

He grinned. 'Only in an amateur way. I told you I was in the motor business. My father was a great believer that a young man should have a trade so he got me an apprenticeship as a mechanic with a firm in Pearse Street.' He paused. 'I ended up owning the company.'

'Really? I'm very impressed.'

He shrugged. 'I was lucky and I made some good business decisions. But when things began to turn nasty in 2008, I realised that the motor trade was going to take a hiding so I sold the company and got out.'

'And you have no regrets?'

'None. Now I can relax and spend time with a beautiful woman like you.' He smiled and raised his glass in a toast.

It was half past three when they left, and Marrakech had emptied. Mick had settled the bill and left a generous tip. He walked with Ellie up Grafton Street to the car park at St Stephen's Green. 'I had a really nice time,' he said. 'Thank you for coming.'

'Me too.'

'Do you think we might do it again?'

'I don't see why not,' she replied. 'Why don't you give me a call and we'll work something out?'

'Okay, I'll do that.'

He drew her close and she thought he was going to kiss her, but instead he brushed her cheek with his lips. 'Goodbye, Ellie. Safe home,' he whispered.

When she got back to Clontarf, she slipped out of her dress and lay down on the bed. Details of the lunch were still vivid in her mind. It was strange being courted again after all this time but she had certainly enjoyed it. Mick Flynn had been the perfect companion: polite, witty, gracious, charming. And handsome, she thought. He really was very good-looking. Mags had spotted it the first time they met. Why had it taken her so long?

Her reverie was disturbed by her phone ringing. When she answered, it was Dee, asking if she would mind looking after Josette in the morning while she took the baby to the health centre for a check-up.

'Not at all,' she trilled. 'It would be a joy. I'd love every minute of it.'

'Are you all right, Mum?' Dee asked. 'You sound tipsy.'

'Not tipsy,' she replied. 'Just happy.'

***

She decided not to ring Mags to tell her about the lunch. She would wait till Mags called her and by then, hopefully, she would have information about her next date with Mick Flynn. The following day, her time was taken up with Josette, who had now grown tired of her new brother and regarded a visit to Ellie's house as a special treat. They played in the nursery and had a picnic in the garden, where Josette ran around chasing the starlings that were foraging on the lawn. By the time Dee called to pick her up, Josette was tired and didn't want to go home. Ellie smiled to herself at this sudden turn of events.

But in the days that followed, she began to find herself anxiously waiting for the phone to ring and to hear Mick Flynn's voice. However, the phone remained silent, and a sneaking doubt entered her mind that he might not call her at all. What was she going to do then? She remembered something similar happening with Joe at the beginning of their romance and how she had worked herself into a tizzy, wondering whether she should pick up the courage to ring him.

That sort of thinking was no good. If she had any sense, she should put Mick Flynn out of her mind. But, no matter how hard she tried, thoughts of him kept creeping up on her. She recalled the lovely lunch and the glorious feeling that had come over her as they strolled together up Grafton Street to the car park. Then that gentle kiss on the cheek as they parted.

What was happening to her? She was behaving like a silly schoolgirl after a first date. It was ridiculous. She was a middle-aged woman and should have more self-respect. Finally, after a week had passed, she reluctantly decided he wasn't going to call. It was time to forget about Mick Flynn and move on. She threw herself into a frenzy of housework, going around the house cleaning windows and polishing ornaments that were already spotlessly clean.

Then one day, her phone rang and when she lifted it, she heard Mags on the line. 'I was wondering if you ever got round to seeing that golfer we met in Marbella,' she began. 'What was his name again?'

Ellie panicked. How could she tell her the truth – that she had been waiting all this time for Mick Flynn to invite her out on a second date and he hadn't called? 'I'm working on something right now,' she said quickly. 'Can I ring you back?'

'Sure,' Mags said.

Ellie gave a sigh of relief as she ended the conversation. That had been a close call. But immediately, the phone rang again and this time when she answered, she felt a wave of relief.

'It's me, Mick, I wondered if you'd like to go to a concert with me? It's Christy Moore. I'm sure you'll enjoy it.'

She didn't even pause. 'Of course,' she said. 'I'd be delighted.'

Chapter Thirty-nine

After that, they began to see each other several times a week. But unlike Joe, who had favoured dates in fancy restaurants, Mick had much broader interests. He took Ellie to bars, clubs, theatres and concerts. He even brought her on a walking trip across Bray Head one weekend. And he introduced her to singing clubs.

'What are they exactly?' she asked, when he first suggested it.

'They're for people like me who sing as a hobby. We meet in the backroom of a pub or a hotel and have a few drinks. Then, the chairman calls each person to sing a song.'

'Is there music?'

'Sometimes.'

'Are the singers any good?'

'You'd be surprised. Some of them are very good – retired professionals. It's great fun and an excellent way to make new friends. Singing clubs have become so popular, I could take you to a different one every night of the week.'

'Okay,' she said. 'I think I might enjoy that.'

The next evening, he took her to a session in a club in Parnell Square. When they entered, there were about fifty people sitting around the room. Most of them were middle-aged but some were young people in their twenties. They seemed to know Mick and waved or came to their table to shake his hand. He bought drinks for himself and Ellie, then a hush descended on the room and the session began.

A man stood up and sang an old music-hall song. Then a woman sang a sad, romantic lament. Someone else gave 'Nessun Dorma' in a fine classical voice. When it came to Mick's turn, he offered a rousing rendition of 'Dicey Riley', a humorous Dublin song that had people clapping their hands and joining in the chorus. By the end of the evening, the whole room was laughing and singing.

Once they were outside in the fresh air, Mick asked her what she'd thought of it.

'It was great fun – I really enjoyed myself.'

'You'll have to learn a song for the next session.'

'I told you once before,' she said, 'that I only sing in the shower.'

***

As she got to know him, he told her about his personal situation. He had been married to a woman called Maria for twenty years. It had been a teenage infatuation, but as time went by, they had realised the marriage was a big mistake. By then, though, they'd had two young children.

'We discussed it calmly and agreed that the best thing to do was to wait till the boys had grown up before getting divorced.'

'That must have been difficult.'

'Yes, indeed. There were times when it was very awkward. We lived in the same house but led separate lives. We had separate bedrooms. But we never had arguments in front of the children. Thank God, Maria is a sensible woman. I told you she got married again – I've met her husband. He's a nice guy, an airline pilot.'

'And the boys?'

'They're both doing well. Colm is the eldest. He's married and has one child. His brother, Noel, is a trainee accountant. I see them regularly. We go to rugby matches together. It's all worked out very well.'

Mick had an apartment in Blackrock, not far from the one that Ellie had once lived in. It was a new-build, a smaller version of the apartment Joe had owned, just a master bedroom and a guest room, a bathroom, a kitchen and a living room. It was nicely decorated and furnished.

'When I split with Maria, I let her have the family home and bought this,' he explained, when he showed it to her. 'It supplies all my requirements and it's cosy. I didn't see any point in buying a large place and paying exorbitant heating bills and property taxes when I'm the only person living in it.'

She thought of the recent bill she had just received for her own house in Clontarf. 'Very sensible.'

Soon she was spending a lot of time in Mick's apartment. One evening, when she got up to leave, he took her hand. 'You don't have to go back,' he said. 'Why don't you stay the night?'

She hesitated. She had known this was going to arise sooner or later. 'I'm not sure.'

He put his arm around her waist, drew her close and kissed her. 'Oh, c'mon,' he said. 'We should get to know each other a little better.'

***

At last she felt confident enough to tell Caroline and Fiona about Mick. Mags had known from the start, and everyone agreed that it was good news, a very positive step for her. Now she had a new interest in her life.

'When are we going to meet him?' Caroline wanted to know.

'Soon,' Ellie replied. 'I'll arrange something.'

It was spring again and the weather was getting warmer. She thought of the children. She should tell them, too, about the new man in her life. Then she had a bright idea: she'd organise a cook-out and invite them all.

There was a lot of excitement when she told the family about Mick Flynn.

'You've kept this very quiet,' Dee said. 'I had no idea you were seeing someone.'

'I didn't go looking for him. We just happened to stumble into each other.' She explained about meeting Mick in Marbella, then in Paris, how he had called her unexpectedly and invited her to lunch. 'It just progressed from there.'

'I should have guessed,' Dee said. 'Recently, you've been going around looking like the cat that got the cream.'

'Really? I had no idea.'

Alice, Mollie and Jack all helped with the cook-out. There was an old barbecue in the garage that hadn't been used since Joe's death. Jack got it out and cleaned it and soon had it in fine working order. He went with her to the supermarket to get the food and wine and helped her carry it into the house. Meanwhile, the girls had trimmed the lawn and tidied up the garden.

The cook-out was arranged for Saturday afternoon at two

o'clock. Now they just had to pray for good weather. When she drew back the curtains on Saturday morning, she was delighted to see a clear sky and the sun beaming down.

She had asked Mick to come in good time. When he arrived, in casual trousers, open-necked shirt and pullover, he found the family waiting in the kitchen to meet him. Ellie made the introductions, watching carefully for their reaction.

'Would you like something to drink?' Alice asked.

'I wouldn't say no to a beer.'

She got a bottle out of the fridge, and soon they were all chatting amicably as Mick asked about their careers and talked with Jack about golf and rugby. So far, so good, Ellie thought. They seem to like him. Just then, the doorbell rang and Caroline and Freddie came waltzing in.

'Darling,' she said, throwing her arms around Mick's neck and planting a warm kiss on his cheek, while Freddie stood and grinned. 'What a perfectly adorable man. I didn't think they made them like you any more.'

Eventually, they all moved out to the garden where Mick and Jack lit the barbecue. By now, Fiona and Mags had arrived with their husbands, soon followed by Dee, Tony and their children. In no time, the party was in full swing.

Later, Caroline drew Ellie aside. 'I really like him,' she said. 'I think you've fallen on your feet. But do tell me something. Are you in love with him?'

Ellie smiled. Trust Caroline not to beat about the bush. 'I'm very fond of him.'

'I'm not talking fondness. I asked about love.'

'A little,' she admitted.

'Don't be ridiculous. There's no such thing as "a little". With love, it's all or nothing.'

***

One evening as they were relaxing in Mick's apartment, he said, 'Tell me about Joe. What was he like?'

She felt herself tense. Apart from Tom Matthews, only Fiona and Christine Palmer knew what had happened. Was she ready to tell Mick?

'Perhaps some other time,' she said. 'My memories of my husband are a little mixed.'

'If you don't want to talk about him, that's fine. I won't mention it again.'

'You don't understand. Joe was a wonderful husband. He died suddenly from a heart attack in a London hotel room. He was on a reporting assignment.'

'My God, I had no idea. That must have been an awful shock.'

'It was terrible,' she went on. 'But there was worse to come. He wasn't alone. There was a young woman with him called Emily Tobin. She was an intern with the *Gazette*. I only found out about it after his death.' The words caught in her throat.

Mick's arm went around her and held her close. 'That's enough. You can tell me some other time.'

'No,' she said. 'Now that I've started, you might as well hear the whole story.'

Over the next few minutes, she recounted her visit to London and the confrontation with Joe's boss, Tom Matthews. 'He tried to convince me it was innocent. He said that Emily Tobin was besotted with Joe and he was simply helping her with her career.'

'But you didn't believe him?'

Ellie hesitated. 'Well ...'

'Why don't you give Joe the benefit of the doubt?

He sounds like he was a good guy. Life's too short to be carrying resentments. You'll feel much better if you can forgive him.'

A few days later, he returned to their discussion. 'I've been thinking about what you told me. Perhaps you need a change of scenery.'

'Where?'

'Some place warm and sunny, some place like Marbella.'

Her face fell. 'Marbella is where Joe and I spent our honeymoon.'

'But it's also where you met me, remember? Was he dead then?'

'Yes. I'd been visiting a grief counsellor. She recommended I go back to a place where I had pleasant memories of him. But that was before I found out about Emily Tobin.'

'If it would be too difficult, perhaps we can go somewhere else.'

'No,' she said. 'Give me more time to consider it.'

**

The next morning, she rang Fiona. 'I need to talk to you. When are you free?'

'Five o'clock. Is it urgent?'

'Sort of. I need your advice. I could drive over to the hospital, if you like.'

'No, it's easier if I call to you. Expect me about half five.'

It was twenty-five to six when Fiona arrived. They went into the kitchen and sat down.

'How is the marvellous Mick? Still keeping you entertained, I hope.'

'Yes, he's wonderful. I'm growing very fond of him. That's

really what I want to ask you about. He's suggested we might go for a break to Marbella.'

Fiona rolled her eyes. 'And you need my advice? Are you nuts or what? Of course you should go.'

'I'm sorry,' Ellie said. 'I'm not making myself very clear. It's not the holiday I'm concerned about. It's the destination.'

'What's wrong with it? I thought you liked Marbella.'

'I do – or, at least, I used to. But it holds a lot of memories for me. Joe took me there very early in our romance and it's also where we spent our honeymoon.'

Fiona stared at her. 'And you think if you go there with Mick you're going to see Joe's ghost on every street, making you resentful and angry?'

'Not resentful, sad.'

Fiona took a deep breath. 'This situation calls for some straight talking. You've managed to find a nice man. You've just said he's loving and caring and you like him. He invites you to Marbella and you're not sure if you should go because it might hold memories of your dead husband.'

Ellie tried to interrupt but Fiona silenced her. 'Hear me out. Every corner of this house holds memories of Joe Plunkett. So do your children and grandchildren. Every time you see a copy of the *Gazette*, it carries memories of him. When will you understand that you can't escape him?'

'But—'

'Listen to me. Don't you think the time has come to make peace with Joe, whatever he did? And bear in mind that you have no proof he did anything, apart from being stupid. You've asked for my advice. Now I'm going to give it. The sooner you let go of the past and move on, the better for everyone concerned – but especially for you.'

Chapter Forty

The sun was hanging like a great red ball above the blue expanse of the sea. Ellie leaned on the balcony rail of their terrace at Hotel Majestic and breathed in the scent of the roses in the garden below. An elderly couple dozed in the shade of the palm trees, straw hats pulled down across their faces. From the swimming pool she could hear the laughter of excited children. The hotel had hardly changed in the years since she had first come here with Joe Plunkett.

She let her eyes roam further, over the rooftops and spires of the town and out to sea, where some yachts were tacking in the breeze. At last, she turned away and sat down beside Mick, who was pouring gin and tonic. She put her hand across her mouth and yawned. It had been a long day: up since six o'clock to get to Dublin airport for the flight to Málaga, then the drive to Marbella.

'Flagging?' he asked.

'I am a bit.'

'Travelling is tiring, and so is the heat. We'll have an early night. You'll feel much better in the morning.'

She leaned across and kissed Mick's cheek. He turned to her and smiled. 'Feeling amorous already?'

'Grateful. Thank you for bringing me here, Mick. I love this place. I know I'm going to enjoy the holiday.'

'Of course you are, particularly when I tell you it's raining in Dublin. I've just checked the weather channel.'

They sat on the terrace sipping their drinks till the sun had gone down. Then they went into their room to get dressed. It was half past eight when they set off down the hill towards the town. As they got closer to the sea, the sound of music and laughter increased till they found themselves at last on the Paseo Maritimo.

The mime artists and hucksters were out, the latter with their trays of cheap watches and jewellery, plying their trade with the tourists thronging along the promenade. Above the ocean, the stars hung like jewels in the dark sky.

'Are you hungry?' Mick asked.

She was ravenous. All she had eaten since breakfast was a sandwich on the plane. 'Yes.'

'Me too. Any idea where you want to eat?'

'Yes. Just keep walking and hopefully we'll come to it. That's if it's still here.'

They walked for another ten minutes, then Ellie's eyes lit up at the sight of a little restaurant set back from the street in a shaded patio. On the wall a wooden trellis was festooned with brightly coloured flowers. 'Here it is,' she said.

They were lucky to get a table for two at the back. A dark-haired young man appeared to ask them what they wanted to drink. Mick chose a bottle of Rioja. The waiter was back a minute later with the wine and took their food order. As he turned to leave, Ellie said, 'Is Francisco still working here?'

The waiter stopped and looked at her inquisitively. 'Did you know him, Señora?'

'I met him years ago, here at the restaurant.'

'He is my father.'

'Really? And where does he live?'

'In Córdoba. He is a teacher there.'

'Does he have other children?'

'I have three sisters. They are at school.' He bowed and went off.

'Now you're making me jealous,' Mick said. 'Who is this Francisco?'

'He was a young student who was working here when Joe and I first came. His father was the owner. He was so friendly and polite. When we were leaving he came after us and presented me with a red rose. I thought it was the most romantic thing.'

'You must have made an impression on him.'

'I'm sure he's long forgotten me. He must have seen plenty of women when he was working here.'

'But none as beautiful as you.'

She smiled. 'You really are a flatterer, aren't you?'

The meal arrived: succulent turbot for Ellie and a fillet steak for Mick. They fell on it with relish. When they had finished, Ellie declined the offer of a dessert but accepted a glass of brandy as a *digestivo*. It was eleven o'clock when they set off once more along the Paseo for their hotel.

Once they got back, Ellie went into the bathroom and had a shower, then dried herself and slipped under the duvet. Five minutes later, Mick joined her. He took her in his arms and kissed her. 'Are you happy?' he asked.

'Absolutely.'

'That's good. I want you always to be happy. I love you, Ellie.'

'And I love you too.'

'Why did you change your mind about coming to Marbella and to this very hotel where you spent your honeymoon with Joe?'

'I realised the truth of something I was told, that I would never be content till I had forgiven him. So now I have.'

She felt Mick roll over and gradually fall asleep. But she still lay awake, staring at the moonlight spilling in from the window. A thought came hurtling into her head. That terrible day when she had been told that Joe was dead, she had known that two more things would happen. All the important events in her life had come in threes.

And it had turned out to be true. She had gone through the trauma of his death, then the shock of Emily Tobin, and now she had found a new man to love. She was at peace again.

She cuddled closer to Mick and held him tight till she, too, drifted off to sleep.